I

Riot of the Living Dead

Vol. 1: Escape from Detroit

By Sam Elkins

©2014

This is a work of fiction (well, mostly). Names, characters, places, and incidences are either the product of the author's imagination or are used fictitiously. Any resemblance to any persons living or dead is either entirely coincidental, or, I think you are such an awesome person that you needed to be in my book. I love you, so please don't sue me.

This book is dedicated to Army SFC William "Kelly" Lacey, KIA 04 January, 2014 in Nangarhar Province, Afghanistan; he is credited with saving the lives of 55 of his men.

"I love the smell of Detroit in the morning;
it smells like… house fires."

Day 1: Saturday, 0502 hrs

In a quiet Midwest town, beneath the cool, dark skies of an early June morning, sat a tightly clustered row of old, wooden houses. They loomed in the frigid silence of 5 am, long before the songs of waking birds, or the bustle of the morning commuters. All of the houses were dark and sleeping … all but one.

It was a small, peculiar, green abode that was beginning to stir, with the light from its kitchen window providing the only sign of life at this early hour. As the curtains of this quaint, clapboard home blew open, the smell of freshly brewed espresso slowly drifted, and the eerie silence of the street was interrupted by the clink of a ceramic mug and the washing of a dish.

Far to the south, rising through the morning air, came the distant call of a train whistle announcing its approach to the sleepy little town. After a moment's pause, the whistle called out again, slowly building and gaining force as the train drew nearer. Gradually, the little wooden house began to vibrate, and then shimmy, and then creak and rumble as the heavy train approached, barreling through the dark morning.

The whistle's volume steadily grew from a melodic wail into a trumpeting blast of air as the train roared by, carrying newly manufactured cars from Detroit to places far and wide, shaking the very foundation of the house as it thundered past.

As the train rolled away, the back door of the house creaked open and out stepped a lanky, long haired man in blue hospital scrubs. Toting a brown suede briefcase in one hand, he searched through his keys for a moment before finding the correct one, and locked the door securely behind him. Kneeling down, he paused to pet the cat that had taken up residency in the pole barn out back.

"Good morning, White Kitty. It's a chilly one."

The cat purred loudly in response and gave a squinty-eyed smile as the man scratched him behind the ears.

High above, the stars shone bright, and the morning chill brought a passing shiver; his paper thin hospital scrubs offered little insulation, but the afternoon promised to be a hot one.

Typical Michigan summer, he thought to himself.

1

Hopping into his red Subaru wagon, he tossed his briefcase into the passenger seat and turned the key, sensibly allowing the car to warm up for a full 30 seconds before putting it in gear (this allows the oil to thoroughly lubricate the engine before driving, thus prolonging the life of the motor). Adjusting his powered seat and electric mirrors, he began the one hour commute to St. John hospital in Detroit.

Sam had been living downtown on Main St. in the little rural town of Milan, MI for seven years now. Intending it to be a starter home, the real estate collapse of 2008 had sealed his fate to ride out a 30 year fixed sentence. Fate, however, could have been much worse: the house was small, and the quirky green paint was peeling, but the young couple fell in love with it on sight. It was built in the typical farmhouse style of the 1920's, with a wide front porch, large windows, high ceilings and original hard wood floors. It was enough space for the couple and their three year old son, Simon, but with Jessica expecting a baby girl any day, things would soon be very tight.

His neighbors were all good people, but mostly kept to themselves. The houses were close together, purportedly to protect one another from "Indian attacks." At least that's what the old timers say. Mature, old growth maples lined the street. Directly across from his house was the local funeral home, landscaped with beautiful flowering trees. His neighbors immediately to the left, Carol and her two sons, were their only close friends in town. They shared each other's back yards and got together to play board games. Milan is the rural sort of town where everyone either owns a pickup truck, a motorcycle, a rifle, or some combination of those three. It's the kind of neighborhood where you never have to lock your doors, but you do anyway.

Pulling onto the highway and throwing it into fifth gear brought an inner sigh of contentment, and Sam melted a little deeper into his heated leather seat. The journey to and from, the daily commute, this was his morning and evening respite. Friends always asked with pity, "How can you drive so far for work, on top of a 16 ½ hour work day?" But this quiet time of driving was his time to wake up and his time to wind down; both meditative and relaxing. Working 6:30 am to 11:00 pm means he sees no real traffic coming or going. A book on CD, NPR news, the BBC World Service, music, daydreams; these are his copilots.

Ten minutes north near the city of Ann Arbor, he merged east onto I-94, a straight shot into the heart of Detroit. His morning cup of espresso was finally crossing the blood/brain barrier, and the false dawn of early morning was beginning to show in the eastern sky.

Cruise control set, radio on:

> "... local officials are not speculating if the rioting at the North American International Auto Show is related to the outbreak of violence on the Korean peninsula, but unconfirmed sources at the Auto Show stated that delegates from the Korean automaker assaulted the German booth as they were unveiling their new compact SUV..."

What!? A riot at the Auto Show?

Reaching down, he turned up the volume.

> "... There are reports of several fatalities, and Detroit Police have been unable to contain the violence overnight which has now spilled out into the city streets. Detroit Chief of Police Deon Kelly is advising area residents to stay at home and local businesses to remain closed until the situation is under control. Reporting live in Detroit, this is Aaron McDowell, NPR News. Meanwhile on Wall Street, stocks are remaining flat as investors ... "

Turning the volume back down, the lean, long haired man sat up a little straighter and rubbed the sleep from his eyes.

> *Wow, the last thing this city needs is another riot. Sometimes I feel like the city just has no hope ... and those who live here don't even care ... blah.*

Attempting to clear his mind of such thoughts, he turned the dial to the rock station and heard the wails of David Bowie singing "Panic in Detroit." It then cut away to the two morning radio guys cracking jokes about this once fair city, jokes that stung, but were oh so true. No jobs, no hope, no future ... but please, no more riots.

The Motor City has a long history of civil unrest, usually centered on issues of race. The first Detroit Race Riot took place back in 1863. The genesis of that riot remains murky, but it ended with two confirmed deaths and 35 buildings destroyed. While not as destructive or deadly as the riots that followed, it was a significant event for the young, growing city. Years later, the Race Riot of 1943 began on the picturesque island park of "Belle Isle," with an altercation between a white and a black youth. The brawl escalated as others joined in, and it eventually spread throughout the city as groups of whites and blacks responded to rumors of a white man assaulting a black woman, and a black man raping and killing a white woman. The riot lasted for several days, and Federal troops were eventually brought in to restore the peace. The final tally was 35 dead, 600 injured, 1,800 arrests, and several storefronts were looted and burned. But it was the Race Riot of 1967 that in many ways signaled the beginning of Detroit's downfall. The spark that ignited the city was a routine police raid on an unlicensed, after hours bar (then known as a blind pig) on the corner of 12th and Clairmount streets. Detroit Police Officers only expected to find two dozen patrons, but instead found a party of 82 celebrating the return of two local veterans from the Vietnam War. Police decided to arrest the entire party, including the vets, as an angry crowd of locals looked on in protest. As the last of the Police cars pulled away, the gathered crowd became violent, smashing the windows of nearby shops. Shortly thereafter, full scale rioting erupted and eventually spread throughout the entire city, resulting in 43 dead, 467 injured, over 7,200 arrests, and more than 2,000 buildings destroyed. Large swathes of the city were razed to the ground. It was the largest, most destructive riot in American history, only being eclipsed by the 1992 Los Angeles/Rodney King Riot. This city changing event brought fear and blight, leaving the population reeling and even more racially divided than before. It signaled the beginning of the 'White Exodus' from Detroit proper. The 'White Flight,' as it was also called, took all the real money and jobs with it as educated professionals and skilled workers fled to the suburbs. This exodus created a vacuum in the city's tax base and property values, triggering an economic domino effect. Several automotive related businesses relocated to the outlying communities, leaving vacant buildings and unemployment in their wake.

Never fully recovering from the 1967 disaster, Detroit was left vulnerable to the social plagues that accompany poverty and unemployment. In the 1980's, crack cocaine began to flood the city, followed by heroin in the 90's. Illicit drug use and crime kicked the city hard, ruining the lives of many. The post-September 11th recession was followed by the collapse of the real estate market, and the bankruptcy of the big three auto companies, which had been Detroit's lifeblood for more than a century. There is no more "motor" in Motown. Mayor Kilpatrick has been sent to prison for corruption, and the city council is no less corrupt then he. Prostitutes walk the streets, virtually uncontested by local police. Isolated pockets of prosperity do exist, but the majority of Detroit is a failed, dead city, populated only by burnt, vacant houses, boarded up businesses, pedestrians standing at bus stops with hard eyes and lines of anger creased in their faces. If they make eye contact it's because they don't trust you. Their walk says "I got my guard up," always on the defense, and with good reason. Many good people try to hang on to the "D," but the chips are stacked against them in this crumbling metropolis.

Thoughts of the failing city drifted away as a river of brake lights came into view.

Whoa ... there must've been a wreck up ahead. I've never seen traffic like this at 6:00am on a Saturday.

Scratching his red beard as he brought the car to a stop, Sam craned his neck to look ahead.

Traffic ... barely moving. Looks like I'm going to be late. Better make a call to work.

Flipping open his phone, he scrolled down the contact list to "St. John MRI" and pressed "SEND." Silence ... no ringing ... more silence ... and then a recorded message: "All lines are busy, please try your call again later. This is a recording, message number one three eight." He chuckled to himself.

This is going to be a long day.

One hour and only ten miles later, he could see the cause of the snafu: a car was flipped on its side with police on the scene. Three

5

lanes of traffic merged into one as the commuters navigated around the wreckage. Rolling past the broken glass, Sam glanced toward the twisted metal and saw a bloodied man staggering away from his car. One arm was hanging limp and he had a vacant, blood stained stare...

Holy crap! That guy needs to sit down! He needs help!

Glancing into his rear view mirror he considered stopping, then he noticed several cops surrounding the man with guns drawn. He averted his eyes back to the road and without a second to spare slammed his brakes hard to avoid rear ending the stopped car ahead of him.

Suddenly from behind: BAM-BAM-BAM! Shots were fired.

Instinctively Sam ducked and gripped the wheel tightly, trying to keep his head down. He peeked into his mirror to assess the situation.

Did they just shoot that guy?!

Then a salvo of honking horns behind him prodded the cars ahead to move along, and the highway opened back up into three lanes. Speeding away and breaking a sweat, Sam kept looking over his shoulder in disbelief.

Did that just happen!? I think they SHOT him ... he was in NO shape to resist! Maybe he drew a gun on them? He shook his head and focused on the road. *Seriously, I have GOT to stop coming to Detroit! I think I'd feel safer driving through Fallujah ...*

Pulling away, leaving the incident far behind him, he put the hammer down to make up for lost time. Winding out fourth gear and slamming it into fifth, singing David Bowie at the top of his lungs:

"He looked a lot like Che Guevara, drove a diesel van,
He kept his gun in quiet seclusion, such a humble man,
The only survivor, of the National Peoples Gang,
PANIC IN DETROIT...!"

6

Day 1: Saturday, 0730 hrs

The sun was breaking the horizon as Sam pulled into the hospital parking lot. Coming to a stop, he tied his long hair back into a ponytail while looking at the clock, "One hour late means several dollars short."

Walking double-time into Radiology, he headed straight to the MRI suite and saw Roland and Lloyd sitting at the desk watching videos on YouTube.

"Sorry I'm late guys, there was a wreck on 94. I tried to call, but I think the lines are down."

Roland looked up from the video entitled "signed in the author's blood" and said, "No worries, man. The first patient didn't show. But hey, what's a 'CODE ORANGE?'"

"CODE ORANGE?" he replied with a puzzled look. "You mean like: CODE RED, CODE BLUE … CODE *ORANGE*?"

"Yeah, they called a 'CODE ORANGE' about an hour ago," Lloyd said.

"Hmmm, good question. I don't know, let's grab the book and look it up."

Sam has been working with Roland and Lloyd for a couple years now. Roland is a tall, young black male in his early 20's, working as a TA (Tech Assistant) to pay his way through the paramedic program. His partner in crime, Lloyd, has been a staple of the MRI department for over 20 years. Although he is in his early 60's, the man honestly doesn't look a day over 45. He has close cropped reddish brown hair and sports a handlebar mustache. With a deep booming voice, a lean carriage, and Popeye forearms, he carries himself like a military man.

Flipping through their binder labeled "Hospital Protocols," they found the emergency code page and skimmed down the various colors till they reached orange. Lloyd read it aloud, "CODE ORANGE: External disaster. All hospital employees must remain on site until 'ALL CLEAR' is announced."

"What?" Roland asked, "That means we can't leave?"

Sam cleared his throat, "Yeah, I think they usually call that code when there's a plane crash or some natural disaster, like an earthquake. It basically means they are expecting a lot of casualties to come in and they want every hand available to help out- receptionists, housekeeping … everybody. They're probably even calling people in."

"Damn, I wonder what happened."

"No idea," Sam said, and then after a little more thought, "I heard on NPR that there was a riot over at the Auto Show. Maybe that has something to do with it. Regardless, you and I are here till eleven anyways. I'm sure they'll have it all straightened out by then. What time are *you* supposed to be off, Lloyd?"

"Three! And I've got plans!"

"Sucks to be you," Roland quipped.

They all laughed and the guys got back to their YouTube clips while Sam unpacked his briefcase and began powering up the MRI machine.

The MRI (Magnetic Resonance Imaging) scanner is basically a large, tube shaped magnet that manipulates a powerful magnetic field to make diagnostic images of the human body.

Sam emptied his pockets on the counter and opened the heavy, copper lined door labeled "WARNING: STRONG MAGNETIC FIELD." He put a fluid filled testing device called a "phantom" in the bore of the magnet and then exited the room, closing the scanner room door behind him. Sam returned to the helm and after a few keystrokes he looked through the observation window at the machine as it began making the loud knocking and clicking noises familiar to anyone who has had an MRI scan.

Sighing deeply, he nestled into his seat. The fully adjustable, plush black, high-end chair in front of his computer was like an old friend. He kicked his feet up on the desk and cracked open a book while the five minute calibration scan began to run.

Glancing up at the monitor when he finally heard the scanner stop, he reviewed the test images and declared, "All systems are 'go.' Do you guys know if the next patient has checked in yet?"

"I'll walk up front and take a look," Lloyd said as he headed for the reception desk.

"Alright, thanks." Sam swiveled his chair toward the tall, light-skinned black man next to him, "So, how've you been, Roland?"

Roland cracked a sly grin, saying "Man, you would not even believe," then proceeded to tell the story of his most recent sexual exploits. Being a married man, Sam found these conversations to be the highlight of his day.

After some time, Lloyd returned saying, "Well, both the 8 o'clock and 9 o'clock patients are no-shows, but the E.R. just placed an order for a brain scan. Do you want me to bring her down now?"

"Sure, we've got to earn our keep *somehow*. But take your time, I'm going to walk next door first and pick up some coffee."

"No prob, mate. I'll see you in twenty. Roland, you have the bridge," Lloyd said as he strolled back down the hall.

Roland hopped to attention and saluted smartly, "Aye-aye, sir."

"Do you want anything from next door, Roland?" Sam asked.

"Naw, man, I'm straight. I'm just gonna jump onto Facebook."

"Ha… and talk to your girl?"

Roland cracked another sly grin, "Which one?"

The morning sun blasted Sam's senses as he stepped out of the back employee entrance. The day was shaping up nicely, and the mercury had risen well past 75. As he cut through the parking lot he began to take note of the sound of distant sirens... several of them. He tuned his ear to pick up the patterns:

> *... police ... fire ... AND ambulance. All three, huh?*

As a child he had a toy megaphone that bolted onto his BMX bike. It had a switch to cycle through each of those three siren patterns and a bullhorn. He has remembered the separate, distinct calls ever since.

He then noticed several muffled "pops" punctuating the background of sirens and road traffic. They seemed to be coming from several directions.

> *That sounds like firecrackers... or maybe gunshots?*

The morning's events flashed back to him and he vividly saw the bloody man swaying vacantly on the highway. The policemen ... the guns ...

> *Did they really shoot that guy? I didn't actually see them fire, but it sure as heck sounded like gunshots to me. Come to think of it, it sounded a lot like these "pops" in the distance...*

Then he remembered the CODE ORANGE.

> *Oh, crap! I forgot, we weren't supposed to leave! Better double-time it. I've never had to observe a CODE ORANGE before.*

Entering the café, Sam breathed deeply the aroma of freshly roasted coffee; it brought a tingling surge of endorphins, and his inner calm began to return. Looking up at the chalkboard menu, he

10

scratched his beard in contemplation as he read the hand drawn sign:

"Trivia! Ten cents off your cup! Name the only 2 countries that are 'doubly landlocked.'"

The barista approached and greeted the brooding man, "And what will it be today, sir? A double shot espresso with an inch of hot water?" She knew him too well.

Sam paused in thought, his wheels visibly turning, "... nooooo ... not today ..." He was torn, the success of the day may very well hinge on this pivotal decision.

"I'll have a medium cap ... non-fat ... dry ..." he paused briefly, hesitating, and then continued with authority, "... with a half dose of hazelnut syrup." *Perfection.*

"Fine choice, sir."

"Oh, and the answer to your trivia is Lichtenstein and Uzbekistan."

"Correct, sir! You're the first one today who's got it." Monies were exchanged, and the barista rolled up her sleeves and went to work.

His mind drifted back to summer school, 8th grade Geography, Mr. Dickey. He was one of the cool teachers; he would just sit at his desk reading the newspaper and grading papers while sipping coffee rumored to be spiked with Bailey's. He left the students to toil away at their only assignment for the summer school semester, which was to write a one page paper on each and every country in the world, totaling approximately 190 at that time. The report didn't have to be elaborate, just the facts: capital, major cities, type of government, land & water features, chief industries and exports, population, and any unusual facts. When Sam encountered these two countries whose most notable facts were being the only two doubly landlocked countries (a landlocked country that is bordered entirely by other landlocked countries) he never forgot them, primarily because he thought their names sounded hilarious. *Liechtenstein and Uzbekistan.*

Exiting the café, Sam walked back toward the hospital carrying his precious cargo with two hands, sipping it lovingly when a speeding ambulance raced past, shattering his bliss. Several other cars were whizzing by in different directions, driving abnormally erratic even by Detroit standards. In the distance a steady but intermittent pop-pop-pop could be heard, and the wails of even more sirens. He picked up his pace.

Something is going on ... something serious. I really better get back to my post ...

Ahead on the sidewalk was a disheveled looking homeless man, the same man that hit Sam up for spare change every time he made a coffee run. However, today he looked unusually haggard. He lifted his head as Sam approached, and reached both arms out. From this distance he appeared to be too drunk to speak, and having no time for dealing with a drunken interaction, Sam side stepped down an alley.

Approaching the hospital, he could see a large crowd surrounding the E.R. entrance. Many people seemed panicked, and it appeared that a fight was about to break out. Swiping his I.D. card at the employee entrance, he was nearly run down by three nurses running full tilt out of the building! Jumping aside, he looked back and saw that one of the nurses was bleeding profusely from her side.

"Hey! Are you alright!? What's going on!?"

There was no answer, they just ran.

Sam sprinted into the building, trying hard not to spill his coffee. People were running in all directions, and over the intercom a woman's voice calmly repeated three times, "CODE GREY, E.R. ... CODE GREY, E.R. ... CODE GREY, E.R.."

A fight in the emergency room? This is getting bad!

Swiping his card at the door labeled "Radiology," he returned to the MRI suite and quickly shut the door behind him. Roland looked up from his laptop saying, "Lloyd called, and he's on his way down with that E.R. patient ..." but after seeing Sam's face he asked, "... whoa, what's up?"

"I don't know, man. I've got to call Security, I just saw a bloody nurse running out the back door," he said, more to himself than to his assistant.

"Wait, what?" Roland asked, but Sam didn't answer. He had the phone to his ear and was dialing frantically.

Ringing ... ringing ... ringing ... no answer.

He hung up the phone and tried again, but still no joy.

The intercom clicked on overhead, and the woman's voice

12

came back on, this time not so calmly, "CODE GREY, E.R. ... CODE GREY, E.R. ... CODE GREY, E.R.." There was a lot of audible commotion in the background of her announcement.

"What's a 'CODE GREY'?" Roland asked.

"A combative patient ... unarmed. If they're armed, it's a CODE SILVER."

"So? We get combative patients all the time. Why don't *we* ever call a CODE GREY?"

"No, this means a serious fight broke out, one that requires Security. When I was walking back from the coffee shop, it looked like there was an angry mob in front of the E.R."

Roland grinned, "Were they carrying pitchforks?"

Sam smiled and relaxed his shoulders a little. "And brandishing torches? No, not like that. But it looked bad."

Shaking his head, Roland said, "Every time some thug gets shot, his whole damn family shows up in the E.R., yelling and causing a scene."

"No, really, I don't think it's like that. Something serious is going on over there."

The door opened and Lloyd pushed in a patient on a large stretcher. Almost instantly, a wall of stench hit both men in the face. They looked at each other, struggling to keep their composure as they reached for the box of rubber gloves. Hospital workers become very accustomed to unpleasant odors, however this went far beyond anything they had previously encountered. The usual smells of sour B.O., stale urine, and poor dental hygiene were all there. However, there was another smell ... not gangrene, nor infection, but the smell of death ... decay... rot.

Sam flipped open the patient's chart and skimmed over the doctor's orders.

"Hi, Mrs. [confidential], my name is Sam. I will be performing your exam today. Hello?... Mrs. [confidential]?"

The patient was non-responsive, so he performed a quick assessment. She was an 82 year old African American female, approximately 110 lbs. Her eyes were half closed and unfocused; she was neither alert nor oriented. Her breathing was shallow and labored. He put his gloved hand across her forehead: she was extremely feverish and sweating profusely.

"Lloyd, this patient is *not* stable, are you sure they want this done right now?"

Lloyd was visibly struggling with the smell, "I couldn't even *find* the ordering doctor or her nurse to ask them. It's a madhouse over there; Security was all over the place."

Sam rifled through the patient's chart. "Has she even been screened for metal?"

"Yeah, the screening form should be in there, I saw it. No metal implants, no injuries involving metal."

The standard MRI machine has a magnetic force of 1.5 Tesla (or 15,000 times the magnetic pull of the Earth). Any ferromagnetic metal (metal containing iron) brought into the room will be pulled at 40 mph into the bore of the magnet. Metal implants can shift in the body or become dislodged, causing major internal trauma. Loose metal objects in pockets or on clothing will become projectiles and fly across the room. Any person entering the scanner room, day or night, must be thoroughly checked for metal, as the magnet is always on.

"Here it is," he said, reviewing the form. "It looks good, but I'm going to try to get the ordering doc on the phone. This patient is *not* stable and should have been accompanied by a nurse, or a sitter, or someone!"

He dialed the phone and let it ring for quite some time. "No answer in the E.R."

Lloyd was holding his forearm across his nose, trying in vain to shield himself from the overpowering smell. "I told you, man, people are going crazy over there. One of the E.R. techs told me that Dr. Remus nearly got her ear bit off when she was trying to help restrain a patient! People were fighting in the lobby … I just picked up this patient and got the 'eff out of Dodge!"

After a moment of contemplation, Sam said with resignation, "Alright, let's just get her in and get her out. Is she *wearing* anything with metal?"

He rolled down her bed sheet and was taken aback by what he saw: several deep bite marks ran down the length of her arm, they were festering and looked infected. Looking further down her arm, he saw soft Velcro restraints around her wrists.

"Lloyd, did you know she was in restraints?"

"No. She isn't supposed to be! I didn't see an order for that in the chart," Lloyd said, double-checking the doctor's written orders. "Nope, no order."

"Good, because they'll have to come off anyway to get her in the magnet."

Roland stood up to help them get the patient into the magnet and saw her arm. "Whoa, I thought we were scanning her brain?"

"Yeah: MRI of the brain with contrast, diagnose mental status changes," Sam replied.

"Then what's going on with her arm?"

The three men looked down at her arm for a long, silent moment; it looked bad. The bites were obviously human, and there was one particularly horrific one with exposed muscle tissue. To their surprise, it wasn't actively bleeding, but there was a lot of dark, dried blood.

"The chart mentioned she was assaulted ..." Sam muttered, and they stood over her a moment longer before he finished, "... let's just make this quick."

They removed the Velcro restraints and slid her over onto an aluminum stretcher to bring her into the scan room. She moaned loudly as they transferred her from the aluminum stretcher to the MRI table.

Sam spoke slowly and clearly, "It's OK, Mrs. [confidential], we're just going to take some pictures of your head. Try to hold very still. The machine is going to be very loud, so we're going to put some earplugs in your ears."

"Do you think she can hear you, Sam?" Roland asked under his breath.

"Probably not, she seems pretty out of it."

After positioning the patient in the magnet, they stepped out of the scan room and pulled the heavy door closed behind them. Sam nestled back into his comfy chair and pulled up the patient's information on his computer. After typing in a few parameters for the first series of images, the magnet went to work. He sat back and watched the patient through the observation window. It would be three minutes before the first images began to appear, so he kicked his feet back up on the desk, adjusted his headrest slightly, and drew deeply from his cappuccino.

"Assuming the position?" Roland asked.

"You know it. Pimpin' ain't easy," Sam said as he put his coffee down and picked up his book, *Marine Sniper: 93 Confirmed Kills*.

Three minutes later, the noise of the magnet stopped, so Sam looked up to review the images. They were all a blur.

"Crap, she must be moving." He leaned over and pressed the intercom button, "Ma'am, it's very important that you try to hold still. That first picture did not turn out, so I am going to repeat it. Please try to hold *very* still."

Her only response was a productive, phlegmy cough and a soft moan.

A few keystrokes later the scanner was repeating the first set of images while Sam reached under his chair to adjust his seat height a fraction of an inch. He let out a frustrated sigh and buried his nose back into his book.

Once those scans ran their course, Sam looked up and saw that these images were no better. MRI exams only work if the patient can hold perfectly still. Even one slight movement during the three minute scan will ruin the entire sequence.

Without removing his feet from the desk, Sam looked over his shoulder and said, "Hey, Roland, will you go in there and try to talk to this lady? Try to get her to hold still?"

"No problem, man. I'll try, but do you think she'll even understand me?"

"I'm not sure, but we have to try *something*. If she doesn't hold still this time we'll just document it and send her back."

Roland got up and opened the heavy door, releasing the sour smell back into the control room. Sipping his coffee with one hand, Sam used the other to set up another repeat scan. He could hear Roland pulling the exam table out of the magnet and talking to the patient.

Sitting several feet behind Sam, Lloyd gasped as the cloud of stench drifted his way. "How the hell can you just sit there nonchalantly and drink your coffee with that ... *smell*?"

"Game face, I only *pretend* that it doesn't bother me," he said coolly.

Sam wiped the cappuccino foam from his mustache. His mind was still in his book: belly crawling through the jungles of Vietnam with the legendary sniper Carlos Hathcock, surviving off a small tin of peanut butter, tracking the Vietcong ...

A loud thump drew his attention from his book, followed by a gargling, wet, gasping sound. He glanced up through the observation

16

window to see Roland staggering backwards with the elderly patient biting viciously at his throat.

Sam almost fell backwards out of his chair, yelling for Lloyd to help! The two men barged into the scanner room and grabbed for the patient's arms. They tried to pull her free, but her teeth were holding fast to Roland's throat. Pulling harder, they heard the gut wrenching "crunch" of cartilage in Roland's neck as his trachea and voice box collapsed. His eyes opened wide and were filled with panic and rage as he began raining down hard punches to the side of Mrs. [confidential]'s head.

The elderly woman's mouth tore loose from Roland's neck, taking a wad of soft tissue with it. The young black man dropped to the floor, clutching the gaping wound, his legs kicking involuntarily. A large puddle of blood was forming on the floor beneath him, growing rapidly.

Sam twisted the old woman's arms behind her back and fell forward on top of her, pinning her face down onto the floor.

"Lloyd! Call the E.R.! CODE BLUE! And call Security! NOW!" Then he turned and looked at Roland, "Hang in there, man! We'll get you fixed up!"

The young man was grasping his throat, trying frantically to stop the bleeding. His eyes locked onto Sam's, and began to change from panic to peaceful resignation as he smirked and shook his head, knowing full well the prognosis of such a terrible neck wound, arteries severed, trachea torn.

The woman beneath Sam was thrashing wildly, her movements jerky and unnatural.

"Don't you give up, Rol'! The cavalry is on its way. You're gonna be just fine." Sam tried to sound calm and reassuring, but his voice wavered each time the old woman bucked. Her stench was unbearable at this proximity, and Sam was amazed by how much physical strength was in that frail looking body.

Lloyd rushed back into the room and opened a large package of gauze which he applied to Roland's neck. "They're still not answering in the E.R., or Security! I can't even get the operator to pick up!" He turned his attention back to his wounded co-worker. "Look at me Roland ... *look* at me!"

Roland had stopped kicking, and the gargling sound was becoming weak, barely audible. His eyes were beginning to glaze over.

"Sam, we don't have the supplies to deal with this! He's going to bleed out!"

"Then just *run* to the E.R.! Go get help! Grab any doctor you see and bring the crash cart!"

"Alright... you got that crazy bitch under control?"

"I got her, man. Go! Go!"

Lloyd took off down the hall, and it became eerily quiet in the room. Sam tightened his grip on the old woman's arms and looked up at Roland, who was lying motionless on the floor. There was an alarming amount of blood soaked into his scrubs, and a massive puddle on the floor.

"Roland? Roland?"

The filthy woman's head began to absently rear back, her blood stained teeth gnashing blindly into the air.

"Roland!"

There was no response, no movement.

The smell of this foul, sick body underneath him was beginning to become overwhelming. His stomach was turning and his mouth was watering. He knew he had to get fresh air soon or he would vomit.

Struggling to keep her pinned, Sam surveyed the room for something to restrain her, but there was nothing within reach. A roll of cloth medical tape was on the far side of the room, it would have to do.

He shifted his hips to get up onto his knees. Trying to lift the patient up with him as he stood, he suddenly felt the woman's brittle forearm bones snap in his hand. In reflex to that horrible feeling, Sam inadvertently loosened his grip, and the crazed woman began flailing her broken arm violently. Sam's stomach turned as he saw her splintered white bones pierce through her paper thin, brown skin. The old crone seemed totally unaffected by the trauma, and she lurched forward with her shattered arm extended. Sam stumbled as he back-peddled, vomiting a little in the back of his throat: stomach acid, coffee, and toast.

He threw a halfhearted kick at the advancing woman as he fell backwards through the door. Scrambling to his feet, he slammed the heavy door shut, trapping her in the scan room. The deranged woman limped over to the observation window and pressed her face against it,

18

clawing mindlessly at the glass.

Catching his breath, Sam looked in horror at the woman. Her mind was gone. Her eyes were vacant and milky white, her mouth and hospital gown were covered in Roland's blood. Her bony right hand banged incessantly on the glass in a jerky, robotic motion, while her broken forearm and left hand flailed about, hanging loosely from the compound fracture. It was painfully nauseating to watch.

Looking down and inspecting his ungloved hands, they were greased with the putrid smelling pus that came from the woman's bitten (and now broken) arm. He grabbed some foaming hand sanitizer and began scrubbing them vigorously.

For the next hour, Sam sat in shock listening to the deluge of desperate intercom announcements: doctors pleading for security personnel; codes GREY, BLUE, and ORANGE; a panicked operator reading a message to lock all doors and "remain where you are until further notice;" a pre-recorded message to disregard the fire alarm; a screaming woman who was begging for help.

Lloyd flew back into the control room, slamming the door behind him. His eyes were wide with panic and his shirt was torn and disheveled.

"Sam! There's a riot in the hospital! There are … *crazy* people attacking *everyone*! They look … sick! Like out of a horror movie! There was blood everywhere!"

"What?! What do you mean? Did you find any help?" Sam asked desperately.

"No! Security is *shooting* people! They said to go back to my department and lock the doors."

"Did you tell them we have someone dying in here?"

"Yeah! They didn't care. There are *lots* of people dying in the halls!" Lloyd looked down at his hand, "and one of the bastards bit me!"

Sam took a look at Lloyd's hand. There was a series of small puncture wounds in an arc across the heel of his right hand, a perfect dental impression.

"You need to clean that up, who knows what these people have." They dug up some alcohol and some fresh gauze.

Lloyd paused briefly, "Is Roland …?"

Sam shook his head in response, and then looked down at the floor. "He didn't make it."

19

"And that lady…?"

Sam pointed to the observation window, "She's locked in the scan room … She's out of her flippin' mind." They approached the window to get a better look. It was truly horrifying to look at her blood spattered face, wild hair, sunken cheeks, and dead, milky eyes.

"I'll be damned if she doesn't look like a freakin' *zombie!*" Sam said in joking disbelief.

"That's what they all looked like in the E.R., too." They stared silently for a moment longer, and then Lloyd spoke again, "Is Roland still in there?"

"Yeah," Sam replied quietly. "So, what was happening out there? How'd you get bitten?"

Lloyd sat down and let out a long sigh. His hands were shaking as he ran them through his hair. "People were running everywhere, some were bleeding. I got to the E.R. and Security had the hall barricaded with overturned stretchers. They were shooting at the people trapped inside, there must have been a hundred of them… they looked sick, like *that* lady…" he pointed to the gore smeared window, "… cataract eyes, moaning, grabbing at anyone within reach. And the *smell* …" Lloyd's head shook involuntarily, like he just took a shot of whiskey. "I yelled to Dave from Security that we had an employee down and needed help in MRI. He said to go back to the department and lock all doors; they would send help when it was safe. Then about five of those things came down the hall behind us. I socked the first one in the jaw, and tossed the next two over the barricade, but they just kept getting back up for more. I saw one of them take a dozen rounds to the chest and he just kept coming … he bit off Dave's thumb. When I tried to help, the bugger latched onto *my* hand! Then Dave blew its frickin' brains out …"

Lloyd had to stop to compose himself, his eyes were welling up and his hands would not stop shaking.

"It's alright, man. We'll just stay holed up here till they get this under control. No one can get through that door without a badge." He looked down at the phone and his eyes lit up. Snatching up the receiver he dialed 9-1-1.

No ringing … silence … then a recorded message, "All lines are busy. Please try your call again later. This is a recording. Message number one three eight."

20

Damn...

He reached into his briefcase and pulled out his cell phone, pressing 9-1-1.

"All lines are busy. Please try..." Click. He closed the phone then flipped it back open, dialing his wife's number. He was met with the same recording. Returning to the hospital phone, he picked up the receiver and dialed an internal extension number. The phone rang once and was picked up immediately.

"Hello?! This is the Lab! Hello?" Her voice sounded desperate.

"Hi, this is Sam from MRI, is Josh working today?" Josh was Sam's brother-in-law.

"Um... yes... hold on! Josh! It's someone from MRI!" There was some jostling of the phone, then: "Hello? Sammy?"

"Hey, bro! Are you guys OK down there?"

"Well, I guess so. There are a couple of crazies outside banging on the door. Have you seen Security?"

"It sounds like they're pinned down in the E.R. trying to quell a riot! We had a patient go crazy and attack my assistant. He's... dead. The psycho patient is still trapped in the magnet room."

"Well don't let her out, man! These people are sick, and probably contagious!"

"What do you mean, Josh? What do you know?"

Josh paused, "Well, the I.V. team called us to a patient's bedside this morning, which *never* happens. They were trying to start an I.V. on one of these... *crazies*... and couldn't find a vein. There was a doctor there from the Center for Disease Control who wanted a blood sample and was *adamant* that he needed it *now*. There was no time to send the patient to the O.R. to get a central line placed, so we ended up using a big 14 gauge needle to tap into an artery! The whole situation was highly irregular, but the CDC guy was breathing down our necks. We finally got access, but the patient's blood looked like thick sludge. We tried to run the sample, but it kept clotting, so I put some on a slide to view it in the microscope. It appeared to be infested with... some... I don't know... *pathogen*, or *parasite*. I've never seen anything like it. And then about an hour later we received some samples from the morgue. They wanted us to run some tests and prepare a sample for toxicology... but the supposedly 'dead' tissue

21

was still active, maybe even metabolic. It had the same parasitic activity we observed in that blood sample."

"Wow ..." Sam wasn't sure what that implied, but at least there was some medical explanation behind all of this. At least it ruled out his "living dead" theory ... or so he hoped. In all probability this was some sort of disease process, or parasite, or swine flu; something like that. "Just stay in the Lab, Josh. My co-worker said that the halls aren't safe. We're going to stay here on lock down until they get this thing sorted out."

"Oh, don't worry, we're not going anywhere. I don't think we could even if we wanted to. We'll be fine here for now. But hey, how's my sister?"

"Oh, she's doing well, man. The baby should be here any day now. I've been trying to call her but the lines are all tied up."

"Well, be careful. Just get home safe to her, you hear me?"

"Loud n' clear, bro. You be safe, too. And call me at this extension if you hear anything."

"Will do, Sammy."

They hung up the phones, and Sam updated Lloyd on what his brother-in-law said. There weren't many options. They would have to just sit tight and wait it out.

Day 1: Saturday, 1330 hrs

Several hours had passed with no more announcements and no sign of Security. They checked the phone lines every so often, but to no avail. Both men were in shock and found it hard to grasp the reality of their predicament. Their friend and co-worker lay dead in the next room over, and the hospital appeared to be under siege by a dangerous group of sick, psychotically ill patients.

The trapped woman's knocking persisted, unyielding. The window was now thoroughly smudged with a glaze of pus and thick, dark blood. The smudge would periodically be streaked by the old hag's face as she pressed it against the glass, trying to look through it.

"That's it, I've had enough of her!" Sam pulled a ream of paper out of the printer and began taping sheets of 8 ½ x 11 over the window. "I'm gonna need to eat soon, and I can't keep looking at … *that.*"

"Eat? You packed your lunch?" Lloyd asked hopefully.

"Peanut butter and jelly, you want half?"

"Thank god, I am starving!" Lloyd said, wincing as he pushed himself out of his chair.

"What is it, your hand?"

"Roger that. It hurts like bloody hell; I think it's getting infected."

Sam paused, looking very concerned. "Tell you what, let's clean it up again and re-dress it before we eat." And they did just that.

Lloyd's hand *did* look bad. It was swollen and red near the bite mark, and was weeping pus. It had a faint but ominous odor, very similar to the foul smelling woman on the other side of the door. Both men smelled it, but neither spoke of it aloud.

They washed up, and then ate in silence, lost in their own thoughts.

Unexpectedly, the slow, persistent banging on the glass window was interrupted by a loud "thunk" … followed by another …

The two men looked at each other, then at the window … thunk! … and then there was an intense, frantic banging from within, causing the glass to strain.

Lloyd's face was pale. "What the hell is she doing in there?"

Sam slowly got up and approached the glass, "She sounds

pissed about *something*." He reached up and carefully peeled off one sheet of the paper. Inching his face toward the window, he squinted to see through the gore tinted glass when …

BAM! A large black fist pounded heavily on the window!

"Lloyd! Roland is up! He's alive! We have to get him out!"

They jumped to their feet and scanned the room for something to use as a weapon. Sam took the fire extinguisher off the wall and brandished it in the air, instructing Lloyd, "You open the door so Roland can make a run for it, and if that lady tries anything I'll bash her in the face!"

Lloyd acknowledged with a nod and said, "Alright, on my count:

"One… two… three!"

The door swung open and Sam took a half step in. Roland and the old hag were standing by the observation window, and they both craned their heads in a puppet-like motion toward the open doorway. Roland looked like a living nightmare: the hole in his neck was enormous, and his tongue hung limply through the bloody opening. His dead, milky eyes locked onto Sam and he began staggering toward the door with bad intentions. He raised his arms and bubbles began gurgling from his throat as he tried in futility to make a sound. He looked like the walking dead.

"No … no … Something is not right with Roland! Close it! Quick!! Close it!!!" Sam babbled as he jumped back and Lloyd secured the door. "He has it, too! He's infected! He's sick!" Sam was talking so fast that Lloyd could barely make out his words.

"Wait, are you sure? He was up on his feet, right?" Lloyd had not seen into the room.

"Yes … but … it wasn't *him*! He looked like … one of *them*!" Sam couldn't catch his breath.

Lloyd said slowly, in a level tone, "Sam, are you *positive*? Because if not, we can't leave him in there."

There was no hesitation in Sam's response, "Yes! I am sure! He looked like a damned ZOMBIE!" The beating on the window returned with renewed vigor, and several cracks began to form. Sam reached for the phone and dialed the lab, but there was no answer. Suddenly glass shards burst from the window and Roland's swollen, bloody hands reached through the opening. It appeared that he had broken several knuckles while pummeling the heavy glass. Large

24

sections of the window fell away and the old woman began crawling through the jagged opening.

Sam dropped the phone and rummaged through his briefcase, "Grab whatever you need, Lloyd! It's time to go!"

Cell phone ... wallet ... car keys ... my book ...

The two men darted out of the door and into the Radiology lobby. It appeared deserted. The receptionist was gone, and the T.V. was blaring loud static. Advancing slowly, they peered through the next set of doors that led into the main corridor. Down the hall there were two bodies lying on the tile floor, but no movement. They could hear distant cries for help and agonizing screams echoing through the sterile looking hallway.

"Let's go for the employee entrance, it's closest," Sam suggested.

"No," Lloyd whispered, "the stairwell up ahead, by the elevators, it has a doorway that leads to the parking lot." With his decades of service, Lloyd was far more familiar with the hospital layout.

"Sounds great, you lead!" and the two were off; swiftly, silently.

They approached the first intersection of hallways and could hear screams in all directions. To the left they could see a dozen people fighting in the hallway. With all the blood it was hard to discern who was infected and who was not. To the right they could see the east elevators and the entrance to the stairwell. They turned right and ran hard for the stairs, slowing their pace as they got closer, then stopping cold in their tracks as they heard several pounding fists on the other side of the door. Slow, methodical pounding. *Lots* of pounding.

The men froze.

Lloyd's voice wavered as he said, "Plan B: we'll use the employee entrance."

The sound of shuffling feet behind them sent their hearts racing and the cornered pair turned to see three elderly women in hospital gowns lunging at them! Arms extended, bony hands reaching, covered in blood ...

Sam raised his fists and roared, "STOP! DON'T COME ANY

CLOSER!"

The women cowered and screamed with fright. His eyes darted from woman to woman, re-assessing these elderly patients. He could see their eyes were panicked but clear, no sign of the sickness.

With his guard still raised, he asked, "Who are you? Are you OK?"

Lloyd grabbed Sam's shoulder and pointed down the hall at the ongoing melee. Their screams had attracted the attention of four hideous looking individuals who were now limping toward them. There was no mistaking the sickness in their eyes. They looked desperate, starving ... *undead.*

It was too late to back track, for the advancing ghouls had already passed the intersecting hallway, and the door at their backs shook with the pounding of unknown assailants. There was no good option.

"Lloyd! The east elevator!"

There was only one button, with an arrow pointing up, and Lloyd began pumping the button furiously. The three women huddled around him, looking like frightened, caged animals, screaming incoherently. They could hear the elevator whirring, and the clack-clack-clack of the "Up" button being thoroughly worked over. The slow, plodding pace of the advancing attackers made the wait for the elevator seem torturously long.

Waiting ...

Hearts pounding ...

Palms sweating ...

Women screaming ...

Then ~DING~ the doors slowly opened and the group piled into the elevator car. Lloyd dove for the control panel, literally climbing over one of the women to slap at the buttons, and inadvertently lighting up several different floors before he zeroed in on the "Close Door" button. He worked the button over meticulously.

Clack-clack-clack-clack-clack-clack-clack...

Just as the stench of the attackers assaulted their senses, the elevator doors casually slid closed and the car began to move.

Catching his breath, Sam asked the women if they were OK.

"*We're* fine," one said, pointing to the other African American woman, "but *this* lady needs help!" She pointed to an elderly Greek looking woman who was leaning heavily on her I.V. pole. Detroit has

26

an historic Greektown, which has steadily been on the decline, but remains one of the few neighborhoods with any real commerce or bustle. However, most of the Greek immigrants and their descendants have moved to the suburbs, and the remaining Greek restaurants are now mostly staffed by Hispanic immigrants and local African Americans.

Sam was perplexed; he looked at the Greek woman, then at the other two. All three patients were completely covered in blood, gowns soaked.

"Wait a sec, *you two* are fine? Then where did all this blood come from?"

Pointing at the Greek woman, she answered, "It's hers! She was gettin' attacked by some maniac, and the nurses just ran! So we pulled that S.O.B. off and tussled with him …" Her words tapered off as the elevator slowed. Muffled screams could be heard through the heavy doors.

~DING~

The doors opened and a screaming nurse fell into the elevator car! There was a large, nude, elderly man tearing and biting into her legs with his false teeth. Her scrub pants were torn to ribbons and her exposed legs were covered with savage wounds.

Sam reared back and kicked the man in the head, over and over, as Lloyd went to work on the "Close Door" button.

Clack-clack-clack-clack-clack-clack …

It was unbearable listening to the poor girl scream, her legs looked beyond repair. Sam was kicking hard but gaining no ground; the man seemed oblivious to his blows. His bloated, pale body looked cyanotic blue, and his face had the same vacant look of death that Roland had.

The doors tried to glide closed twice, then re-opened each time as it met the resistance of the two bodies lying in its path. Then ~whoosh~ the nurse was pulled back into the hallway and the doors slid closed.

The elevator gently lurched, and then continued its upward course.

The group was in stunned silence … panting … glancing around at one another … speechless. They were all in disbelief. The elevator slowed to a stop as it reached the next floor, and the group braced themselves, minds racing as they prepared for what horror

27

awaited them at this next stop.

~DING~

The doors slid open and a security guard stood there with his gun drawn on the elevator, his eyes wide and filled with fear. Behind him were several nurses, huddled like frightened sheep.

"FREEZE! DON'T MOVE!" The guard's voice sounded young and unsure. His uniform was disheveled and his face dripped with sweat.

Sam spoke up first, showing his opened hands, "It's OK! We're not sick! But we need help!"

The young guard looked around at the blood splattered group before him, hands shaking. "S-s-stay where you are! ... Have any of you been bitten?" He tried to sound authoritative.

"Yes!" our older spokeswoman said, again pointing to the desperately wounded woman, "She needs help!"

The young man's eyes hardened as he drew a bead on the bleeding woman's head and fired! The sound was deafening in the elevator, and time stood still.

Sam's ears were ringing. The metallic smell of blood and cordite mingled in the air, and he turned to see the old Greek woman's lifeless body fall to the ground. Her head was no longer intact, but was in globs of bone and tissue dripping from the back wall.

Time and sound returned abruptly as the guard yelled repeatedly, "IS ANYONE ELSE BITTEN?! IS ANYONE ELSE BITTEN?!"

The elevator's occupants all yelled in chorus, "NO!" as the doors slid closed. The elevator calmly resumed its upward climb as the two remaining patients began screaming hysterically. The two men looked at each other, and then down at Lloyd's bandaged hand. Lloyd reached down and hit the elevator "Stop" button, and the lift jerked to an abrupt halt.

The two hospital workers tried to calm the screaming women, but they were inconsolable. Sam adjusted the dead woman's gown to cover the few remaining bits of head still attached to her neck. The men tried to converse about their plan of action, but it was nearly impossible over the wailing and calls for "Jesus" coming from the distraught patients.

"What now?" Lloyd asked.

"Well ... I'm in no hurry to find out what's behind door

28

number three… I say we stay right here and wait it out." Sam flipped open his cell phone and said, "No signal," then slid to the floor and held his head in his hands.

Day 1: Saturday, 2030 hrs

The hours ticked by slowly in the cramped and blood stained elevator. The air was hot and stale, and Sam was beginning to suspect that *someone* was having bladder control issues. By now the women's cries had slowly melted into whimpering sobs. Lloyd had fallen asleep but awoke with a start, as if having a nightmare.

"Are you alright?" Sam asked him.

"Pshhh, not really. My hand is killing me and I feel like I have a damn hangover." Lloyd paused, obviously in deep thought, and then asked, "Do you think I'm infected, too?"

This caught the attention of the more vocal patient. "Wait, what do you mean? Are you sick, too?" Then she looked at Sam while pointing her ancient, arthritic finger at Lloyd, "Is he sick, too?! He ain't gonna turn into no zombie, is he?!"

The word "zombie" caught Sam off guard a little, and he chuckled to himself, saying, "No, ma'am. I can assure you that nobody is going to turn into a 'zombie'." His calm tone did little to reassure the woman.

"You better look around you, boy! This ain't no joke! Them people out there are *zombies*! And if *that* white boy is going to turn into one, *we* need to know!" Again with the pointing.

Lloyd looked at Sam nervously, hoping he would say something reassuring, enlightening … something to give him hope.

He thought for a moment, almost spoke, and then thought some more.

"Ma'am, something very serious is going on out there. A plague … rabies … a virus … I don't know; something horrible. But what I *do* know is that there is no such thing as zombies, or werewolves, or Santa Claus, or unicorns … these people are just sick … and dangerous. One of them bit Lloyd's hand today and it's getting infected …" everyone turned their head toward Lloyd, "… but that doesn't mean he's going to turn into one of them. We just don't know. We don't know what is happening and we don't know how it's spreading. If it's in the air, or in the water, we may already be infected. *All* of us."

"Well I don't want that man in here. That's all there is to it!" She crossed her arms defiantly and held her chin high.

Sam sighed with frustration, "I know, ma'am, I understand …"

The group paused for a moment and listened as several muffled gunshots fired from somewhere within the hospital campus.

Sam looked up at the emergency escape hatch on the roof of the elevator, then at Lloyd. "We really do need to find out what's going on out there. It's been several hours and the shooting hasn't slowed down a bit. I don't think we're gonna be able to wait this thing out in an elevator; it could be *days* before they get this under control. Do you think you can climb?"

Lloyd rubbed his hand, "I sure as hell will if I have to."

"Alrighty then," Sam turned to the two women, "Lloyd and I are going to climb up the elevator shaft and look for help. If we don't make it back in two hours … we probably *won't* be coming back. You'll have to continue on your own. We've already stopped at the 3rd and 4th floors, which were obviously not safe. I would try the 6th floor, pediatrics. They usually do a real good job at keeping that floor on lockdown, so no one can just walk out with someone else's kid. Our best chance for safety is probably there. Do you ladies think you'll be OK for a few hours here?"

The women looked down at the dead body on the floor. This was a bad situation, but again, there were very few options.

"Yes. We'll be alright."

"Okay. But if we aren't back in two or three hours, DO NOT wait for us. Either something bad has happened to us, or we just can't safely make it back."

The women nodded but said nothing.

"Alright Lloyd, let's do this."

Sam tucked his paperback book into his waistband and stepped onto the handrail to reach the top hatch. It wouldn't budge. There was no handle, no key hole, no visible screws or fasteners, just a ¼ inch gap tracing the outline of the hatch.

"How do they expect people to escape an elevator if they seal the escape door closed?" he asked in frustration.

Lloyd offered up an explanation, "I saw an interview with the guy who was locked in an elevator for 41 hours. Apparently the door is for emergency personnel to get *in*, not for the occupants to get *out*."

"Really? Hmmmm …. We'll see about that; hand me that I.V. pole."

Progress was slow and difficult, but after a half hour of

banging and prying, the loud sound of snapping metal announced that the door had been freed of its fasteners.

The bent hatch lifted easily, exposing the dark shaft that lead to the roof. There was a single incandescent bulb illuminating the top of the shaft, only two or three stories above them.

"I've always wanted to climb through one of these," Sam said as he pulled himself up through the opening. Sam has been an amateur rock climber for several years. He climbs at a local indoor climbing gym twice a month, and has climbed on the roof of every house he ever lived in, every school he attended, some local water towers, and most places of employment he worked at. This would be his first trip to the roof of the hospital, seven stories up.

He reached back into the elevator to lend Lloyd a hand, who was looking pale and feverish. Once on the roof of the elevator, they stood there for a few moments to allow their eyes to adjust. There was a service ladder leading up the shaft, so up they went.

Pausing at each set of doors along the way, they could hear screams coming from every floor, including pediatrics. It appeared that the entire hospital had been overrun. Every so often a volley of gunfire would echo up the shaft from some unseen drama taking place below.

Reaching the top of the ladder they stepped onto a small metal platform. Once aboard the platform, Lloyd paused and got down on one knee. After trying to suppress a few raspy coughs, he began to dry heave.

"Are you alright, man?" Sam asked.

"… Just give me a second to pull it together … this thing is kicking my butt… it feels like the damned stomach flu …" Lloyd was struggling with each word. Eventually his stomach heaved and the peanut butter and jelly sandwich made an appearance, which in turn brought a little color back to his pale face. Lloyd returned to his feet, shook off the whole episode and asked, "Alright, twinkle toes, what are you waiting for?"

Sam laughed, "Oh, nothing, man. Sorry I was holding you up."

They followed the platform to a flimsy, hollow core door, far too thin to be an access door to the roof. Creeping up closer, Sam pressed an ear against the door. There was a faint hum that sounded like a motor, but nothing else. Testing the handle, he found it to be locked. After a brief, whispered discussion, they formulated a plan:

32

(1) kick in the door, (2) charge in like gangbusters, (3) be ready for a fight.

They both took a step back, and then Sam gave a hard, stomping front kick to the door. His foot passed straight through the thin wood, *up to his knee*, but the door didn't budge! He panicked and thrashed about chaotically, trying to pull his foot out, all the while envisioning diseased teeth biting into his shoe.

He finally freed his foot, and then felt a little embarrassed by how silly he probably looked struggling with the door. Upon further inspection, they quickly realized that the door opened *toward* them, not away. There was no way they could kick it open from this side. Oops.

Lloyd cautiously looked through the busted opening and could see a dingy engineering room with faint, natural sunlight illuminating the room via skylight. He could tell by the purple-orange hue that the sun was setting. He saw no movement and heard no sounds save that of the humming motor.

"Well … it looks clear but I can't see the whole room. I can see the roof top access straight ahead … and it looks like there are two open doorways to the right." Lloyd reached through the crude hole and tested the doorknob. "Crap ... It feels like it's locked with a key."

"And you don't see anybody in there?"

Lloyd looked back through the hole and gave a loud, shrill whistle that broke the silence, startling them both. After looking and listening for a few more moments, he said, "No, I think we're all clear."

"OK, then. Stand back, I'm going to kick this hole a little bigger so we can slip through."

Sam took a few steps back and did a few simple stretches to limber up his legs, then charged forward with another heavy front kick. The door split nearly in two with a large, jagged crack, yet it remained intact. He wound up for his next kick, and just as his foot met the wood, a large black man crashed through the door! His bulk absorbed both the kick and the splintering door as he fell forward onto Sam.

The two men rolled backward as Sam struggled to push the man's face away. His eyes were crazed and he reeked of death. They rolled dangerously close to the edge as the large man, apparently a maintenance worker, tried repeatedly to bite at Sam's hands and face.

Lloyd ran up to them and grabbed the big man by the scruff of his grey overalls, hoisting him up high and socking him in the jaw. The big man stumbled backwards with arms flailing wildly as he tumbled and fell over the ledge! Seconds later they heard the nauseating thud of dead weight striking hard metal, as it echoed up the elevator shaft.

Looking down the shaft they could see the man's right leg and back were contorted into crumpled, unnatural positions, obviously broken. Then to their surprise and horror the broken man began to move, writhing about on the roof of the elevator car. The elevator occupants began shrieking in terror as the man pulled himself to the opening and ungracefully flopped into the suspended car!

"Oh God, no ..." Lloyd said under his breath.

The screaming intensified and they could hear the women struggle with the infected man! Lloyd and Sam jumped back when they heard the elevator motor engage, and the car began traveling down, down the shaft, all the way to the ground floor. The motor powering the elevator stopped, and a faint ~DING~ echoed up the shaft as the doors opened and the screams abruptly faded.

After a few moments of silence, Sam spoke first, "I hope they got out of there ... without getting bitten."

Lloyd looked distraught. "I didn't mean to knock him down the shaft ... I didn't intend to ... dear God, those poor ladies."

"I know man, I know ... but you saved my butt. Thanks. I just don't understand how that guy kept moving after that fall! His back *had* to be broken in *several* places. He should have been paralyzed, or dead!"

Lloyd looked down at his bandaged hand, and then said soberly, "Do you think I'm going to turn into one of *them*?"

"I honestly don't know, man ... I hope not. How do you feel?"

Lloyd sighed deeply, "Like crap: headache, nausea, I'm febrile ... my hand is burning like hell. Do you think... do you think those people can be cured?"

Sam smiled and suggested jokingly, "A stake to the heart? Garlic?"

Lloyd chuckled, "No, man, that's for *vampires,* these are *zombies*."

"Oh yeah, I forgot, *zombies* ... a bullet to the brain, right?"

"Works every time, mate," Lloyd grinned with a wink.

34

"Alrighty then: a bullet it is. Let's go find you some medicine." Both men forced a half-hearted laugh. "Wow does this day suck. But seriously, we have to get out of here. Let's go check out the roof, maybe there's a fire escape."

Day 1: Saturday, 2115 hrs

Turning a deadbolt, they stepped out onto the hospital roof. The sun was setting and there were several thin columns of black smoke streaking up from throughout the surrounding neighborhood. It smelled like burning rubber.

"House fires?" Sam asked rhetorically.

Police sirens could be heard in all directions, as well as gunfire, both single shot and fully automatic. It sounded like a war zone. But more ominously, a chilling, human sound was also being carried along in the wind: moans, emanating from the infected people below. The voices sounded tortured and mindless.

Stepping closer to the edge, they could see that their circumstances were dire. Hundreds of infected people were congregating around the hospital entrances, and there were several unfortunate people struggling in mortal combat with large groups of attackers. They were being completely overwhelmed by the rabid mob, and it appeared as if those who fell were being eaten alive. Their screams could be heard seven stories up on the roof. The scene was surreal.

"We've got to get away from here," Sam said. "How far do you think this has spread?"

"It looks bad as far as the eye can see." Pointing to the western horizon, Lloyd said, "Those smoke contrails are near the Ambassador Bridge to Canada, which is probably ten miles away."

"That doesn't bode well for my commute. I've got over *fifty* miles of real estate to cover. I just hope this hasn't reached home, yet. Where did you park?"

"Over in the parking structure. You?"

Squinting, Sam scanned the parking lot for his car. "I'm in the employee parking lot ... right there." He pointed to his red Subaru wagon. There were a few suspicious characters standing about the parking lot, slowly swaying, oblivious to the mayhem around them. They were obviously infected.

Pacing the roof's perimeter, they found no external fire escapes, no service ladder, no easy route of egress. They did find three doorways leading back into the hospital, but they were heavy steel doors, and all were locked from the inside. Aside from returning to

36

the elevator shaft, the only other possibility of escape was several runs of 3" conduit pipe that ran down the length of the building. The prospect of climbing down one of these pipes was terrifying, and they agreed that it would be a last resort.

Hoping for a safer route, they circled the roof once more, pausing to witness the unfolding drama below. Periodically, they would watch as someone would try to escape the hospital and make a run for it, only to be dragged down and ripped apart by the slow moving throng. There was nothing that could be done to help them.

"These ... 'things' don't seem to be very fast, nor do they seem too bright," Sam said. "I haven't seen one of them run yet, or even move faster than a walking pace. They seem to just stumble forward like they're drunk."

Near the main entrance, they watched as a group of the poor bastards tripped on a short set of steps, one after another, falling face first before they fumbled on their hands and knees up the remaining steps. It was only a string of three steps, but none of them seemed to have the coordination to navigate them without spilling comically once or twice.

"These guys are chumps," Sam said, "I bet we could easily outrun them, or out maneuver them."

"*Right* ... like Barry Sanders?" Lloyd balked.

"No, I'm serious! Watch them! I bet I could speed walk circles around these jokers."

Stopping above the Emergency Room entrance, they observed this hell in silence; all joking had stopped. On this side of the building there must have been a thousand "zombies." The sheer number of bodies was reminiscent of a concert, or a violent protest. Many just loitered in place, swaying and empty eyed, while others stomped forward aggressively, looking agitated and enraged. However, most of them appeared to be herding together like cattle, migrating toward any uninfected person they saw, moaning, arms raised, looking like starving, sunken-eyed refugees. It was terrifying, and the two men felt hopelessly trapped.

The sound of an opening door caused the men to turn abruptly, ready for a fight. They saw a group of hospital workers cautiously stepping out onto the roof from one of the previously locked doors. It appeared to be a few nurses and another man from maintenance. Lloyd and Sam ran over to greet them.

The group was startled to see them approach.

"Hold it right there! Are either of you two … injured?" one of the nurses asked hesitantly.

This caused the guys to stop in their tracks, remembering what happened the last time that question was put to them.

Lloyd slowly raised his bandaged hand saying, "I'm okay. One of those bastards bit me on the hand, but so far I'm okay."

The women looked at each other nervously as the maintenance man stepped forward, brandishing a bloody hammer, but he was stopped short by one of the nurses.

"Lloyd? Is that you?" she asked.

It was 'The Braid'.

'The Braid' was a nurse of legendary beauty. She worked on the 7th floor in the ICU (Intensive Care Unit), and the guys would often make a detour to pass by her nursing station with hopes of catching a glimpse of this girl with the face of an angel. She wore her long brown hair in a thick braid that reached her rear, hence the nick name.

"At your service," Lloyd replied with a graceful bow and a sharp nod. His suave gesture relaxed the women, and they all gathered around to inspect Lloyd's hand. He glanced over at Sam and gave a sly wink, appreciating the attention of these young ladies.

The two groups exchanged stories.

Apparently, several bite victims were brought to the ICU when their vital signs began to deteriorate. The first one rose from his bed around noon and began attacking the staff, injuring several before they could restrain him. Hours later, those who were injured became infected and killed the only two ICU doctors on duty before the maintenance man, Andy, bludgeoned them to death with a hammer. It was at that point that the charge nurse ordered all patients to be restrained in their beds, several of whom had now succumbed to the infection. They had not heard from Security since noon, and had been unable to reach anyone by phone. So, after hours of waiting for help to arrive, they decided to send a small group to check the roof for a way out.

The sun had now fully set, and the besieged group circled the roof together, confirming that there was no easy way down. The hospital's main building was a beautiful old structure that was designed long before helicopters existed, so there was no suitable landing pad, no hope for a medevac flight. After walking the perimeter and seeing how many of the undead had surrounded the hospital, the women were visibly shaken.

The maintenance man, Andy, spoke up, "We're wasting our time up here. There's no way we'll be able to leave. What we need to do is get back inside and barricade the doors until the police arrive." They all agreed. Escape seemed hopeless; they would have to hunker down and wait for help.

Approaching the entrance that led back down into the building, horrific moans could be heard from the open doorway. Lloyd put his hand out, halting the group.

"Don't worry," Andy said, "There's a bunch of them at the bottom of the stairwell, but they haven't tried to come up the stairs ... yet. Earlier it sounded like they had someone cornered down there." He paused for a moment, his face looked pained. "Whoever it was ... they stopped screaming for help a couple hours ago. But I think they're still distracted by something, they've been going berserk down there."

Entering the stairwell, they descended to the first landing and Sam leaned over the railing to peer down the shaft. Indeed, dozens of zombies were crowded together at the bottom of the stairway. They sounded more agitated than some of the others, and were banging on the doors and moaning loudly. The acoustics provided an unsettling effect to the sounds that echoed from below. Hurrying along quietly, they opened the door marked with a large red "7".

Stepping into the brightly lit ICU, the nurses pulled Lloyd aside and went to work cleaning his wound properly. The charge nurse, Yvonne, came over to greet them. After seeing Lloyd's injury and his morbid complexion, she stated very matter-of-factly that we would have to put Lloyd in Velcro restraints in the likely event that the infection overtook him. Sam's heart sank upon hearing this, but Lloyd took it like a champ.

"I've got no problem with that, Yvonne. To be honest, I really need to sit down before I fall out. Just park me by the T.V., and keep my nurse here with me in case I need to be released to make a run for it," he said, grinning and pointing hopefully to The Braid.

Yvonne grinned back knowingly, "I can't spare my best nurse right now, Lloyd, she has *real* patients to attend to. However, *Ruby* is free, so I'll have her keep you company."

Lloyd's hopeful grin came crashing down when a short, beastly woman stepped forward, sporting a hopeful smile of her own. It was very apparent that she suffered from some sort of thyroid condition, or maybe she had just let herself go. Regardless, she led the heart broken man over to the employee lounge and strapped him into a wheelchair.

Sam stayed at the nurse's station, trying to find out what he could. Andy was giving Yvonne an update regarding the stairway and roof.

"Well, there is no way to get down from the roof, and even if we *could* get down, the building is surrounded by hundreds of those heffers. *Thousands*, even. It's a LOT worse out there than we thought; I think we're stuck here for the duration. And the ones in the stairway are still there … but I didn't hear that guy screaming for help anymore."

Sam cut in, "Yvonne, do you have any idea what on earth is happening?"

"Only what they've been saying on the news. This whole outbreak seems to be centered in Detroit, but a few other cities are starting to report incidences of assault and cannibalism …"

"Cannibalism?" Sam interrupted.

"… yes, maybe you haven't noticed but there are several hundred people surrounding the hospital who are trying to *eat* us; that's called *cannibalism*."

The Braid leaned toward Sam and apologized for Yvonne's sarcasm, "Don't take offense, she's always like this."

Yvonne looked briefly appalled, then smiled at the young woman's gall, countering, "Do you not have patients that need tending to, young lady?"

The Braid saluted, turned smartly, and sauntered away, her lovely braid swaying as she walked. Sam's eyes glazed over.

Wow… that girl sure knows how to fill out a pair of scrubs …

"Snap out of it," Yvonne said, returning the smitten man to earth.

"Oh … uh … sorry. Where were we? Cannibalism?" Sam blushed.

"Cannibalism. The infected people are eating their victims.

40

Some people are saying it's a mutation of the Avian flu, some are calling it Zombification, and some religious zealots are calling it the End of Days. All I know is that we are trapped here until help arrives, with a highly contagious disease running rampant around us."

"Where are you hearing all this information?"

Yvonne smiled at the young man, "There is this new invention, maybe you've heard of it, it's called 'television.' And on this 'television', they have programs, one of which is called 'the news.' We happen to have one of these televisions in the lounge."

Sam smiled back at her, appreciating her Quinton Tarantino reference. "I like you, Yvonne. *You* are going to make it out of this whole thing in one piece." Yvonne truly was a force of nature, large and in charge. "I'm going to go check on Lloyd and get my news fix. Let me know if there's anything I can do to help."

"Alright, but let me be honest with you, your friend's prognosis is not good. Everyone who has been bitten has succumbed to the infection within hours. *Everyone.* If your friend takes a turn for the worse, you need to come get myself or Andy."

Those words hit home. In the back of his mind Sam knew that Lloyd was probably infected, but to hear it spoken so freely made it seem real. His friend would soon be dead.

Seeing Sam's face, Yvonne added, "Let's not think about all that right now, we can't afford to let ourselves get distracted. Just take each moment one at a time. Focus on getting through this with your butt intact. There will be time to mourn later."

"Yes, ma'am. I'll let you know if he takes a turn for the worse."

Walking down the hall, Sam was lost in his thoughts. The now familiar moaning sound could be heard from several of the patients' rooms. The doors to those rooms were shut, with hand written notes taped up stating: Infected Patient - DO NOT ENTER.

The Lounge was crowded. It was a small room with vending machines, a kitchenette, a long table, and several chairs. It was standing room only as there were several people gathered around, their attention glued to the T.V. mounted on the wall. The local news anchorman, Ray Wallace, was in studio, dishing it out fair and balanced:

"… Detroiters are being asked to stay home and to remain indoors. The Auto Show Riot has not yet been contained, and there have been wild reports and accusations from throughout the city of assaults and *cannibalism* (the dapper man shook his head and chuckled in disbelief). Channel 4's own Piper Simmons is on the scene LIVE from Joe Louis Arena, where police have established a 'Green Zone' to base their operations. Piper?"

"Thank you, Ray. The Eastern Market district is *in flames,* and Fire Department officials are saying they are unable to reach the areas in need due to rioting. Several firemen and First Responders have reported that they have been attacked by the very people they are trying to save. We are expecting Police Commissioner Deon Kelly to make a formal statement within the hour. In the meantime we caught up with a local man who said that rioters *broke into his home* and assaulted several members of his family. He escaped by climbing through a bedroom window and is here to tell his story."

She extended her microphone to a young black man in a red bandana, who grabbed the microphone and said, "Well, *obviously* we have some danged *maniacs* out here, in *Detroit,* dey climbin' in your windows, dey snatchin' your people up, so ya'll need to n..." the interview was interrupted as an older man grabbed the microphone with both hands and blurted, "Dis ain't no riot, dis is a Gawd-damned zombie hi-pocalypse! These people ain't sick or crazy, dey's DEAD!" he crossed himself before continuing, "I can tell you right *NOW*, dat man was *dead*, ya see? I saw him *die*, ya see? Sure as Jesus. Only to

42

rise up an ..." he crossed himself again and backed away from the camera. The younger man snatched the microphone back and addressed the chipper blonde reporter, "So you can run an' tell *THAT*, homeboy." He then dropped the mike and crossed his arms high on his chest, cocking his head sideways and nodding like a gangster.

Without batting a lash, Piper looked back at the camera saying, "You heard it here first, Ray. Back to you!"

In the Lounge, the group collectively sighed and shook their heads, one of the nurses saying what they were all thinking. "Why is it that when reporters go downtown, they find the most *ignorant* man standing to put in front of a camera and represent the city of Detroit?"

Yvonne came into the lounge, panning the room with a stern look. "Alright ladies, we have patients that need monitoring. Let's just leave Lloyd and Ruby in here to keep us current with the news updates. Sam, I want you to go with Andy and make sure this floor is secure, he mentioned trying to block the elevator and stairwell."

"Alright, Yvonne. I'm on it."

Sam found Andy over by the west elevator; he was stacking several boxes of printer paper in the open elevator's doorway to prevent it from closing.

"Hey, Andy. Yvonne asked me to give you a hand."

"Sure, grab some of those boxes. If we can keep these doors from closing, the elevator will stay stuck on this floor so we don't get any more surprises."

"Surprises?" Sam asked.

"Yeah, an hour or two ago a wounded doctor came up, bringing three infected patients with her. They spilled out of the elevator fighting, and two more of our people were bitten before we could put the bastards down."

"What happened to the doctor? And the other people who were bitten?"

Andy stopped for a moment, and gave Sam a cold, hard stare, and then returned to stacking the boxes.

Andy was a tough looking character in his mid 40's, square jawed and broad shouldered. His grey overalls were splattered with blood, as was the hammer hanging from his tool belt. Sam was glad they were on the same team.

"What about the east elevator? Did you secure it also?"

"No. The east elevator's been on the ground floor for the past hour. I pressed the button earlier to try to summon it, but it hasn't budged. Something's probably propping those doors open also, or maybe someone hit the 'Stop' button."

"Speaking of that," Sam said as he leaned into the elevator and pressed the "Stop" button, "That should help."

Andy glared at him, "Oh. A smart guy, huh?"

Sam shrugged innocently, and then related his story of the three women in the elevator car, and of the maintenance man who fell down the shaft and attacked them.

Andy thought for a moment, saying, "That sounds like Bill, the Maintenance Supervisor," and then continued dismissively, "but that's alright, he had it coming. I guess what we need to worry about is the possibility that it's a dead or injured person lying in the elevator doorway down there. If they happen to rise from the infection, the doors will close and the elevator is going to be on its way *here* since I pushed the button. Hopefully it will be empty when it arrives."

Having secured the west elevator, the pair moved on to the other point of egress: the stairway. Opening its door unleashed the echoed moans emanating from below, causing the hair on the back of their necks to rise. This was not fun.

Andy gave a serious look and said, "I want to sneak a few flights down to see how many of them we're dealing with, and to see how close they are. Do you have a weapon?"

Sam patted himself down and produced his worn paperback copy of *Marine Sniper*, holding it up proudly.

Andy gave him a deadpan look. "I'll take that as a 'no.' So here, take my Maglite. It's not much, but just aim for the head, and don't stop swinging until you see brains." He was serious.

Sam took the heavy flashlight and gave it a few practice swings. Andy was correct: it wasn't much, but it would have to do. This was going to be down and dirty. "Alright, man. But the plan is *recon*, right? We aren't looking for a fight."

"That's right, don't let any of those suckers hear or see you."

They slowly crept into the stairwell and looked down the shaft. There did not appear to be any zombies on the next few landings, but the view beyond that point was blocked by the winding staircase. Far

44

below, on the ground floor, dozens of them could be seen moving about.

Sam grabbed Andy's shoulder, whispering, "Wait a sec, *why* do we need to go down there? To *count* them?"

Andy flashed an impatient scowl. "Not an exact count, just a rough idea of how many are down there. But more importantly, we need to see if any of them are wandering up the stairs… getting closer. Now keep quiet."

Descending the stairs, they approached the door labeled "6" and pressed their ears against it. It was impossible to hear anything over the echoing voices from below.

"I can't hear a thing in there. Should we take a peek inside?" Sam whispered.

"Hell no! Now keep quiet!" Andy hissed.

They listened closely for a few more moments, and then continued down.

Past door "5"…

Past door "4"…

The chorus of moans was deafeningly loud now. Crouched like tigers and moving as slowly and quietly as they could, they paused upon reaching the 3rd floor. There were a dozen zombies on the 2nd floor landing, and several more than that on the 1st. They were all reaching upward, clawing at the air beneath the landing where Sam and Andy were now perched. The two men went prone to avoid being seen, and it was then that Sam noticed a leather strap tied around the hand rail and draped down off the edge. Inching forward to investigate, he made eye contact with a man who was suspended in the air just beneath them! The man looked emotionally beaten and exhausted, but his eyes lit up and he began screaming in a hoarse voice, "THANK GOD! HELP ME! THEY'RE TRYING TO KILL ME! HELP!" Somehow the man had managed to climb over the railing and use his belt to secure himself up and out of the reach of these things, like a carrot dangling by a string.

"Shhhhhhh!" Andy tried to warn the man to remain silent, but it was no use. The desperate man was panic stricken and delirious. He would not stop pleading for help.

"PLEASE HELP ME! THEY KILLED MY WIFE! YOU GOT TO HELP ME!"

"Be quiet, dammit! You're going to blow our cover!" Andy

45

scolded in a coarse whisper.

"YOU GOT TO HELP ME GET DOWN! I HAVE MONEY! I WILL PAY YOU!"

The infected victims on the second landing apparently got wise to the conversation and began stumbling up the stairs. In seconds both Sam and Andy were spotted and the enraged zombies began to scramble on all fours, banging their way up the hard tiled stairs with a purpose. Andy stood up and tried pulling on the leather belt, but before he could make any headway the first of the angry creatures cleared the top step and was lunging forward.

"RUN!" was all Andy said, and he took off up the stairs clearing three steps with each stride. With thighs burning, both men flew up the stairs and were at the 7th floor before they even knew it. They stopped to catch their breath and look down the shaft at their pursuers. The entire horde was slowly giving chase, but was several floors behind them. They hadn't noticed previously, but the suspended man's belt and leg were visible from here. He continued screaming for help in a hoarse, psychotic voice, and was thrashing about. Nothing could be done for him, so the men bolted back into the ICU.

Andy barked commands at the few nurses that were nearby, "Listen up! We have to block the stairwell! They're coming! Help me grab anything large to throw down the stairs!"

A bucket brigade of terrified nurses was hastily formed from the hallway to the door, and the group began throwing anything and everything to dam up the staircase that led downward to the approaching ghouls. Office chairs, mattresses, gurneys, trash cans, wheel chairs, computer monitors and file cabinets. Even after the passage was filled from steps to ceiling, they continued to throw everything they could find: blankets, sheets, medical supplies and anything else that was within reach.

The tangled barrier was truly formidable, and it took a full 15 minutes for the horde to reach it, confirming Sam's theory that these infected people had difficulty navigating stairs. However, what they lacked in agility was compensated for by a single minded persistence. Upon reaching the barrier, they became enraged at the obstacle and began to tear away at it blindly, pulling, pushing, hitting, and haphazardly knocking loose items down the stairwell. This makeshift barrier would not hold indefinitely.

Yvonne stepped into the stairwell to check on the progress, and her face went pale when she saw the nightmare that was ascending toward them. The top three flights of stairs were overflowing with pursuers, who were now close enough to be seen clearly. All bore horrific wounds, mostly bite marks on their faces, necks and arms. Some had been disemboweled, with ropes of intestine dragging behind them, being stepped on and entangled in the ghouls that followed. Most of the undead were in street clothes, but many wore hospital gowns or blood soaked scrubs. Chillingly, many of the faces were recognizable from working in the hospital: Jill from C.T., Lauren from NICU, Dr. Van Der Spek, even Dr. Remus had succumbed to the plague.

Yvonne took a moment to compose herself, and then asked, "How long do you think it will hold them off, Andy?"

"Not long enough. But even *I* would have a hard time dislodging those gurneys. Hopefully it will buy us enough time to ..." Andy's words were cut short by screams coming from the ICU.

The group ran back inside to see the two previously "dead" doctors ripping off a young nurse's scrubs and tearing at her flesh. One of the doctors was unbelievably tall, and was trying to pull the girl apart limb from limb. With a gut wrenching sound, one of her arms tore free from her body and she fell to the ground screaming, landing in a pool of her own blood. Other nurses had gathered around and were throwing charts and books at the two doctors, trying in vain to help their colleague. Two other women lay writhing on the floor nearby, apparently wounded by these men.

Andy charged the two infected doctors, whose backs were turned, and brained them both viciously with his hammer. One fell instantly, while the tall one took several more blows before crumpling down lifelessly on the injured woman.

Yvonne ran to the fallen woman and tried to stop the bleeding, but it was futile. Her wounds were too severe and she bled out within minutes. Without missing a beat, Yvonne turned her attention to the two other women who were on the ground bleeding. They had both been bitten.

One of the younger nurses standing by could take no more and her mind cracked. She let out a crazed sob and blubbered almost unintelligibly, *"Wh-what in the hell is happening!? Why is everybody crazy!? Dr. Klos was DEAD! I saw him DIE! I checked his vitals! He was dead! The dead don't walk! This isn't a freaking zombie*

47

movie! Dr. Klos was dead! HE WAS DEAD!" The girl collapsed, sobbing uncontrollably.

Sam leaned on the closest counter and closed his eyes. He felt as though he was losing his mind, too. This day was like living in a horror movie, it was all too fantastic to be real.

Maybe this is all a dream... maybe I'm lying at home, in bed with Jessica, dreaming this whole damn thing. The alarm clock will sound off any minute now and this whole nightmare will be over. I'll just get in the shower, grind some espresso and head off to work. Or maybe I'm just going crazy and this is all in my head ...

After a few deep breaths, Sam lifted his head and saw the hospital phone sitting on the counter. He thought about his brother-in-law, Josh, who was working in the Lab earlier that morning. Picking up the phone, he dialed the in-house extension to reach the Lab. After several rings, the answering machine picked up. The young man rubbed his weary eyes and sighed with a heavy heart.

I hope you made it out of there, Josh.

Andy approached Yvonne, kneeling next to her. "You know what this means, right Yvonne? They've been bitten." His voice was dead serious.

Yvonne continued to work on the bleeding women, "Andy, why don't you and Sam go secure the stairwell. I'll take care of things here."

Andy softened his voice. "Yvonne, we ..."

"I will take care of it, Andy," she interrupted, "just go and make sure those things can't get up here. *NOW,* please."

Grunting his disapproval, Andy relented. It was no use arguing with Yvonne; they were on *her* turf, and *she* wore the pants around here. If the unthinkable had to be done, she was certainly strong enough to do it.

Walking toward the stairs, Andy and Sam were brainstorming.

"After we check the stairs, I want to go barricade the east elevator, too, the one that's stuck on the 1st floor. We don't want any more surprises," said Andy. "But I don't think we should barricade

48

the stairwell *door*, because we may need to fall back to the roof if things get out of hand. We just need to jam up the *descending* staircase air tight so none of those things can reach the door in the first place. I say we toss the patients who have 'turned' down the shaft and use their beds to block the stairs."

Sam forced a chuckle, "I'll let *you* run that idea past Yvonne. But I think you're on to something; those beds would do the trick."

Opening the stairwell door, they were shocked to see a young black man just standing there mindlessly with glazed, milky eyes. Without a thought, Andy pounced on the man, caving his face in with his trusty claw hammer. Lifting the pulverized man up by the shirt, he then tossed him over the railing and down the shaft.

Sam scanned the landing for any more surprises, but it appeared clear. The debris pile in the stairs had shifted, but was largely intact. Somehow this one had squirmed through it. Leaning over the railing, Sam looked at the body seven floors below; it was no longer moving.

"Dear God, Andy. You are one scary mo-fo."

This finally got Andy to crack a smile. "Why the hell does everybody say that? I'm actually a nice guy!"

"Hey, whatever you say, man. I'm just glad you're on my side."

The men were alerted by the sound of a falling chair in their barricade. As the two watched, the entire pile began rocking side-to-side from the relentless assault of the infected crowd behind it. It shifted again, and a large gurney slid over the side, bouncing like a pinball on the railings as it fell down the shaft. Nearing the bottom, it struck the belt-suspended man and he fell to the floor screaming in pain. He was quickly overwhelmed by several zombies who had been waiting patiently beneath him all day.

Andy's smile vanished and his hard features returned. "That's not going to be *me*. Come on, let's go grab those beds."

Running down the hall, they stopped at the first door bearing the sign "Infected Patient- DO NOT ENTER." Opening the door cautiously, a wave of stench blew past them. The room was dimly lit, and lying strapped to the large hospital bed was an emaciated elderly man, still intubated and hooked up to an I.V. and several monitors. When they unlocked the bed's wheels, he lifted his skeletal head and began to let out a feeble moan through the intubation tube that was

49

inserted down his throat. The moans became louder and angrier as Andy began ripping out the I.V. and various lines.

"I guess this isn't the time for polite bedside manner," Sam tried to joke.

"You're damn right! This sick bastard is holding a one way ticket to the bottom of the stairs!"

They wheeled the bed down the hall, but were intercepted by Yvonne. She was bleeding from the side of her face.

"Where the hell are you taking my patient!?" she demanded.

"To the stairwell, we need his bed! But what happened to *you*?"

Yvonne hesitated. "Apparently one of my nurses was hiding the fact that she'd been bitten. She was in the bathroom when I found her ... she was infected and attacked me."

"Is that a bite on your face?" Andy asked empathetically.

"I'm afraid so."

Sam and Andy's mouths dropped.

"Noooo, Yvonne ...." Andy's voice was pained.

"Don't worry about me; I'm sure I have a few hours. There is a lot to do between now and then," she cleared her throat and brushed away a tear, "... and when the time comes, I'll make sure I'm not in a position to endanger any of you."

Andy had stopped listening; he was looking past Yvonne, down the hall. "Wait ... who the hell is *that* guy?"

There was a cadaverous looking old man in a hospital gown just standing at the far end of the hall, swaying ominously. A urinary catheter bag was still tethered to him, dragging behind him on the floor like a dog on a leash. As the group watched, an unsuspecting nurse rounded the corner closest to him and the old man attacked!

Before the men could react, the stairwell door behind them opened and two infected women staggered in, grabbing hold of Andy from behind. As he spun around, they sunk their teeth deep into his shoulder and upper arm. He grabbed the smaller woman by the hair and tossed her over the restrained patient's bed. Sam circled around the bed and began cracking the woman in the head with Andy's Maglite. After the fourth or fifth hit, the woman's skull caved in and she stopped struggling. Turning back around, he saw Andy standing over the other woman's crumpled body, hammer in hand.

"Dammit! She bit me!" Andy yelled, looking at his wounds.

He dropped his head, saying, "Whoever isn't bitten needs to get the hell out of here. After I retire that old bastard down the hall, I'm gonna go down to our little barricade and brain anyone else who tries to squeeze through. You need to round up anyone who's left and get to the roof. Once I feel the infection setting in, I'm going to do a half-gainer down the shaft."

"Dude, you can't ..." Sam tried to say.

"I'm *NOT* going to let myself turn into one of them. I'd rather take a nose dive than turn into one of *them*. To hell with all this." With that, Andy charged down the hall and decimated the old man's head, then turned and brutally finished off the mortally wounded nurse. This caused Yvonne to lose it, and she charged Andy screaming.

Sam stood there speechless. The world was falling apart around him, and the building was being overrun. One by one, they would all eventually be infected and the hospital would fall.

As he stood there bewildered, a faint ~DING~ echoed down the hall, coming from the un-barricaded east elevator. The door slid open and several infected patients tumbled into the hall, including the two elderly women who were trapped in the elevator with him earlier that day. To his horror, most of the flesh from their arms and abdomens had been eaten away, *cannibalized*, yet here they came, walking toward him with bad intentions.

It was time to go. Sam ran down the hall yelling, "There are zombies on the floor! Everyone to the roof!" He burst into the lounge to grab his co-worker Lloyd, finding him both unrestrained and unguarded. The room reeked of cigarette smoke and death. At first glance Sam thought his friend had turned, but he was mistaken. Lloyd was just sitting nonchalantly in the wheelchair, legs crossed, watching the news and smoking a cigarette.

"Wha? ... You're *smoking*? In the *hospital*?"

Lloyd flashed a huge grin, stretching his handle bar mustache from ear to ear. "Why not? What are they gonna do? Fire me?" He took a drag and blew three perfect smoke rings. He looked awful; his eye sockets were dark and sunken in, and his skin looked shriveled and grey.

"What happened to Ruby? She was supposed to be keeping an eye on you!"

Lloyd struggled to focus his eyes, and then snickered, "I guess

51

she couldn't take a joke."

"Christ, Lloyd. You … you look like a zombie!"

"Yeah, well, I'm starting to smell like one, too. What can ya do?" He drew deeply from his cigarette, grinned again genuinely, and then coughed up some phlegm.

Sam shook his head, panic returning. "Man, we got to get out of here! There're zombies everywhere! I'm going to the roof, are you in?"

"I'm in. Do you mind giving me a push?" Without answering, Sam spun the wheelchair around and they were off.

He yelled as they sped down the hall, "Everyone needs to evacuate or hide! It's no longer safe here! We're going to the roof!" But the nurses they passed were all running in the other direction, toward the sound of Yvonne's screams.

Reaching the stairwell door, they were confronted with an ominous banging sound coming from the other side. This sound was becoming very familiar, and it did not bode well for their escape.

Lloyd looked up from his wheelchair, "I don't think this tale is going to have a happy ending, Sam. Let's go down with a fight, eh?" The two men exchanged a look of camaraderie, like brothers in arms.

"When they pull this Maglite from my cold, dead hands," Sam agreed, brandishing the gore splattered flashlight in the air.

Behind them echoed a woman's scream, "The patient in 720 bed 2 is loose!" It was immediately followed by the screams of others, then the sounds of a scuffle.

Sam looked back at Lloyd, "Alright, we have to go NOW. If we clear the stairwell can you make it to the roof?" Lloyd stood with some effort and nodded. "Alright then, help me push that bed!"

They grabbed the empty bed parked in the hallway and rolled it up against the stairwell door, locking its wheels in place and pumping the bed up to nearly chest height. Then carefully reaching over the bed, Sam pushed the door open just enough for their visitor to get hold of it and jerk it open the rest of the way. It was a blood covered man in O.R. scrubs, and he mindlessly charged into the bed which blocked his path, arms reaching out as he tried to latch onto one of the men.

Sam leaned over the bed and cracked the man hard in the head, causing him to stagger. He swung again and again, each blow cracking the man's thick skull a little more and a little more, until finally the flashlight broke through, causing the crazed man to seize violently and drop, propping the door open with his convulsing body.

They listened closely and could hear the barricade in the stairs crumbling, but as of yet no other zombies met them in the doorway. They dared to lean forward and peer over the bed and down the stairs. There was lots of shifting of the debris pile but no other creatures appeared to have broken through, so they unlocked the bed and pushed it aside. Running at full steam the two men raced up the single flight of stairs and were back on the roof, slamming the door behind them.

It was now dark out, and the cool evening air felt great. Both men were out of breath and sweating profusely. They kept their backs pressed firmly against the door, expecting at any moment that the ham-handed banging would resume.

Lloyd spoke in a raspy, winded voice, "Well, the good news for *us* is that the ICU door is being propped open by that surgeon, so with any luck those bastards will go *that way* instead of heading straight for the roof."

"Yeah, and fortunately they don't seem too adept at working a door knob either, so even this closed door should slow them down for a little while. I guess it's time to seriously consider climbing down one of those pipes now. Let's go take a look."

Running toward the edge of the building, they were quickly reminded of how utterly surrounded the hospital was. Climbing down into that infected mob was beginning to seem suicidal.

Sam looked out across the parking lot, eyes wide and shaking his head, "I can't believe how many there are. How could this all happen so fast? Did you hear anything on the news?"

"Yeah ... a lot. It's bad. *Real* bad, but none of them seem to have a clue as to what's really going on. They closed Detroit Metro Airport this morning due to an "undisclosed security incident," and now they've closed Memphis International, LaGuardia, and JFK. The conservative news channel is calling it a biological terrorist attack perpetrated by North Korea, and the liberal network is claiming that it's an unknown illness originating from a chemical gas attack against South Korea. Only the local stations had any real footage of what *we've* been seeing; deranged maniacs attacking and *eating* people in the streets." Lloyd paused, shaking his head with a disturbed grin, "The sportscaster from channel 4 was torn apart in front of the Renaissance Center live on the air ... it looked like the camera was on a tripod because it never flinched or turned away. They finally cut

53

away to a 'technical difficulty: please stand by' screen."

The sound of an approaching ambulance averted their attention. It came into view two blocks away, approaching from the north, and was swerving wildly to avoid infected pedestrians and the several abandoned vehicles that now littered the street. It pulled into the hospital campus with sirens blaring, attracting the attention of the gathered horde. Approaching the emergency room entrance, the driver began to honk and alternate his siren call, attempting to part the crowd. This proved to have the opposite effect, as every infected person within an earshot of the sirens advanced on the ambulance. Even the ones who seemed lethargic before became excited by the noise and commotion, closing in around the van.

The ambulance's siren went silent and was replaced by a steady beep-beep-beep as the driver attempted in vain to go in reverse. By now they were completely surrounded on all sided, 20 bodies deep, and from around the building more kept coming.

"This might be our best chance to climb down, Lloyd! Let's go to the other side and take a look!"

They ran back to the side of the building that faced the employee parking lot and looked down. The height was dizzying, but they could see that very few zombies remained on this side. Most of them were slowly making their way around the building toward the ambulance, while a few others looked to be confused by all the commotion and were walking in circles.

There were several conduit pipes and down spouts that ran down the wall, and the two desperate men approached the edge to inspect them. They all appeared to be securely fastened to the brick wall, and neither of the men weighed more than 155 lbs. soaking wet. However, the 80 ft. drop was unnerving to behold. It made their heads spin.

"Wow … vertigo …" Lloyd said.

Sam looked over to Lloyd, and there was no more denying it, he looked haggard. His eyes were glazed over and sunk deep within their sockets, and his complexion was sickly pale.

"Are you alright? Do you think you can do this?"

"I don't know … I feel sick, my hand hurts like hell, and *that*…" he said pointing, "… is a long way to fall!"

He was right, they were *very* high up. Sam was a rock climber, but even *he* did not feel comfortable at this height. The brick wall was a sheer vertical drop of seven stories, with no window ledges within reach, and only a cement slab of sidewalk to catch them if they fell. There was only one way to approach this descent, so Sam put on his climbing hat to instruct Lloyd on the proper technique: "Just lay on your belly and grab the conduit pipe, then swing your legs over the side. Hold on tight and ease your upper body off the roof. Then begin a reverse hand-over-hand climb all the way, just walking your legs down the wall."

Lloyd stared at Sam with a blank expression.

Sam gave a crazy-eyed grin, "Sounds easy, right? An 80 ft. climb, all arms, over a sea of frickin' zombies!" He paused for a beat, and then asked more seriously, "Do you think you can do it? With your hand?"

Lloyd sighed and looked down at his hand, rubbing it, "What's the plan if we get halfway down and they spot us, and start congregating at the bottom of the pipe?"

Sam answered honestly, "Well, I don't think I would have it in me to climb back up at that point. This is a one way trip. If any come over and wait for us at the bottom, we're just going to have to deal with them. But I think our odds are a lot better climbing down here than going back into the hospital … especially while the bulk of them are distracted by those poor paramedics."

Lloyd stood there in deep thought, looking worse by the minute. He appeared to have aged 20 years in these past 12 hours. Even in peak health this would be a challenging climb, maybe even impossible, but they both agreed that going back inside meant certain death.

"You could just stay up here on the roof and wait for help to arrive … but it might be *days* before they get this under control. And if any of those things start pouring out onto the roof, you'll have to attempt this climb regardless."

"To be honest, Sam, I don't believe I *have* a couple days. I think I'm going to turn into one of those things if I don't get help soon," Lloyd's voice sounded weak and hollow, a far cry from his usual deep baritone.

"But falling to your death won't be much better for your health, either."

Lloyd looked at Sam square in the eye, "It would sure as hell beat turning into a zombie."

"Hmmm … good point." He knew this was a bad idea, but they were fresh out of good ideas. "Okay, then. Down we go."

Sam crawled up to the roof's edge and grabbed the pipe. His hands were sweating and he had butterflies in his stomach; the fear was close to overwhelming him. He looked over at Lloyd, who was positioning himself over a pipe about eight feet to his left. He appeared to be having as much apprehension as Sam.

Looking down the wall made his head spin, but he could see there were only a handful of zombies remaining on this side of the building. It was now or never.

"Let's just do it. Don't think about it. One … two … three … go!"

Both men swung their legs over the ledge and went to work. Sam was surprised by how light his body initially felt, surely due to the adrenaline coursing through his veins. His heart was racing and his palms were sweating, but his grip felt sure. The first thirty feet flew by, and his hopes of surviving this climb were beginning to soar. But looking over, he realized he was rapidly outpacing Lloyd, so he slowed his descent.

"Are you hanging in there, man?"

Lloyd had been in great physical shape, but this infection was taking a toll on him. His legs were shaking and he was breathing heavily.

"I'm… not sure… my hands… are sweating."

"No worries, man, you got this. Just go slow and steady." Sam waited for Lloyd to catch up before continuing, "We should really do this more often, maybe on our lunch breaks, like all those nurses who walk the stairs. Hey, have you ever watched that show 'Ninja Warrior'?"

Lloyd chuckled softly, "Dude, don't make me laugh…"

And then he fell.

Everything seemed to go quiet.
Sam looked down and saw his friend …
drifting through the evening air,
slowly turning,
falling further and further away,
and then bounce silently.
A split second later the sound reached his ears.

A heavy, wet, smack.

And now Sam was alone.

A wave of guilt hit Sam in the chest.

I shouldn't have been talking to him ... distracting him ... I am so sorry, Lloyd.

Looking back down at his fallen friend, his guilt was soon replaced by fear. Two obese black females staggered over to his body and began tearing at it, ripping his shirt off and clawing at his chest. And from across the service road another group of them were coming, maybe five or six in number.

There was no time to mourn, he had to act fast.

He climbed down the pipe with reckless speed. His hands were sweating profusely from fear; however his grip was strong with anger. Anger at what they had done to Roland ... and Lloyd ... Yvonne ... Andy ... and the women in the elevator. He was going to get away from here, that much he knew. He was going to make it home to his wife and his son. Nothing was going to stop him.

He paused ten feet above the ground to plan his landing. The two women who were now eating Lloyd's entrails had not yet seen him, but the approaching group had their dead eyes locked firmly on him, belting out excited moans and gargles. They were only twenty feet out and closing fast, so Sam just dropped.

The landing wasn't too hard, but Sam scrambled to his feet so fast that he nearly stumbled. Initially, he had to run *away* from the parking lot to circle wide around the approaching group. They gave chase, but even the fastest one in the group had no more than a toddler's speed or grace. He easily outdistanced them in his wide detour but could now see there were dozens of their ilk roaming between the parked cars. He had to be careful.

Slowing his sprint, he continued on a convoluted route between cars to avoid the infected. It appeared that he could easily out reason and out maneuver them, so he took no chances approaching his Subaru wagon. He circled around to the far side of the car, looking between each row of cars before he felt sure that he could safely advance.

Reaching into his scrub pocket, he readied his key for the door lock. He did not want to attract any more attention by using his wireless key fob to unlock the car with its loud, audible beep.

Scanning the perimeter during his final approach, he saw that many of the things were slowly working their way toward him but were several car lengths away.

Don't panic ... just turn the key and hop in ... they won't reach me fast enough if I just stay calm and DON'T PANIC ...

His hands were shaking but the key turned easily and he closed himself into the relative security of his vehicle. As soon as his butt hit the seat, the car was in gear and launching out of the parking lot.

Heading for the main road, he had to skillfully navigate around several attackers. They all bore horrible wounds that should have incapacitated any sane man, and many looked as though they should have been dead: gaping wounds to the face and neck, disemboweled abdomens, broken limbs, torn faces ... it all seemed so surreal and impossible. How could they survive such trauma? Why haven't they bled out? Their pain threshold seemed limitless.

Turning toward the campus exit, he encountered a dozen of them in the road, blocking his path. They were immediately drawn to the moving car. The urge to plow his car through the mob was great, but he thought about the damage a single deer strike does to a passenger car, and he couldn't risk it.

He slowed the car to a jogger's pace and bumped into the first two, pushing one aside as the other fell across his hood and rolled off the other side. The next few were not dispatched as easily. Several fell to the ground and were run over, jostling the vehicle violently as another one dented the hood before falling backwards under the front bumper, becoming lodged beneath the car.

Sam turned onto the main street, dragging the pinned man beneath his car for several hundred feet before he broke free. The back left corner of the car bucked up as the rear wheel rolled over the freed man. Apparently this damaged the muffler, which began to rumble loudly.

Third gear was pushed hard as Sam tried to put the hospital far behind him. There wasn't much traffic on this road, but there were several abandoned cars and a few characters roaming about aimlessly. All were wounded or sick.

It was hard to grasp what was happening around him; some

sort of epidemic plague, mass hysteria, a riot of homicidal maniacs…
this was just too fantastic to be true. Surely this must be a nightmare,
or a hallucination.

Gripping the wheel with sweating palms, he looked down at
the dashboard:

2:35am   62°F

The road leading from the hospital was a straight shot north to the highway. The posted speed limit was 35mph, but when the road was clear Sam wound-out his turbo, hitting 110mph before traffic forced him to resume at a safe speed. Several cars crossed the grass boulevard and drove against opposing traffic. There were multiple fender benders, but no one bothered to stop. The panic was palpable.

As he approached the highway, he could see that the traffic was bad for 2am, but still moving. He turned at the sign reading "I-94 West." Traffic in both directions looked grim, and he began the slow merge onto the downward sloping on-ramp.

This stretch of highway was cut into Detroit like a narrow canyon. The six lane tarmac lay about 16 ft. below the surrounding city streets, cutting through rundown neighborhoods of once grand houses, abandoned factories and industrial parks. The sides of the canyon alternated from steep grass embankments to vertical walls of poured concrete.

Traffic was stop and go, but mostly stop. There was lots of honking, and cars jockeying for position. The torturously slow drive was punctuated by rude hand gestures and verbal outbursts. Drivers looked wide-eyed and desperate to prod the procession along.

Ultimately they slowed to a crawl, and then stopped entirely. He had been on the highway for nearly 45 minutes, but had only traveled six or seven miles. Sam looked around at the gridlock that entrapped him. He was in the left lane of three westbound lanes. To his left was a 4 ft. high concrete divider that separated him from the opposing traffic. In the car to his right was a young black female who appeared to be a college student. She was sitting up straight and looking around nervously. They made eye contact and exchanged a polite, uneasy smile.

Movement caught his eye and he looked up beyond the girl and her car to the steep grassy embankment. He thought he saw something roll down it, but now there seemed to be nothing there. He rubbed his eyes and looked again. Squinting hard, it appeared that the dense row of shrubbery at the top of the embankment was rustling about, when suddenly three men pushed through the foliage and tumbled end over end down the steep grade. Then another man burst through and took the plunge, and then another.

Unexpectedly to his left, the sound of shattering plastic caused Sam to jump in his seat as his left rear view mirror was folded forward and crushed by a white SUV squeezing between him and the concrete divider! He began to lay on his horn and cuss at the vehicle, but it just kept on going, revving its motor and side swiping several more cars as it forced its way past. Sam tried to take note of the vehicle's license plate, but he missed it. He only caught the bumper sticker on its rear window which read, "I lift Detroit in prayer."

Several cars behind him began to honk incessantly, and the young woman in the car next to him started shrieking in terror. He looked over and saw scores of bloody people plowing through the bushes and tumbling 16 feet down onto the highway! Like water overflowing a dam, a sea of humanity poured down onto the interstate.

Uninfected people around him began to abandon their vehicles and flee on foot. It was then that he saw the first infected man approach his car. He was a tall, black male in his early 20's, wearing a torn, blood stained white T-shirt, oversized cargo shorts, and new looking high tops. As the man got closer, Sam could see that his nose and cheek were missing, exposing his teeth and gums. With the push of a button Sam locked his doors, but the attacker didn't even try the handle. He pressed his mauled face up against the passenger window and made eye contact, then began to pound wildly on the glass.

Before Sam could react, the crazed man was knocked down and swept away by a stampede of screaming people, rushing forward between the stranded cars. In his rear view mirror he could see the highway was entirely filled with blood covered individuals attacking motorists as they abandoned their cars.

I need a weapon ... where's that Maglite!? Did I leave it on the roof?

He frantically checked the seats and floorboards but couldn't find it. Thinking back, he remembered using it on that surgeon's head in the ICU, but couldn't recall having it after that. Opening his glove box and briefcase, he rifled through his belongings looking for anything that could be used as a weapon. With a loud crash, his back windshield shattered from the torrent of bodies now careening into his car, and he decided it was time to abandon ship, weapon or not.

61

Opening his car door, he jumped out and filed into the stream of fleeing people. They screamed and shoved and fought to keep pushing forward. The smell of sweat, adrenaline, and death was thick in the cool night air. Hands grabbed and tore at his hospital scrubs, and he felt the bodies of trampled people beneath his feet. He ran and ran like a man possessed, over cars, over people, clawing to keep from being pulled down and crushed, all the while being battered by elbows, fists, and feet.

The steep grassy embankment gave way to vertical cement walls, which funneled the surging mob into a concrete bottle neck. There was nowhere to go but forward, and those in the front were being crushed and buried by those in the rear.

Ahead Sam could see an off ramp: exit 217, Mt. Elliott. He locked his eyes on that ramp and scrambled his way forward, at times on all fours. Over more cars, over more people, tunnel vision guiding his way. Stepping on faces and stepping on backs, like a single minded animal fighting to survive, he no longer heard the screams of those behind him or those beneath him.

He felt his feet finally touch pavement again as he rushed up the shoulder of the exit ramp. Jumping over two guard rails to cut the corner, he turned left onto the overpass. Looking back down at the recessed highway, it looked like a turbulent river of bodies, bubbling and flowing around the parked cars, churning forward slowly, a river of death.

There were 20 or 30 people huddled together on the overpass. They were screaming and talking to one another, trying in vain to get cell phone reception. Most were injured and bleeding.

Sam just ran past them.

Arriving at the first intersection, there was a gas station on one corner, a diner on the other, and several vacant lots. From within the gas station he heard multiple gun shots ring out. Between the lotto sign and cigarette ads in the window he could see several black men struggling in a fight. There was more small arms fire from within, and the front windows of the store crashed out into the pump lanes giving him a clear view of the wounded men fighting for their lives. There were at least eight zombies in the store, and the two men making a stand were bloodied and bitten, but they fought on.

Looking across the street at the diner, he saw men barricading the doors and windows with table tops and kitchen appliances.

Glancing up he read the street signs: Mt. Elliott and Grand River. He had no idea where he was, but he knew he had to get away from the highway, try to find a spot to hide where there weren't so many people. Ahead the street looked relatively quiet and poorly lit, so that's exactly the way he went, running on into the night, heading south.

After putting several hundred yards behind him, he felt as if his heart was going to explode, so he slowed down to catch his breath. This entire city block was dark, as there were very few working street lights. The buildings were mostly old businesses that were either boarded up or burnt down; five and dime stores, muffler shops, vacant chapels and watering holes. At some point this had been a bustling street, but that was decades ago.

Far behind him at the stoplight he could see several zombies now staggering from the highway. The gunfire from the gas station had stopped, and he knew those two men were now dead.

A shuffling sound caught his attention, and he turned to look back in the direction he was heading. There was a lone man walking slowly up the street. It was hard to tell from this distance if he was sick or not, so Sam slinked back into the shadows along the sidewalk and backed up against a six foot wrought iron fence. The man was steadily approaching, but had not yet seen him. Sam searched the ground around him for a stick, a rock, a brick, or *anything* that could be used as a weapon, but again he found himself empty handed. He looked through the wrought iron fence and could faintly make out the silhouettes of large, ornate tomb stones: it was an old cemetery.

A voice from down the street called out, "Hey! You!" It came from an unlit house near the walking man. The man grunted and turned mechanically toward the voice, and then began moving double time toward its source. A single gunshot hit him in the chest and dropped him, but he got right back up and was met by a hail of bullets. Two young men stepped out into the street firing, and their bullets chipped away at the man without effect until a large chunk of his head went flying. He then dropped, never to move again.

Dear God ... I have to get off the street before someone

63

mistakes me for a zombie and tries to shoot me!

Looking over his shoulder and between the iron bars, the cemetery appeared still and quiet, so Sam stealthily climbed the fence and dropped down onto the other side.

There shouldn't be ANYBODY in this old cemetery, especially at this hour, in an abandoned part of town. This seems kinda crazy, but it just might be the safest place to hide for the night ... unless of course the dead begin to rise, in which case I am totally screwed. He chuckled to himself. *If this were a horror movie, I would be yelling, "Don't go in there!"*

The young man walked deeper into the old, historic graveyard. It was immense, and judging by the knee high grass it appeared that it was no longer in use. He took refuge behind a large, elaborate tomb to catch his breath and collect his thoughts.

How could all this happen in just one day? At this time yesterday he was lying comfortably in his own bed, and tonight he was huddled in a dark, cold, graveyard in an abandoned part of downtown Detroit. His car was stranded on the highway, and he had no hopes of retrieving it until the police got this outbreak under control. He was now presented with the prospect of a 50 mile walk to get home. Obviously, he had to avoid the highway at all costs; however that was the only route he knew. But the overriding dilemma was that apparently the city has been overwhelmed by some sickness that was reminiscent of "Night of the Living Dead." This was all too much to believe.

Looking up at the stars he began to realize how cold he was. He had broken a healthy sweat when fleeing his vehicle, and now that he was at rest the chill was beginning to set in. He would have to find a better spot to wait out the night, so he stood up and began walking further away from the road. The muscles in his legs were stiff and sore from his purge of effort. Never before had he experienced such a visceral episode of fight or flight syndrome, and he now felt exhausted and spent.

Distant sounds of gunfire could be heard echoing in the night sky, but this cemetery felt like a peaceful sanctuary. Surely those things did not have enough dexterity to climb that iron fence, and he doubted that any other "live" person would be crazy enough to hide in a graveyard when, by all appearances, the dead were now walking the earth. However, Sam was never one to have an unnatural aversion to graveyards, ghosts, or the dark. He loved visiting cemeteries, and would try to find the oldest tombstone there, or the memorials of war dead. This particular one must have been magnificent in its day, but even in the dark he could see the signs of neglect and disrepair, unchecked weeds and overgrown hedges.

Walking out into a clearing, he beheld the silhouette of an immense industrial building that seemed to reach to the horizon in both directions. This graveyard backed right up to the building's dilapidated brick wall, being separated only by two rows of rusting train tracks. Stepping over the weed ensnarled tracks, he approached it cautiously and could see that it was graffitied and abandoned, with no intact windows or doors to bar his entrance.

Crouching at an open doorway, Sam listened intently for any noises coming from within. The only sounds he could perceive were coming from the direction of the highway, being carried along by the wind: screams, sirens, and gunfire.

Spurred by the cold, he took a step inside and strained his eyes to make out any shapes in the room. It takes approximately 40 minutes of darkness for a person's eyes to reach their full night vision potential, and the young man's keen eyes were beginning to adjust. He could see that the room was littered with debris, and that there were two doorways leading to adjacent rooms. It smelled like a mildewy machine shop. There was just enough ambient light coming through the large, glassless windows to make his way, so he moved toward the door to his left.

The room he now entered was long and wide, with dozens of stout, square pillars of cement supporting the low ceiling. It was more difficult to see in this room, but the white pillars formed a grid that made it easy to keep his bearings. Upon reaching the far side, he discovered a large, open, industrial elevator shaft. It was large enough to accommodate three or four full size automobiles. Next to it was a cluttered work bench and a control panel. A light bulb turned on in Sam's head and he reached into his pocket, pulling out his cell phone. He flipped it open and used the display light to look around. On the bench was a heavy, water damaged book. He brushed years of dust and mold off the cover, and could faintly make out the words, "Packard Motor Car Company – Hydraulic Service Log."

Sam had inadvertently found his way into the long abandoned 3.5 million square foot Packard Plant. Built in 1903, this cavernous half mile long complex was the most modern automotive factory of its day. In an era when cars were selling between $375 and $1,500, Packard was building cars that started at $2,600. It was Detroit's premier luxury brand, outselling Cadillac and Lincoln *combined*. Their slogan was, "Ask the man who owns one." They pioneered many innovations, such as air conditioning, a production V-12 engine, and the modern steering wheel. During World War II the factory was retooled to build Rolls-Royce engines that powered US fighter planes during the war. After the war they introduced a line of "middle-class" cars, which initially sold quite well. However, this change of focus tarnished the prestige-factor of the name plate, and marked the beginning of a downward spiral. The company shut down the factory and folded in 1956, leaving the building to the mercy of the elements, homeless squatters, and metal scrappers.

There was nothing else of value on the workbench, and the shivering man was at risk of being overcome by exhaustion. He had to find a safe place to rest for the night before his body collapsed, someplace warm.

Using his cell phone to light the way, he quietly walked deeper into this vast industrial complex. Initially he felt safer being back inside a building, however that shred of security was rapidly fading as he moved through the dark, dank factory. Passing through a series of smaller rooms, he began to feel that something menacing was lurking ahead of him in the dark. A rush of fear was beginning to build in his chest.

And then he heard a sound …

His senses went on high alert and his heart rate went through the roof. He crouched against the closest wall and closed his cell phone for fear that the light would betray his position. He was now engulfed by total blackness. With wide eyes and ears he whipped his head one way and then the other, trying to pinpoint the source of the sound. The silence had become deafeningly loud, and no matter how hard he strained his eyes he could see nothing in this inky blackness; he had ventured too far from any windows.

Had he imagined the sound? It sounded like a single foot fall;

like a pebble being crushed beneath a boot. He *knew* that he had heard it, and felt positive that it wasn't just the old building settling. He was not alone in this old factory.

Panic began to gain the upper hand and the room started to spin. He was losing it, and was ready to run for the graveyard screaming, but he was too terrified to move. Freezing to death outside in the cemetery now seemed far preferable to creeping around this godforsaken factory. Like an animal trapped in a cage, he cowered in the darkness, waiting for some unknown assailant to descend upon him.

Seconds ticked by, then minutes, then perhaps an hour. The only sounds that met his ears were the occasional drip of water and a few isolated gun shots from far away; whatever had made that sound had either stopped for the night or crept away unheard. Opening his phone was like igniting a torch, and he stepped boldly into the next room: it was empty.

The young man was now emotionally wrecked and decided to press on and face whatever lay ahead. Feeling like a zombie himself, he plodded on with far less care than he had previously demonstrated. It was time to lay down *anywhere*. He wanted to just curl up in a corner and endure the cold, but he decided it would be far safer to sleep on an upper level, where the stairs would help act as a barrier to any creature that may wander his way. He had passed a few dark stairways while exploring the building, so he turned back to seek out the closest one.

Without much care, he recklessly walked straight up to the third floor. The stairway continued upward, but this floor seemed to have good natural light, so he closed his phone and stepped into the massive, open space. There were large open windows on all sides, providing enough light to make out most of the room. Rubble littered the entire floor, and he could see a large, peculiarly shaped object in the middle of the room that begged his attention.

Approaching it, his frazzled brain couldn't process what he thought he was seeing, so he flipped his phone back open to illuminate the view. There was a medium sized, fiberglass sailboat sitting up on cinder blocks. Its hull was light blue, and it appeared that at some point, someone was attempting to repair the derelict craft. It was tagged with multiple layers of graffiti, the most legible script reading, "Ask the white man who owns one."

There was an old wooden step ladder alongside the boat, so Sam climbed up to the third rung to peek over the gunwales. Inside were two fiberglass bench seats molded into the rear deck, and an open doorway that lead to a small cabin. He couldn't imagine how on earth someone managed to get this boat up onto the 3rd floor.

Knowing he had found his bed for the night, his sense of reason returned and he began to worry about his back trail. He didn't want anyone catching him off guard in the night, so he returned to the stairway and quietly spread some of the small bits of rubble across the top few steps. He then did the same in a small perimeter around the boat. He figured he would hear the rubble crunching under foot if anyone approached.

Defensive measures now complete, he climbed back up the ladder and boarded the craft, pulling the ladder up behind him. Illuminating the ship's cabin with his phone, he entered someone else's world. There was a well-made bed consisting of a single mattress on the floor of the ship's bow, with sheets and a blanket turned down with military precision. Next to the bed was a two liter pop bottle filled with water, and a plastic cup perched upside down on top of the two liter. On the counter that served as the ship's galley was a row of neatly arranged vodka bottles, an ashtray, and a deck of cards. The walls were covered with pin ups of RUN DMC, Grand Master Flash, and vintage Playboy centerfolds. There was also a signed Polaroid of legendary Detroit boxer Tommy 'Hit Man' Hearns, posing with two dapper gentlemen. The signatures read, 'The Motor City Cobra,' 'Maserati Rick,' and 'Emanuel Steward.'

Worries of the occupant returning disappeared as he began to check the cabin more thoroughly. The bedding was covered with a powdery mold; the cup and playing cards had an impressively undisturbed layer of dust; the artwork was of 1980's vintage; and the two liter was an old bottle of Tab diet cola. No one had been in this boat for decades, so without giving the matter a second thought, Sam collapsed onto the moldy bed and was out in seconds. As he drifted off into sleep, his exhausted mind wondered:

Do they even MAKE "Tab" cola anymore?

Sam awoke to the sound of helicopters passing by overhead. He tried to sit right up, but his body was slow to respond. He had slept like a brick; however, it felt as if he were sleeping *on* a brick. Reaching beneath him, he pulled his paperback book from his waistband. It was now crumpled and dog eared, but he grinned knowing that he still had it with him.

The morning light in this sailboat was beautiful: a dim, golden glow that filtered through the dingy yellow window treatments. His body creaked and protested as he sat up and looked around the cabin. This old boat was an anachronism, a time capsule left by someone who found himself homeless, but had enough pride to make his bed every morning. Why did he leave? Who was he? Surely the boat didn't belong to the man who was squatting in it ... or maybe it did? A wise man once said, "The cheapest part of owning a boat is the day you buy it ... then it starts to get expensive." Maybe this was the purchase that bankrupted the man. And how did this boat end up on the third floor of an abandoned automotive factory? Just another bizarre layer to an utterly bizarre day.

He knew immediately that yesterday was no dream. It even seemed far more real this morning than at any time during the previous day. Pushing the violent visions out of his head, he thought of his pregnant wife. At this hour, Jessica would be awake, probably feeding Simon his breakfast and having a cup of tea (she had sworn off coffee for the duration of her pregnancy). She must have been worried sick to wake up alone.

Pulling out his phone, he tried dialing her number. It was the same message as yesterday, "All lines are busy ..." He closed the phone and collapsed back down on the moldy bed, his eyes resting on a particularly attractive Playboy centerfold. She was holding an American flag, and had a big 80's hair style that was teased up with hairspray. The backdrop was red, white, and blue, and the scene was littered with confetti. It looked like a "political rally" theme she was going for. This struck Sam with an idea and he quickly sat back up, grabbing his phone.

He remembered the 2008 inauguration of President Barack Obama. They were expecting a record turnout for the event, and knew that the cell phone towers in DC were insufficient for the amount of phone traffic that would accompany the large crowd. So, they got the word out for people to *not* make cell phone calls from the event, but to instead send only texts. A text message uses only a split second of bandwidth, and can more easily trickle through if the lines are clogged with traffic.

He typed in a message to his wife, "r u ok?" and pressed send.

His display read, "sending... sending... sent."

Whoa ... Did that actually go through?

Almost immediately, Sam's phone beeped. Jessica responded with a text, "yes, why? where the hell r u? i've been trying to call."

He smiled, mostly because he could tell that Jessica was ticked off. She *never* texted in shorthand unless she was *really* mad. It was also apparent that she was oblivious as to what was going on. She rarely watched television, so she must not have heard the news reports about the riot. She was probably mad and worried, wondering why he didn't come home last night.

He replied to her text, "i'm ok. lock the doors & turn on the news. i'm safe, but my car is stuck on 94 and i am walking home" send.

She replied, "what? did u call a tow truck?"

She had no idea what was going on. He answered, "no babe, just turn on the news, theres a riot in Detroit. i cant get back to my car" send.

About two minutes passed before she responded, "OMG... is this for real? ZOMBIES? WHERE ARE YOU?"

"exit 217 off i-94, i slept in an old car factory. the highway is not safe so i'm gonna try 2 cut thru town and hitch a ride" send.

"can i come pick you up?" she responded.

"no! its not safe! just lock the doors and stay inside. i'm gonna start walking now, and my phone will be on silent so i can be sneaky. i will text again at noon," send.

"oh baby please be careful! i love you!"

"<3" send.

It felt great to hear from his wife. Their marriage had been strained recently, nearly to the point of breaking, but the past 24 hours had put a lot in perspective. His spirits were lifted and he wanted to win his wife's love back. Invigorated with hope, he was ready to start walking. He just wanted to get home and hug his son, kiss his beautiful wife, and brew a double shot of espresso. Fifty miles to go.

He gave one final look around the cabin before leaving, but found nothing of use. He was both starving and parched, but did not trust the contents of the dusty old Tab bottle. Sam was a huge boxing fan, so he grabbed the Polaroid of Tommy Hearns and put it in his book. Stepping out of the cabin, he stood on the aft deck and gave his sore back a much needed stretch. The large room looked far less menacing by daylight. There was even a bit of tragic beauty in the old, abandoned building. *So much wasted space,* he thought.

Nature was calling, so he bellied up to the port side gunwale and relieved himself off the side of the boat. The sound of urine striking pavement was far louder than Sam anticipated, and it echoed throughout the cavernous room. He had to remember to practice better noise discipline while hiding out.

Lowering the ladder, he climbed down and proceeded to head for the stairs. As he approached them, another helicopter flew over the factory, slow and low, so he decided to hustle upstairs to the roof and possibly summon some help. There was a lot of debris on the steps, and he tried hard not to disturb any of it. He didn't want to make any more noise than he already had.

The stairway terminated at the top floor, and there was no apparent access to the roof. There was, however, a long corridor that led several *hundred* yards in the direction of the highway and the helicopter. He thought that it might provide a vantage point on the highway to check and see if the police had secured the area yet, so he headed that way.

The dimensions of this building were awe inspiring. This oversized hallway seemed to reach the horizon, and an old track for a conveyer belt ran down its entire length. The floor was tiled with small wooden tiles, cut against the grain of the tree, leaving visible tree rings. He remembered hearing about such tiles being used in old machine shops, because the tree rings absorbed the oil, making for a good non-slip surface. Most of the building had been thoroughly gutted; however there were a few random car parts, piles of trash, and some rusty old machinery. Checking each pile as he passed, he found nothing that could be used as a weapon.

Another helicopter buzzed over the factory, so Sam broke into a quiet jog, running toward the highway and the direction of the chopper. As he ran, there were sections of the hall that crossed over the streets below through a series of enclosed bridges. Apparently they were used to move cars from one building to the next without having to expose the unfinished car to the elements. These enclosed bridges connected the buildings together from one city block to the next. It was all quite impressive. As he crossed each bridge, he looked out the windows to the street below but saw no cars or pedestrians. This neighborhood was largely abandoned even before yesterday's riot, making it hard to judge what the real situation was like from here.

He finally reached the building's end, which butted up against the recessed highway, towering over it. From this bird's eye view, high up in the factory, he beheld Detroit's apocalypse. The unflinching morning sun illuminated a scene straight from Dante's Inferno. The highway was flooded with slow moving bodies, mangled and disfigured, bumping between abandoned cars; hundreds of bodies, maybe *thousands*. Several of the cars must have had live occupants trapped inside, because there were groups of the undead surrounding them, banging on the windows, trying to get in.

Two news helicopters flew by, following the contour of the highway. Sam tried to get their attention, but there was no way they could see him.

It was overwhelming to look out at the highway. There was *no way* he would be able to get to his car, and this forsaken road was the only route he knew to get home to Milan. He was trying to formulate a plan; escape and evade. His home was roughly 50 miles west-southwest of Detroit, and the only other road he could think of that would put him in that direction was Michigan Ave., also called US-12. It ran all the way from Detroit to Chicago, but passed within about 6 miles of his home. He had no idea how far Michigan Ave. was from here, but he knew that by heading south he would eventually cross it. This was the only option he could think of, and he just had to start going in that direction until some better idea presented itself. With any luck, he could thumb a ride from someone. He turned around and headed back down the long hall.

Sam was flabbergasted that he couldn't find an old piece of pipe in this factory to be used as a weapon, but Detroit is notorious for scrappers picking these old buildings clean. The best thing he found

72

was an old brick to carry around.

I can't believe I lost that Maglite! Argggh... It's either back in my car or at the hospital. It's amazing how well that thing worked to smash that doctor's skull in. His body shuddered. *God, I hope I never have to do that again.*

It was a long walk back to the staircase, and it gave him plenty of time to think about the horrors behind him and the daunting journey ahead of him. Sam was an avid runner, but the distance he had to cover was slightly less than a double-marathon. He had never run more than 13 miles in one shot, so this was going to be a challenging hike. At a walking pace he could expect the cover the distance in less than 20 hours. If he factored in some rest time, a couple detours and wrong turns, he could realistically expect to arrive home late tomorrow night.

A growling stomach reminded him that he had not eaten since that peanut butter and jelly yesterday at lunch, the one he shared with Lloyd. His head hung low as he recalled Lloyd's fall, and Roland bleeding to death on the floor. Two of his friends were dead, and to his surprise and shame, he wasn't even capable of mourning. He couldn't, not now. He was too preoccupied with saving his own skin. If he didn't keep his wits about him, he would be next.

Get home first; there'll be time to mourn later. Just focus on survival ... lay low and keep moving.

He was hungry, but more importantly he needed to find something to drink. A person can easily survive a week without food, but he really needed to find something to drink today, and soon. He was parched, and moreover, he was not accustomed to functioning without his morning cup of coffee. His head was feeling foggy and his nerves were shot.

Before going back down the stairs, he found a window that looked out over the graveyard. To his relief there was no movement among the grave markers, and the burial plots looked undisturbed; none of the dead appeared to be rising from the grave. In the back of his mind he was a little nervous about that all night; he had seen too many zombie movies to not be a *little* nervous. The old iron fence surrounding the cemetery looked secure and formidable, and the entrance was barred by an elaborate iron gate. Trees obscured most of the road that he came in on, but he definitely saw movement on Mt. Elliott, a LOT of pedestrian movement. Judging by their jerky motions and gait, they were all infected. He began to count as many of them as he could see.

Twenty-four.

No … twenty-five. And there were certainly more out there, obscured by the trees. Whatever their number, he had to start walking. Southwest.

Back on the ground floor, he decided to look for an alternate route away from the factory before committing to leaving via the graveyard. There still seemed to be something counter intuitive about spending too much time in a graveyard when "zombies" appeared to be rising from the dead.

The factory looked very different by the light of day. There were mounds of old tires, trash and bricks. The ceiling had collapsed in several areas, and the building looked genuinely condemned. Drawn toward a brightly lit room, he found a loading dock that spilled into a wide alleyway. Creeping toward an open garage door, he saw that the wide alley was full of detritus from a past civilization: an old black & white tube TV, old couches, and a rusting hulk that may have once been a 1970's era Oldsmobile.

Cautiously, he stepped outside onto the crumbling pavement, and again found himself in awe of this monstrous complex. The alleyway bisected the entire length of the factory, and could be more accurately described as a private road, surrounded on both sides by drab factory walls. Several covered bridges passed overhead, connecting the two parallel buildings into one. It was a huge, neglected monstrosity from the automotive/industrial revolution.

Looking north the "road" was blocked by a pile of bulldozed debris, but the southbound direction looked passable. It was littered with broken glass and some rubbish, but still navigable, so south he went.

Quietly through this industrial ghost town he walked, with plastic bags blowing like tumbleweeds, and scraggly vines eroding and reclaiming the neglected brick walls. The cost to demolish this old complex would be more than the land was worth, so here it sat, perpetually "for sale or lease."

74

There was movement ahead, prompting Sam to freeze in his tracks. One hundred paces ahead a large man stumbled into the alley, he was hunched over and seemed disoriented. Slowly craning his head from side to side, the dark figure locked his gaze on Sam and began to limp toward him enthusiastically.

The hospital worker remained motionless, his mind racing …

Is that guy just injured and looking for help? Sheesh, that is one heck of a limp... maybe he's infected? I wish he'd call out or something, to show he's one of the good guys. Hmm ... I guess if he won't, I will, before he gets too close.

"Friend or foe?" Sam yelled, his voice echoing off the factory walls.

The approaching man responded with a terrifying groan and doubled his pace!

Sam wasted no time. He turned and beat feet, running back into the loading dock and through the musty old building, leaping over puddles and trash at full speed. As he distanced himself from the alley, the congested corridors became progressively darker and darker, nearly pitch black, but then thankfully began to brighten as he neared the rooms facing the graveyard, with their large windows and abundant natural light.

Upon reaching the far side he paused to catch his breath and listen for his pursuer. The deep, angry grunts of the man could be heard echoing through the building, but it sounded as if he were headed the wrong way; his animal like groans were fading toward the north.

Sam resolved to escape through the graveyard, so he peered through several windows until he found one that couldn't be seen from the road. Slipping out of the glassless window, he crouched low and sprinted across the overgrown lawn to the nearest tombstone. The road lay 200 yards to the west, and he cautiously worked his way from tomb to tombstone, choosing his path carefully.

Once he was within 30 yards of the iron fence, he went prone and surveyed the road. At this distance he could clearly see the horribly wounded people who were stumbling around aimlessly in the street. These people all needed medical attention, but somehow managed to plod around without showing any signs of pain. Had this disease numbed their minds to the pain... or were these people actually *dead* but still walking?

That's impossible ... this isn't a freaking zombie movie. Are they psychotic, contagious, and oblivious to pain? Yes. But undead? They CAN'T be.

Quiet as a mouse, he worked his way to the south end of the cemetery which bordered a quiet, forgettable street of run down yet still occupied houses. There were cars in most of the driveways, but only half of which appeared to be operational. To his relief, there was only one person roaming this street, and he was heading in the other direction.

After making one final check, he scaled the iron fence and silently headed for the houses across the street, brick in hand. Crouching behind a late model Caprice Classic, he took a better look at the houses closest to him, wondering if he should knock on a door and ask for help. The first house had no blinds or curtains, and no other signs of being inhabited, but the next house *did* have curtains and a full trashcan by the side door. He decided to give it a try.

Staying low, he sprinted across two barren yards and approached the house's side door. Loud music was coming from within the home. It was a great song: a cover of Stevie Wonder's "Living for the City," performed by a local Detroit band called "The Dirt Bombs." He listened for a few moments, hoping to hear any other sounds or signs of life, but there was nothing.

Clenching the brick tightly, he built up his courage and knocked on the door. Waiting for a response, he looked up and down the street nervously. That lone straggler was no longer in view. That was either good or bad news, only time would tell. He thought he saw movement from within the house, but a thin curtain and the glare from the sunny sky made it difficult to see inside the home. He knocked harder, and then cupped his hands to the glass to make it easier to see inside. This door appeared to lead into the kitchen. It was difficult to tell, but he thought he saw movement, again. Looking over his shoulder, he was beginning to get very nervous. He did not want to knock much harder and risk drawing attention to himself, but the music inside was loud and would make it difficult for anyone in there to hear him.

76

Bam-bam-bam!

He knocked so hard that the sound startled him. If anyone was inside they *certainly* heard it that time. Cupping his hands to the glass, he strained to see through the curtain and was *positive* that he saw movement. After a moment someone walked past the window without stopping, so he tapped again at the glass. There was some commotion inside, then a hand reached up and began to fumble with the curtain, trying to push it aside to see who was knocking. The fumbling continued for several long seconds, as he anxiously continued tapping on the glass, urging the person inside to hurry it up. Glancing over his shoulder nervously, he stopped and did a double take; standing in the driveway was an unkempt, middle aged man, staring at Sam with confused eyes and an annoyed look on his face. He just stood there, almost appearing appalled by the young man's presence.

Sam froze. It was hard to tell if this man was infected. He was an intimidatingly strong looking man, probably a construction worker, and he didn't appear wounded, but something about him did not seem right. His posture was off, and he was swaying almost imperceptibly. His gaze stayed locked onto Sam, unblinking and unfocused. This did not feel right …

Slowly averting his eyes to look back at the door, he saw the person inside now clawing at the curtain with both hands frantically. The curtain suddenly ripped free from its rod, exposing a grotesquely mangled face.

Sam took a half step back out of fright, and this single movement seemed to activate the other man. He bellowed out a gargled moan and began to gallop up the driveway at an alarmingly fast trot!

Unable to contain his fear, Sam screamed and ran around to the back side of the house. There was nowhere to hide here, so he ran for the next house. Rounding the corner, he tripped over a man's leg and hit the ground HARD, face first. Instantly he was seeing stars and his head was spinning, but he slowly pulled himself up on to his hands and knees. The blow almost knocked him out, and he wasn't sure if he could stand. He slowly lifted his head out of the mental fog to see who he tripped over, and realized he was laying in the midst of seven zombies; they were on the ground, huddled around the carcass of a large dog, eating its entrails. One by one, they began to notice this living man amongst them and started moving toward him.

77

Alarms were going off in his head, but his body was not responding. He forced himself to his feet, took several steps, and then fell back down to one knee.

Come on, feet, don't fail me now!

He heard the galloping man round the corner behind him and crash into the group that were now rising to their feet, which incited the lot of them to begin moaning loudly and become agitated.

Get up! Get up! Pull it together!

His head was spinning and time was going slow. The moans faded away as white static noise clouded his peripheral vision, progressively getting worse and creating a terrible case of tunnel vision. The tunnel grew smaller and smaller, and then disappeared entirely in a field of white as he fell into unconsciousness, knocked out cold.

Dreamily, his mind wandered back in time, lingering on the only other time he could remember losing consciousness. It was late at night, walking with a friend through downtown Ann Arbor. There was no one else out on the street except a group of three kids wearing Dexter High School wrestling jackets. As he passed them, the biggest one said to him in a mocking tone, "Faaaags." Without missing a beat, Sam replied with an extended middle finger just inches from the bigot's face, accentuating the gesture with a *whip-crack* sound for effect. Of course this didn't sit well with those gentlemen, so heated words were quickly exchanged.

Realizing a fight was unavoidable, Sam began to slide his jacket off. However, before his arms cleared his sleeves, the 220 lb. antagonist executed a perfect double-leg take down, flooring Sam hard on the sidewalk. Unable to get a good angle on the big kid's face, 140 lb. Sam took a few good shots at his ribs, but was quickly wrestled into a pretzel, which flowed effortlessly into a vice-like chokehold. Sam had always been good at taking a punch and giving one, but neither of those two things were happening in this fight. He had never lost a fight in his life, but this one was going bad fast. Both of his arms were pinned, and this guy's forearm was dug in deep across his throat, squeezing hard. He couldn't breathe, and the white tunnel vision was beginning to close in around him, squeezing out his consciousness.

Searching for air, he turned his head slightly to the side and unexpectedly saw these two cute girls he knew, Christina and Amelia, standing there watching the whole thing. His last thoughts before passing out were, "Oh, *great*. Here's the one time I'm getting my butt kicked, and of course there are two cuties standing by to watch. Where did they come from? What are they even doing downtown at this hour?" And then he drifted off … to sleep.

Day 02: Sunday, 1111 hrs

Memories of cute girls fell away as Sam became gradually more aware of something tugging on his leg. Bleary eyes slowly opened to a dirty backyard in Detroit, with a beautiful blue sky overhead. Looking down at his leg, the galloping man had hold of it and was biting into his shoe! Sam kicked hard and scrambled to his feet. There were four of them surrounding him, the rest were still feasting on that dog that was leashed to the house's back porch. His brick was lying on the ground next to him, so in one dizzy movement he snatched it up and bashed in the face of the shoe biter. As the man staggered backwards, Sam took the opening and ran.

What happened!? How long was I out!? ... It must have only been a few seconds, but... it felt like I was asleep for hours! DANG! I think that thing bit my foot! I have to find help!

Running out into the street he headed toward Mt. Elliott. A quick check over his shoulder revealed that several of those ghouls were trying to pursue him, but it was almost laughable when he saw how slow they were moving. The one that had initially galloped at him was a little faster than the rest, but could easily be outrun.

I'm just going to make a run for it! I'll head south on Mt. Elliott, keeping a manageable pace, and I won't stop until I find some help...

He took off down the middle of the street in broad daylight, sneakers slapping pavement at a steady pace. Turning south at the intersection, his heart dropped when he saw that the street was dotted with zombies *everywhere*. There were far more than he had estimated from the cemetery, and they all turned to look as he rounded the corner.

Making a snap decision, Sam steeled his nerves and decided to just go for it, to dig down deep and make this happen.

A chorus of moans began to rise as he approached the first cluster of them. They all turned to face him, the torn and battered people of Detroit, raising their hands and clawing at the air as they staggered to intercept his path.

He zigged and zagged, then zigged again. As long as he didn't let them cut off his corridor, he felt sure that he could out step them. Like a football running back looking downfield, he scanned the street for openings amongst the shambling bodies.

Barry Sanders ... Barry Sanders ... Barry Sanders ... was his mantra.

Speed served him well, and he breezed past dozens of the slow moving freaks. It was like taking a jogging tour through a wax museum. Sickly pale eyes, waxy shriveled skin, open wounds and torn clothing. He began to question his own eyes, his own sanity.

How is this real? How did I get here? How far am I going to have to run? I need to stop somewhere and check on my foot!

Running around cars and over decrepit wooden porches to avoid being grabbed, he thought of the Buddhist principle of being like water, flowing effortlessly to the path of least resistance. He veered right to avoid a cluster of mangled kids, then glided back left to steer clear of an armless and faceless man.

The first few blocks may have been stressful on the mind, but physically they were relatively easy. Since the sick were dispersed across the wide street and were not coordinating their attack in any way, it wasn't too hard to plot a safe course.

Also working in his favor was the fact that this neighborhood was largely abandoned and post-apocalyptic even before the outbreak, so there were very few potential hosts here to become infected. Most of the storefronts on this street were either boarded up or burnt down. However, there was a small muffler shop up ahead that still looked to be in business, and surrounding it was 30-40 zombies who were banging on the barred windows and doors.

Sam hoped to breeze past them unnoticed, but as he drew near the mob turned and attacked. He tried to circle wide, but there were too many of them. As he approached the group, they haphazardly fanned out, clogging the street entirely. Turning around to find a different path, he realized that every zombie he'd passed along the way had filed in behind him and had accumulated into a substantial horde. Panic threatened to overwhelm him as he crashed between two infected women, and then knocked down a disfigured old man, but he suddenly had to stop cold in his tracks. His back trail was completely cut off by scores of the undead.

He turned and ran laterally to a boarded up building and started kicking and pulling at a rotting board, trying to get inside. As a wave of them approached, loud gunshots rang out from the muffler shop. All heads turned as a man came stumbling out of the shop, yelling for help. His shirt was off, and tied around his head. Holding a large, chrome handgun, he blasted his way through the crowd. The recoil on that gun was tremendous, and its effects were devastating; heads vanished in a pink mist, bodies tumbled end over end. The old man was dealing death to any zombie that came close.

As he approached, Sam could see that the man had a substantial head wound, and the shirt wasn't doing a great job at stopping the blood.

"Help! Are you a doctor?" the old man asked as he reloaded his gun.

"What?" Sam was dumbfounded by the question, and then remembered he was still wearing his hospital scrubs. "Um … no! I'm an MRI Tech!"

"A *what*?"

"An MRI Tech! You know, like CAT scans, x-rays … *MRIs!*"

The old man looked confused by his answer, "So … you *are* a doctor?"

"No, man! That's not important right now! Just keep shooting! I've almost got this window opened!"

The man had lost a lot of blood and was delirious, but that didn't seem to affect his aim. He turned and squeezed off three more rounds, dropping three more zombies.

Sam went back to work on the boarded window and wrenched it open, tossing the rotten wood at the approaching crowd. He climbed in first and then helped pull the wounded man in. Zombies converged on the open window and began to tumble in after them.

Sam quickly surveyed the burned out building. It looked like an old hardware store, but it had been gutted and looted years ago. Looking desperately around the dark store, they saw an open door leading to a back stockroom. They ran in and slammed the charred door closed, locking it behind them.

A column of dusty sunlight was beaming down through a burned out staircase, illuminating the scorched room. A smoke damaged couch sat in a corner next to a pile of scrap wood, so Sam immediately went to work barricading the door. As he did so, he could hear their pursuers stomping around in the front room.

After piling the couch and a sufficient amount of debris in front of the door, he turned back and saw that his companion had collapsed to the floor, lying face down in his own blood. Hesitatingly, he approached the man.

"Hey, buddy, are you alright?"

There was no response.

"Hey, man, did you get bit?"

Still no response.

As he pondered his next move, he heard clumsy hands testing the door, softly at first, and then with a little more conviction. Within seconds several more hands joined in and began to bang violently on the frail door. He had to keep moving.

There was an adjoining room that he quickly rummaged through, but there were no windows or doors leading out. Running back into the first room, he peered up the opening where the staircase once stood. The beautiful blue sky could be seen through a large hole in the roof.

Testing a few blackened remnants of wall studs and the old handrail, he deemed it safe enough to climb given these circumstances. Stepping one foot onto the handrail, he reached up and grabbed high on the sturdiest looking stud. With a lunge and a twist he was up and within reach of the second story's wooden floor, so he gripped the edge and pulled himself up.

The second story was thoroughly gutted by the fire and was entirely unsafe to be in. The floor looked as though it could give way at any moment. There were a few intact studs holding up the front part of the roof, but the back half had collapsed, opening up the ceiling and allowing ample light to fill the charred room. There were no boards or glass in the front window panes, so Sam crept closer to see how bad things were looking in the street.

A large crowd of infected people had surrounded the building, with more approaching from farther up the street. The light of day

83

exposed this terrible scene in all its horror. These poor people had been critically mutilated yet continued to function. It defied logic. Superhuman resilience seemed to be an effect of this terrible epidemic.

The sound of splintering wood drew his attention back to the room below. He peered down and could see that the door was beginning to give way to the relentless pounding. The old man was still lying face down, but his chest rose and fell as he let out a deep sigh.

Sam called down to him, "Hey! Are you still with me, man?"

He responded clearly but remained prone, "Yeah, I'll be a'ight … I just need a corpsman."

"A *what*? Oh … do you mean a medic?"

The man rolled over. His face was swollen and his blood soaked shirt was wrapped tightly under his chin and over the top of his head, just like in an old movie. He looked irritated and barked back, "Heck naw, I ain't lettin' no *Army* hack near me! What I need is a damned *corpsman*!"

Sam remembered that Marines referred to their medical personnel as 'corpsmen.' Apparently this cat was a former Marine.

"Hey, Marine, did you get bit?"

"No, shot," he responded.

This man had lost a lot of blood and was possibly delirious, so Sam was hesitant to believe him.

"What do you mean? Who shot you?"

"Some damn punks. I was closin' up the shop and these two little bastards came in and robbed me."

Sam was still reluctant to take the man at his word, so he pressed his inquiry, "Are you sure they *shot* you? Maybe they bit you."

The Marine looking visibly annoyed, "When a man presses a gun up under your chin and says, 'Open the damn register,' you sure as hell don't forget it."

They stared at each other for a moment longer as their attackers continued to assault the old door. The man seemed lucid enough, so Sam took a chance. "Well listen, sir, those things are about to break through that door. Do you think you can climb up here?"

The man got up slowly and walked over to the stairway. Reaching up, he said in a tired voice, "Lend me a hand, Doc."

Taking the man's hand, Sam pulled him up, grunting as he

84

said, "I told you, I'm not a doctor, I'm an MRI Tech."

"Whatever. I just hope 'M-I-R Techs' are good at removin' bullets."

Sam smiled, both at the man's resilience and at his butchering of the acronym "MRI."

After hoisting him up, they went to the front of the room near the windows and sat with their backs against the wall. Peeking out the window, he saw more and more sick people coming, attracted by the excited mob beneath them. As was becoming the norm, there was no good plan. Finding himself in a building surrounded by homicidal maniacs seemed to be his lot in life.

Extending his hand to the wounded man, he said, "My name's Sam."

The man hesitated, then returned with a vice-like hand shake, simply saying, "Clarence." His face looked grotesquely swollen, but he spoke very clearly. He was a well-built black man, probably in his 50's or 60's.

"Well, Clarence, it's a pleasure to meet you. So what happened, how bad are you hurt?"

"Not sure. I was staying late to wrap up some work, and somehow two damn kids got in the shop. The one pressed a gun right up under my chin an' told me to open the register. I *did*, and then the little piss ant shot me anyways. I woke up on the floor this mornin' with a gawd awful headache and dried up blood all in my mouth and 'round my neck. I heard some sounds in the shop, so I went back into the office to get my gun. Sure enough, them two kids were still there... they were lying dead on the floor being *eaten* by some serious lookin' characters, so I shot the whole lot of em'. I tried to call 911 but couldn't get through, so I went outside to find help, but the whole dang street was a mess. Rioting, lootin' people fightin'. Then some messed up lookin' cracker tried to jump me, so I put a bullet in him, too, an' jus' decided to fall back inside the office. Things started quietin' down out there for a minute, and then I heard *your* ass comin' down the street like the damn Pied Piper. But I saw you's dressed like a doctor, an' I need to get this gunshot looked at."

"Like I said, sir, I'm no doctor, but maybe I can help. Let me take a look at it."

He undid the makeshift wrapping, revealing a small entrance wound under the man's chin. The bullet had passed through his mouth, missing his tongue and continuing through his upper palate, lodging somewhere inside his head. There was a lot of dried blood, and a little fresh blood, but the bleeding had mostly stopped.

"Well, Clarence, there's no exit wound, so the bullet is still in there. It must have been a small caliber, like a .22 or a .25, because it didn't blow the top of your head off. The good news is that you aren't bleeding too much now, but with all that swelling and discoloration you may still be bleeding on the *inside*. You really need to get to a hospital, but I just came from St. John, and it is completely overrun. We could try to get you to Detroit Receiving, however it could be bad there, too. Heck, I wouldn't even know how to get there from here. Do *you*?"

"Yeah, jus' head south then turn right on Warren. I got a truck behind the shop, but I didn't have enough bullets t' clear the way. Hell, I got a lot less *now*," he said as he removed the clip from his enormous handgun, cleared the chamber, and loaded it back up. "Two in the clip, one in the chamber."

Sam grimaced. "Well, that won't do. We are in a *bad* predicament, friend." Sam looked out the window before continuing, "Do you have any idea what's wrong with these people?"

Clarence's bloodshot eyes stared off in the distance. He weighed his answer carefully before speaking, "They said on the radio that it's rabies, or some such nonsense," then he turned his gaze to meet Sam's, "but that ain't it. This is judgment day, son. I hope you've made your peace with God."

Sam didn't know what to say, so he just looked back out the window.

There were so many sick people surrounding the building, and an overwhelming feeling of hopelessness was pulling at his mind, dragging him down. Looking down at his foot, he saw the bite marks in his shoe and his heart almost stopped. He untied his shoe and pulled it off, inspecting his foot closely. His toes were bruised, but the man's teeth didn't appear to have punctured his high tops. Letting out a sigh of relief, he smiled at Clarence, saying, "Someone down the street bit my shoe. I thought I was done for." Clarence just gave him a blank stare, and then closed his eyes. His face was grotesquely swollen.

Sam got up to take a better look around the room. After a thorough tour of the upper story, he confirmed to his new companion that they were trapped.

"We're stuck. I don't know what else to do but sit tight and wait for an opportunity to present itself. If we hide long enough, maybe they'll forget about us and move along."

Clarence didn't open his eyes, he just said aloud, "I shoulda stayed in my damn muffler shop."

They sat silently for a long while, listening to the moaning crowd bang on the locked door beneath them. In the distance, sporadic gunfire continued. Sam's hands were blackened from the charred building, and his clothes reeked like that mildew coated mattress he slept on. His nerves were shot, and try as he might, it was getting difficult to ignore his thirst.

Pulling out his phone, he checked the time, 11:20 am, forty minutes before he was due to text his wife. Returning it to his pocket, he closed his eyes and tried to recap the past 24 hours in his mind. It felt like his morning commute was *weeks* ago. His mind began to drift, and he wondered if the good people of Liechtenstein and Uzbekistan knew what was happening in Detroit.

It was at that time that a loud, splintering sound announced that their pursuers had broken through the charred door below. Clarence and Sam both opened their eyes and looked at each other, but neither moved. They could hear the room beneath them filling rapidly with the moaning dead, stomping around and banging at the walls. These creatures *knew* that the men were in here somewhere.

Sam whispered, "I'm not even gonna *peek* down there, I don't want to risk attracting their attention up here. And y'know, I really don't think they'll be able to climb up, so if we just lay low and let them ransack the building, hopefully they'll eventually get bored and leave."

"They ain't leavin', this ain't like the Riot in '67. These fools are zombies, they got the Devil in them," Clarence mumbled in a whisper.

"*Zombies*, huh?" Sam asked.

Clarence glared hard but kept his voice down, "Dat's right: zombies. If it looks like a duck, an' quacks like a duck, what da' hell else you supposed to call it? Suppose I say, 'look out, here comes a zombie,' you sure as hell know who I'm talkin' about! That crazy eyed mo-fo who's walkin' around actin' like a damned zombie! *Dat's* who!"

"I hear ya, sir … I'm just having a hard time wrapping my head around this. I still don't believe in zombies, but here they are," Sam shook his head in disbelief, then added, "And let me just say it right now: if I see a damned displacer beast walking up Woodward Ave., I'm just going to cash in my *own* chips."

Clarence looked at him like he was crazy, "A displacement *what*?"

"Oh nothing, man. It's a mythological creature… like zombies and unicorns."

Clarence just shook his head, "Cash in your own chips? Damn white folks, always the first one to pull your own trigger, t' give up the ghost. Don't ya'll know suicide's a sin? *That* one will getcha a ticket straight to hell."

"Aw, I don't really mean it, sir. I plan on fighting to the end, but if I can't laugh at my predicament or crack a joke, I probably *will* lose it. Besides, I don't really believe in hell … or zombies, or displacer beasts."

"Well, you got two out of three out there in the street right now, so maybe when you see that 'displacement beast' comin' at cha, you'll start to believe."

It was getting hard to hear one another speak, because the angry moans and thumps of the undead below were becoming deafening. Even so, the self-preservation instinct kept both men speaking in whispers. The old burned out store was also groaning and creaking under the weight of so many occupants. It sounded as if there were a hundred of them in the room below, with more piling in through the front window.

Sam was contemplating escape, but getting nowhere. "I can't believe this place did not have a back door! That *can't* be up to code."

"Naw, it sure wasn't up t' code. Dat's why that man died when they burnt it down. He jus' couldn't get out," Clarence answered.

"Seriously? Someone died here?"

"Yeah, this place was white-owned, an' got torched during the riot."

Sam was intrigued, "Wow. Were you here during the riot?"

Clarence was visibly annoyed with the question, but answered anyway, "Yeah, when I heard the trouble was spreading I ran around to all my stores, boardin' up windows. An' when I pulled up to the muffler shop, I saw the hardware store was lit, an' you could hear that ol' bastard inside there screamin' for help. Even though he was a bastard of a racist, I still felt for 'em."

"That's wild, man."

Sam was silent for a moment, thinking about Clarence's words, the burning man, and racism in general.

"You know, sir, my dad was in the military, too, so I moved around a lot as a child. Down South I met a lot of folks who seemed like good, decent people, but you never could tell who was a racist. One day, while I was living in Niceville, Florida, I'm at this kid's house playing Super Mario Brothers, and he mentioned something about being in the Klan. I didn't believe him, so he took me in his dad's room and showed me the closet: they had white Klan robes for him, his dad, his uncle, and his brother. I didn't even know the KKK existed anymore, and here I am playing video games with one of those jokers! It freaked me out.

"I had just moved there from Alabama, where I attended the 'Black' school. It was supposedly desegregated years ago, but since the neighborhoods were still racially divided in practice, the whites still went to the same nice, well-kept school, and the blacks still went to the same old run-down school. And since I dressed like a punk, had long hair and an earring, the white kids there *hated* me, calling me a queer, and a Yankee and what not. I guess they'd never seen a guy with long hair before. So I hung out with the black kids. I was the 'token white boy' in our group.

"So anyways, when I saw those Klan robes I felt like I was about to be lynched! Apparently he didn't know I wasn't cool with that. Needless to say, I never hung out with *that* kid anymore."

"*Niceville*, huh?" Clarence forced a chuckle.

"Yeah, it actually is a nice little town, and it's much better now, but it's in the part of Florida they call 'Southern Alabama,' or the 'Redneck Riviera.' As a matter of fact, and forgive me for using the N-word, but my friend's ma told us that there used to be a hand painted sign by the bridge leading into Niceville that read, 'All Niggers be out by sundown.' Can you believe it? That wasn't even 30 or 40 years ago."

Clarence sat up straight and shook his head, "Pshhh … can I believe it? Listen up, kid. I've got six stores 'dat I own: three drug stores, a party store, a diner, an' 'dat muffler shop, Back in '66, I used t' primarily work at my drug store on Grand River, and I'd always walk next door to the diner t' check on things and do my order. But the po-lice would harass me every time they saw me standing outside my store. They'd say I was loiterin', or trespassin'. I told them I *owned* both these buildings and had every right t' stand in front of them whenever I choose to. I think they didn't like the idea of a successful black man makin' more money than they was, so they'd commence to beatin' on me. Bustin' my eye, bustin' my nose, kickin' me in the nuts, an' then they'd jus' leave an' come back the next day, and we'd fight some more. After a while, I got purdy damn good at fightin', so I started beatin' *they* asses. It finally got t' where they'd just drive by and stare me down. The only times they'd stop is when there was at least four of 'em. And it wasn't jus' me. All over this city, a black man jus' couldn't catch a break, an' if he started t' get ahead in life, the po-lice would come an' beat 'em down. *That's* why those folks rioted. 'Cause 'dat wasn't the country *I* was fightin' for in the Marine Corps. In *my* America, every man is created equal, no matter what color his skin is."

"I'm with *you*, man. That just ain't right." Sam agreed.

Clarence let out an incredulous puff of air, "Yeah, you say 'dat right now, sittin' here with me, but I wonder what you'd say if you was here with a surly ol' white man, an' a room full o' black zombies beneath you. Better yet, what would you say if your own daughter came home wantin' to date some black kid?"

Sam smiled and looked at the floor, "Well, actually I have a 19 year old daughter who lives with her mom out in Illinois. Her first two boyfriends were both black, and I never had a problem with it. As a matter of fact, Jermaine was a really cool kid. I wish she'd stayed with him, but she ended up dating some moody white kid who can't seem to keep his hands to himself."

"The boys never can, and it sounds like neither could *you*," Clarence laughed, giving Sam a sideways glance, "What you' mean you have a 19 year ol' girl? How ol' are you?"

"I'm 34," Sam said.

Clarence gave him a sly grin, nodding knowingly.

"I know, I know," Sam said shaking his head, "I was pretty young and irresponsible. I fell in love with this Thai girl when I was 14. She was 16, real cute, had a car … and she wasn't very shy, if you know what I mean."

Clarence gave a big, toothy smile, "Oh, I know *exactly* what you mean, you fell victim t' white man's kryptonite!"

"What? ... I ... I don't get it, what do you mean?"

"Yeah, man, *Asian* girls. White man's *kryptonite*. With black dudes it's the blondes; we jus' can't say no to 'em. With white folks, it's the Asian girls."

Sam smiled introspectively and laughed, "Ya know, you've got a good point, man. I guess I never really thought about it, but I am a sucker for 'em!"

Both men laughed for a few moments. It was nice to let off a little steam, to talk and laugh, and forget about the menacing plague for a few brief seconds. As their laughter wound down, they looked each other in the eye for a moment, smiling genuinely and appreciating each other's company.

"You got any other kids?" Clarence asked.

"Yeah, I have a three year old named Simon, and the wife is pregnant right now with a girl."

"Well congratulations, Doc," Clarence said, extending his hand.

Sam gratefully took the man's hand, "Thanks, sir. Thanks a lot, but I'm afraid ... things are a little strained with my wife. I'm afraid the only reason she hasn't left me is because of the pregnancy. Her heart's started to stray."

"Well I'm sorry to hear that, son. You jus' hang in there. You seem like a decent man, I'm sure she'll see the light."

"What about you? Have you got any kids?"

"Six kids, and fifteen grand kids," Clarence said with pride, "an' every one of 'em is college bound."

"That's great, man. But six? I think I'm gonna stop at three. Oh! Speaking of family, I need to text my wife!"

He pulled out his phone and checked the time: 11:55, close enough.

Clarence's eyes opened wider than Sam had seen all morning, "Say wha? Are the phone lines back up?"

"No, but I've been able to send and receive text messages," Sam said as he began typing on his cell phone:

"hi babe. i'm stuck in a hardware store on mt elliott, near warren. what r they saying on the news?" send.

He received the reply in seconds, "u need to get out of detroit! the whole city is full of zombies! i'm so worried! R U OK?"

Sam responded, "yes babe, but there r lots of them outside, so we're stuck here for now. did they say if the police r getting it under control?" send.

"no! the police are trying to get out too, they are calling in the national guard! even the news people are trapped in the station!"

"yeah, there r so many sick people out in the street, its gonna be a long walk home. what else is the news saying?" send.

"same thing is happening in a lot of cities, but detroit is the worst. memphis is also real bad. and something big is going on with china and n korea, it sounds like they might go to war"

"wow. ok, i'm stuck here with another man for now but i will try to leave when its safe, or when the national guard shows up. my cell phone battery is low, so i'll turn it off for a while, but will txt again when i leave here" send.

"baby i have been crying all morning, plz be careful!"

"i will, luv. just keep the doors locked and the news on. try to text my fam if u can, i will be home soon <3" send.

"I LOVE YOU be safe!" was her reply.

"I LOVE U 2," send.

After bringing Clarence up to speed with the news report, Sam got up to stretch his legs. He was becoming stir crazy in the small, burned out room. Claustrophobia, the smell of burnt buildings and rotting corpses, fear, it was all very taxing on the mind. After pacing a few circles, he dared to peek out the window again.

Clarence opened one swollen eye and said, "Why don't you give me a SITREP while you're lookin' out there, a situation report? The Corps trained us to recon the enemy usin' the SALUTE format: Size, Activity, Location, Unit, Time, and Equipment. Try it."

"Alright, S-A-L-U-T-E, huh? I can do that," Sam said as he focused his attention to the horde in the street.

"SIZE: I count 37 of them, not nearly as many out there as before.

"ACTIVITY: basically they're just shuffling around in front of the building, moaning like they're sick …. or wounded … or maybe … *hungry?*

"LOCATION: most of them have gathered in front of the store, but they don't seem to be climbing in the window anymore. Maybe we have a full house down there, standing room only. And there are still a few down the street, but not many; I only see … eight.

"UNIT? What does that mean?" Sam asked.

Clarence answered without opening his eyes, "What unit are they from? Are they wearin' anythin' what identifies who they are?"

"Oh, okay. UNIT: most of them are just wearing street clothes … I see some jeans, baggy shorts, a Pistons jersey … but there are two cops out there … a fireman … a couple paramedics … and wait … there's three more firemen." The firemen were severely mutilated, as if wild animals had been gnawing on their heads, exposing their skulls. Sam shuddered involuntarily and rubbed his eyes.

"Where was I? S-A-L-U-T … T? TIME?" he pulled out his phone to check the time, "12:20pm.

"And 'E' is for EQUIPMENT: well, they're not carrying much, just teeth and a bad attitude. One of the cops has a gun in his holster …," Sam craned his neck, squinting, "the other one doesn't. That's about all I see."

Clarence opened both eyes, which were now just puffy, swollen slits, "Good recon, Doc. So what can you conclude with your intel? If there's only 37 of them sons a bitches out there, dat' means there's a whole mess of 'em packed in the room below, 'cause there was easily a hundred of 'em before. An' with only a few out in the street, dat' means we prolly attracted all them what's gonna come, so the rest o' the block is prolly pretty clear. But it's the Unit report I don't like. Eight firs' responders."

"Eight *what*?" Sam asked, not quite understanding the man's old school Dee-troit dialect.

"Firs' responders! Po-lice, Firemen, Paramedics. Them's the boys that are doin' the front line work, an' if they's gettin' chewed up an' bit, there ain't gonna be no one around to help us but our *own* selves."

He was right. These were the people who would be needed right now, the ones who were trained to deal with public emergencies, first aid, and security. Unfortunately, being first on the scene would also ensure that they were among the first to be attacked and bitten by the very people they were coming to help. That would also explain why the hospital was so quickly overrun; all of the bitten and infected victims were being funneled to the ER for treatment, making it possibly the worst place to be in an outbreak of this kind.

Sam felt a little better from having an organized assessment of the situation, however bleak it may be. He sat back on the floor and began to do a few yoga poses to loosen up his tense muscles.

Clarence watched him for several minutes through increasingly swollen eyes before finally chiming in, "What now, you plan on usin' some Kung Fu on they ass?"

Sam was lunging deep into the Warrior II pose, "Naw, man, I'm just doing some yoga to limber up. I want to be ready to make a break for it at the first opportunity."

Taking several slow, deep breaths, he transitioned into Warrior I, and then to Reverse Warrior. Holding that pose, Sam thought only about his breath, clearing his mind of the smells of charred wood and rotting corpses, and the sounds of tortured moans. Holding the pose with a strong core and his right arm extended to the sky, he became gradually more aware of a new sound creeping into his senses. He slowly opened his eyes as the sound became louder and closer; it was police sirens.

Breaking his pose, he rose to his feet and looked out the window; Clarence did the same. The zombies in the street were all looking north, in the direction of the highway and the approaching sirens. As the three police cars came into view, the momentum of the horde shifted in their direction, arms raised with hunger.

"This may be our chance, Clarence! Get ready!" Sam said as he tiptoed to the stairway and cautiously looked down. The room below was packed like the front row of an arena concert, shoulder-to-shoulder, pushing and shoving. He had hoped that they would be moving toward the front window, drawn by the sirens. Much to his dismay, most of them seemed oblivious to the sound. The few that did take notice were looking around the room wildly, apparently unable to pinpoint its source.

The sirens were getting louder as the vehicles drew near, so Sam returned to the window. There were three patrol cars approaching fast, but they slowed to about 15mph as they closed in on the thirty or so zombies that were being drawn toward them. Each car was filled beyond capacity with at least eight passengers packed tightly into each vehicle.

They stayed in formation, a single file line, as the first car's reinforced bumper struck the leading edge of the crowd. A few bodies were knocked into the air as others went over the hood and rolled harmlessly off to the side. However, the majority of them were knocked to the ground and rolled over by the police cruisers. The cars bounced violently as they rolled over torsos, heads, and limbs.

The first two cars cleared the pack and began to accelerate away, but the third car began to lose momentum. It bounced over several bodies as it slowly ground to a halt, revving its motor and spinning its rear tires. The stalled vehicle was slightly propped up and cockeyed, apparently it had high-centered on the fallen corpses and was unable to gain traction.

Like hyenas pouncing on wounded prey, the ghouls surrounded the lame vehicle and threw themselves on it, banging angrily on the windows. A woman's screams could be heard coming from within as the driver alternated between forward and reverse, trying to rock the car free.

For several minutes the car rocked back and forth as the men in the house looked on. A large woman's torso was acting as a chock or a jack stand in front of the car's rear tire, propping it up and preventing it from gripping pavement. The terrified passengers could clearly be seen through the car windows, looking like frightened animals caught in a trap. Then, right before their eyes, they saw a man in the back seat pull out a gun, stick it in his mouth, and pull the trigger.

BLAM!

The back windshield of the police cruiser exploded outwards as the side window went opaque with splattered blood. The poor, doomed occupants shrieked horrifically as diseased hands reached into the now gaping window, pulling a young woman out by her weave, kicking and screaming. She slid off the back trunk lid and was pulled to the ground. As the crowd ate her alive, she screamed and plead for someone to kill her. It was not a quick death.

The driver floored the vehicle mercilessly, red lining the engine and spinning the rear tire against the large woman's torso. Sam watched as the spinning rubber slowly peeled away her blouse, and then her skin, and then began slinging ropes of intestine until it finally caught some traction in her open abdominal cavity, propelling the car forward.

After a few rough bounces, the car broke free and sped off down the street. As the sirens faded into the distance, the two men stood speechless, watching the carjacked woman being eaten in the street. She was still moving, still alive.

Clarence raised his chrome gun and pointed it at the woman's head.

95

BLAM!

She finally stopped struggling.

Several of the undead turned toward the sound of the gunshot and staggered back onto the front stoop of the hardware store. Their hungry determination was renewed knowing that someone was indeed still alive in the building.

"Two rounds left," Clarence said as he sat back down, closing his eyes.

Sam joined him on the floor, feeling defeated. He wondered aloud how much longer he could tolerate this, but his thoughts were rhetorical and Clarence did not bother to respond. He had a splitting headache, most likely from caffeine withdrawal and dehydration. Fear and adrenaline had been keeping him going, but he could feel exhaustion beginning to set in. He leaned his head against the blackened wall and closed his eyes, nodding off in seconds.

They awoke to the sound of splitting wood and creaking timbers. Sam tried to get to his feet, but the floor was shifting and shuttering… then it stopped. The men looked at each other with wild eyes, hoping each other had an explanation. It took a few moments to realize the structure they were in had shifted under the weight of all these occupants.

"You alright?" Sam asked.

"Yeah … but this buildin's about t' *go*. Shoot, it wouldn't take more'n a stiff breeze t' blow this ol' buildin' down, an' here *we* are with a couple thousan' pounds of pissed off dead weight stompin' around down there."

Sam forced a smile, "Maybe I should text the Fire Marshall, tell him we got a maximum occupancy violation, in a condemned building, no less."

Clarence was not amused.

"Pshhh … Go back t' sleep," was his response, as he closed his eyes and rolled over, adding, "Didja notice who it was dat capped hisself in the po-lice car? It was the white boy."

Sam gave a somber laugh, "Yeah, you got a point, sir."

He flipped open his phone and checked the time: 3:47pm. He had been napping for three hours.

Standing up, he slowly walked the perimeter of the 2nd floor. The old building creaked balefully with every step, but didn't appear any different than before the shift. The room beneath them was still full of infected maniacs.

"Boy, you best be steppin' gingerly. I don't wanna fall through this floor," Clarence warned.

"Like a ninja, sir," Sam responded, as he soft-shoed back to the front window. The woman who had been dragged out of the car was now little more than a bony carcass, picked clean of muscle and flesh. The gunshot to her brain apparently worked to keep her from rising from the dead, and Sam knew he would be wise to remember that fact.

"How's it look out there, Doc?" Clarence asked.

"Oh, not good. That big woman that had her guts peeled out by the police car is up and walking around … it's hard to believe my eyes, sir … it looks like the apocalypse."

"Hell, son, that's just Detroit. It's looked like the damn apocalypse for years," the old man chided, "What I'm axin' is how many of 'em is still out there?"

Sam did a quick count, "Thirty eight souls, probably more."

Clarence huffed, "Ain't no souls in *those* poor devils; they already gave up the ghost. Just you let me know if you see an opening, 'cause I mean t' get out o' here an see my family."

"I hear ya, man. If I see an opening, you'll be the first one I tell," Sam joked as he sat back down on the floor. "So are you from Detroit, Clarence?"

"Me? Not really. We moved up here from Montgomery in '43 when my Pa got a job at Chrysler, makin' Army tanks. He was proud t' be doin' it, helpin' with the war effort an' all. 'The Arsenal of Democracy' is what he called it, where a man could git an honest day's pay for an honest day's work. But he was one of the lucky ones. He had a good boss that didn't pay no mind t' the color of his skin. He worked on the factory line, gettin' paid the same as everyone else, white or black. Some colored folks weren't so lucky. A lot o' whites didn't want a black man workin' alongside 'em."

"Wow, how the times have changed," Sam said, staring out the window at the blue sky, "I'm only 34, so it's hard for me to imagine Detroit *not* being a predominantly black city. We have a black mayor, black city council, black police force, black doctors … well, actually most of the Docs I work with are from India or Asia …" his words tapered off, and after a moment of thought he cracked a huge grin.

"What? What is it?" Clarence asked.

"Well, a nurse I work with told me a crazy story. She can remember the very first black patient to come into the hospital, I think she said it was 1970. The patient had come into the ER the night before, and the next day *everyone* was talking about it. That neighborhood was all Polish and Italian, so I guess it was a big deal at the time. Later that week, Human Resources made all the employees attend a mandatory 'sensitivity training' class. They were divided into pairs, and they took turns putting on a 'black' face mask so the other person could get comfortable talking to someone who's black."

Clarence's eyes opened wide for the first time in several hours and he let out a big belly laugh, "You pullin' my chain!?"

Sam laughed back, "No, sir, I swear! That's what she told me! Can you imagine that? They took turns putting on a black face. Do you suppose they tried to *talk* black, too? I just can't believe how inappropriate that sounds by today's standards. Heck, if they tried to pull something like that today, Al Sharpton would be all over them like white on rice!"

"Dat's the damnedest thing I ever heard!" Clarence said, still laughing and shaking his head.

"I know, man!" Sam agreed, "I just wonder what that mask actually *looked* like. I mean, that was back in 1970, when Halloween mask technology wasn't like it is today. I bet it looked pretty freakin' scary!"

"Hell! *I'd* be scared talkin' to some crazy cracker wearin' a damned black-face mask! But that's how things was back then, I suppose a lot o' people just didn't know no better," Clarence mused.

Both men sat there for some time, staring off into the burned room daydreaming. A brief flurry of gunfire echoed in the distance, snapping them out of their moment of tranquility.

"I think we're going to be pinned down for the night, Clarence. I wonder if I can slip out of the window once the sun goes down to try to get us some water."

"Shoot, if you's climbing down, I'm gonna be right behind ya."

Sam peeked out the window again, assessing the viability of his idea.

"I don't know, man, there isn't much to hold on to, and there's still a crowd of them on the front stoop. Climbing out the window might not be my best idea. I *could* try to climb up on the roof and check for a way down in the back alley," Sam offered.

Clarence scoffed, "You got some *stones* if you gonna try to get on *that* ol' roof. You'll fall straight through."

Sam sized-up the burnt, half collapsed roof with a look of doubt. "Yeah, I think you're right. Our best hope is that someone else will come along to draw their attention away from us, but I don't know how long I can wait. I've never been this thirsty before in my whole life."

"When's the last time you had somethin' t' drink?" Clarence asked.

"Hmm … yesterday around 9am or so, I had a cup of coffee."

"Hell, Doc, you got at least another day or so before you know what *real* thirst is. I was in the Chosen Reservoir back in 1950 …"

"Korea?" Sam interrupted.

99

"...yeah, Korea. An' we was surrounded by Chinese soldiers, *thousands* of 'em. Pinned down on the side of a rocky mountain, we was completely cut off from our supply chain. Canteens was either empty or frozen solid, an' they wouldn't let us light fires t' thaw 'em 'cause it'd give away our position t' the Chi-com mortar men. So we ate snow fer about three days till men started droppin' from hypothermia. Ya see, eatin' snow may quench your thirst, but it brings your core temperature down, so we was ordered t' stop eatin' it. It took us three more days t' fight our way outta that frozen reservoir, an' by that time my tongue was so dry an' chapped I couldn't even speak."

Sam thought for a minute, "Wait a sec ... 1950? How old are you?"

Clarence laughed, saying, "Too old for *this*," as he slowly got to his feet and walked over to the gaping stairwell. He looked over his shoulder and gave Sam a wink, and then returned his gaze to the first floor as he unzipped his trousers.

"Hey! Ugly!" he yelled down to the first floor, following it up with a loud, shrill whistle. Several diseased faces looked up at him. "Yeah! YOU!" he said as he relieved himself on several of the undead, cackling as he aimed his stream from side to side, strafing the zombies below with urine. They were notably agitated by this, and it amused the old man to no end. Clarence let out a booming laugh and a loud fart as he zipped back up and returned to his spot on the floor.

"Let's see what dey think about *dat*," he added as he got comfortable and closed his swollen eyes.

The men laid there silently for several hours, listening to sounds of the chaotic city. There were surprisingly few police sirens now, and the gunfire was intermittent, but decreasing steadily. Several helicopters could be heard circling nearby, but they never passed over this block. There was no way out of this old hardware store, and all the men could do was to wait for events to unfold, or for thirst to force them to confront the mob.

Before the sun set, Sam pulled out his paperback copy of *Marine Sniper: 93 Confirmed Kills*, and passed the time reading until there was too little light to see the words. Closing the book, he reached over and gently tried to rouse Clarence, who had been lying motionless for some time. The old Marine did not wake easily, but after some effort he began to grumble and stir.

"You feeling okay, sir?" Sam inquired.

Unmoving, the man tried to speak, paused to clear his throat of phlegm and dried blood, and then answered hoarsely, "Oh, I'm just peachy. When do we move out?"

Sam smiled, "No time soon. It sounds like they're having a house party downstairs. How's your head?"

"Oh, that. I guess I'm feelin' a little groggy ... an' I got a bear of a headache. I'll be fine, I jus' need t' sleep it off."

"That's probably a good idea. Save your strength, I'll wake you up if I hear anything."

Clarence just grunted in agreement. The swelling was getting worse, distorting his facial features like an over inflated balloon. In the moonlit room his face had the appearance of a bloated, discolored corpse. It was obvious that the old man was deteriorating, and Sam began to doubt that he would make it through the night without real medical attention. The bullet wound to his head was far worse than either man wanted to admit.

Resigned to the fact that they would be sleeping here tonight, Sam pulled out his cell phone to text his wife with an update. To his horror, the display was flashing 'low battery'... no bars.

He typed, "hi babe, i will be sleeping in this hardware store on mt elliott tonight. it's too dangerous to leave right now. i'm with a man who has a gun, so we'll be safe," send. Sam didn't want his wife to worry, so he neglected to mention the man's injury or their dwindling ammo situation ... or the dilapidated, zombie filled building that was crumbling around them.

The response was almost immediate, "Please be careful! It is SO bad on the news, Detroit is being quarantined, but they may let you out if the National Guard doctors check you out first. r u ok?"

"yes, just thirsty. we are safe for the night. what else r they saying on the news?" send.

"They are showing videos of zombies in Detroit, Memphis, Chicago, and New York. It looks horrible. I cant believe ur out there! And China is bombing North Korea because of the zombies. Obama is going to be on tv soon"

"wow, thanks. i cant wait to see the national guard! but my battery is dying so im gonna turn my phone off for the night. i'll text u when i wake up. keep the doors locked! i love you!" send.

"Ok, I will be waiting to hear from you. Come home safely!"

101

was her reply.

Sam powered down his phone and stowed it in his shirt pocket. He considered rousing Clarence again to pass along Jessica's update, but decided to let the old man sleep. He could fill him in when they woke up.

The evening was cooling off, so he pulled his lanky arms into his shirt for warmth and nestled against the charred wall, closing his eyes. The haunting sounds coming from those diseased corpses below was enough to induce the worst kinds of nightmares, but exhaustion trumped any chance of dreaming as Sam fell into a deep, hard sleep.

Day 3: Monday, 0138

Again the young man awoke to chaos and motion. The pitch black room seemed to be spiraling out of control as splintered wood came crashing down on him. The floor beneath them slid off kilter then dropped several feet onto the hundred or so squirming zombies in the condemned hardware store. The fall knocked the wind out of him, and the blackened ceiling joists buried him in a pile of twisted and snapped wooden beams. In the dark, arms that stunk of rotting flesh were flailing around between the demolished floorboards, pawing violently at the disoriented man.

Sam kicked and pulled and pushed broken lumber aside as he unburied himself from the collapsed building. Clambering and squirming toward a pocket of moonlight, he pulled his body free of the splintered wood and fell eight feet, landing hard in a paved alley behind the row of buildings. The fall and impact only added to his sense of confusion, and he scrambled to his feet and ran straight into a large, angry, human body.

He yelled and instinctively punched the dead man hard in the face, knocking him down. Unable to see in the dark back street, he ran blindly down the debris filled alley, tripping and recovering multiple times before he reached a moonlit clearing between two abandoned buildings.

Crouching in a defensive stance, he looked for any attackers but could see none coming his way. The dark silhouettes of the undead were all converging toward the woodpile and the buried Marine. Two loud gunshots rang out from beneath the collapsed hardware store, followed by loud, proud singing:

> From the Halls of Montezuma,
> T' the shores of Tripoli;
> We fight our country's battles
> In the air, on land, and sea;
> First t' fight for right and freedom
> And t' keep our honor clean;
> We are proud to claim the title
> Of United States Marine.

103

Sam listened for a few more moments, and could faintly hear Clarence struggle and curse as the collapsed building was overrun. Yelps of pain and more cursing indicated the old curmudgeon was putting up a fight, but from the sounds of the melee it was obvious that the man was being bitten. His voice tapered away and was lost among the loud moans emanating from the infected horde. The commotion of the buildings collapse had worked the infected up into a frenzy.

Crouching low into the weedy, vacant lot, he took a few moments to reorient himself and calm his racing heart. The moon provided sufficient light to see that the way South was relatively clear of zombies, but he was sick to his stomach from thinking about poor Clarence.

I have to keep going ... there is nothing I can do for him; he is as good as dead. I have to survive and get home to my family.

He hated himself for leaving the old man behind, but there is no way he could dig through a pile of rubble in the dark, looking for a needle in a haystack of zombies. There were way too many of them surrounding the building and too many buried *with* the old Marine. Returning to the zombie strewn woodpile would be suicide.

Wading through the tall weeds and the cool night-time air, Sam crept away, south until he came across a bramble of overgrown shrubs that grew alongside an abandoned home. He squeezed his slender frame deep into the bush then sat quietly, trying to regain his breath and clear his head.

His right hand was beginning to throb, and he suddenly began to panic wondering if he may have broken the skin of his knuckles across the infected face of that zombie in the alley. Feeling his hand in the dark, he traced the contour of each boney knuckle and was relieved to find his skin intact, but slightly swollen.

Mental note: do NOT punch zombies in the face. I would be a total IDIOT letting myself get infected like that; I've got to be more careful.

The shrubbery Sam was now hiding in was within 20 ft. of the poorly lit street, which he assumed was still Mt. Elliott, but in his reckless flight from the collapsed building he could not be positive.

Movement drew his attention to the street, and he watched silently as three grotesque silhouettes wobbled by on shaky legs. They were heading in the direction of the hardware store, and as they passed, the smell of body odor, death, and urine passed by with them. He watched for several minutes as they meandered down the street and out of view.

Inspecting his little patch of cover, he was amazed by how much litter was strewn in the weeds around him. There were fast food wrappers, oil containers, spare tires and candy wrappers. He could easily fill an entire trash bag by only grabbing what was within reach. And then his eyes rested on a water spigot protruding from the house's foundation not more than five feet from where he sat. He crawled over to it and gave the handle a turn: nothing. Bone dry, his hopes were dashed. Something had to be done to slake his thirst. Even a pot hole brimming with muddy water sounded divine given his current state.

Having finally calmed his pulse and regained his composure, he was now wide awake and decided it would be best to keep moving south. These bushes offered good concealment, but this was by no means a defensible position. If he were spotted, they would be upon him before he could squirm out of these tangled branches.

Seeing that the coast was clear, he quietly worked his way out of the dense foliage and realized he was no longer on Mt. Elliott, but on some smaller street that was a mix of abandoned residential husks and shuttered businesses. Unable to discern his north from his south, Sam stepped out into the street and looked for a landmark to get oriented.

In the direction that he believed to be west, the red flashing lights of a fire truck illuminated an intersection two blocks away, and a flickering orange glow reflecting off rooftops alluded to a large fire in progress. He was skeptical, but decided to approach it with hopes of finding help.

Like much of the surrounding neighborhood, this street would be menacing to walk even *without* this horrible epidemic. Under normal circumstances, most people would be afraid to merely *drive* down this street at night. The first several homes he walked past were charred and in various states of collapse, victims of arson from years long past. The boarded up and graffiti tagged storefronts were either rough looking liquor stores or sad, hole-in-the-wall chapels with

105

elaborate names like "Holy Church of Jesus Christ the Redeemer II," and "Sacred Temple of Faith in Jesus Name." All were long abandoned with peeling paint and fading signs. Every other building had poorly hand painted advertisements for check-cashing services, lotto tickets, or pagers for sale.

Stopping every hundred feet or so, Sam paused to look and listen. He felt exposed and vulnerable walking down this particular street, there were too many nooks and shadowy porches for assailants to be hiding in. Even with the background noise of chaos echoing throughout the city, he felt that each step on the sidewalk was grinding minute flecks of sand into the pavement with a deafeningly loud crunch, alerting unseen zombies of his presence. It was a struggle to not let his imagination get carried away and lead him to panic, but what could his imagination conjure up that would be worse than this reality?

Nearing the intersection, he could hear the roar of a house fire blazing out of control. Not wanting to approach it hastily, he crept alongside the last few storefronts until the burning structure came into view. It was an old, three story home that billowed bright orange flames from nearly every door and window. In the uppermost window a woman was waving frantically and calling out for help.

As he watched, a disfigured man wearing only blood stained briefs came into view. His uncoordinated and mechanical movements testified that he was infected. The man approached the home's front lawn and gazed up at the woman, becoming immediately more animated. Then without showing any sense of self preservation, the half-naked man staggered up to the home and walked through the open front door, directly into the blazing inferno. The woman inside began screaming hysterically upon seeing this and disappeared inside the window.

Sam was in shock and remained knelt down at the corner building, watching for several minutes as the home became thoroughly engulfed in flames. The heat from the fire was painfully intense, even at this distance. He saw no more signs of the man or the woman who were inside, but the roaring conflagration had erupted into a dramatic crescendo, illuminating the surrounding neighborhood and the night sky.

Faint voices drew his attention away from the burning home and to the adjacent corner, where a single fire engine was in position, red lights flashing but sirens off. Straining to listen over the violently roaring fire, arguing voices could be heard coming from behind the truck.

"Just cut it off, man! Right now! Do it!" The man's voice sounded frantic.

Sam thought for a moment, and then took one last look around, scanning the shadows for any more of the infected.

Well, the coast looks clear... here goes nothing!

He stood up and took off at a full sprint for the fire truck, feet slapping pavement and lungs pumping air. His vision wobbled as his head bobbed from the run, but flicked between his goal (the fire truck) and the numerous dark places where zombies could be loitering unseen.

When he reached the fire engine and rounded the rear bumper, he found one man kneeling down by the truck's running boards, and another man looming over him with a large ax! The two men jumped up into defensive postures when Sam approached. Both were dressed in paramedic uniforms and were splattered with blood.

"WHOA! Hold it right there!" the ax wielder barked, "Are you infected?"

"M-me? No!" was all Sam could spit out when confronted with the ax.

"Wait, are you a doctor?" asked the other man, the one who had been kneeling down unarmed. He was a stocky guy, with a shaved head and glasses, and appeared to be clenching a bloody wound on his left hand.

"Um ... uh, no. I'm an MRI Tech."

"A *what?*" the axman asked with a dumfounded look.

"Never mind!" the other men yelled as he knelt back down and placed his forearm across the truck's running board, "Just cut it off, Hicks! Quick! Before it spreads!"

The man holding the ax, apparently named Hicks, nervously shifted the weapon from hand to hand. It was then that Sam noticed the terrible bite marks covering Hicks' arms; he was as good as dead. But the other man, who was only bit on the hand, was apparently working under the assumption that if he hastily cut his hand off, it would stop the infection from spreading.

"I ... I don't know if I can do this, Dave. I've never swung an ax before! What if I miss!?"

The wounded man, Dave, looked over at Sam desperately, "Hey you! MRI Tech! Do you know how to swing an ax?"

"Um ...well, yeah. We used to heat our house with wood. When I was a kid I had to chop kindling in the morning while I was waiting for the school bus."

"Okay-yeah-whatever, just get over here and grab that ax! You know what those 'people' are, right? One of them bit me on the hand, and I need you to cut it off before the infection spreads. It's my only chance. Can you do it?"

Sam took a step back and raised his hands, "Oh, man, I don't know ... will that even work?! Chopping it off?"

"I don't know, but we have to do it *right now* or I have *zero* chance! Just do it ... please!"

Sam stood silent for a full three seconds before replying soberly, "Okay."

He walked up and accepted the ax from Hicks. It was a large fireman's pick ax, with a bright yellow fiberglass handle and a large curved spike protruding off the back of the ax head. Sam stepped up to the truck and took a good look at the man's stocky forearm that rested on the diamond plate running board. There were two tourniquets wrapped tightly above the elbow, and one more above the wrist. Bloody gauze was wrapped around his injured left hand, while his right hand was clenched tightly around his bicep, with the thumb applying pressure to his brachial artery. He was ready.

"Do it just below the elbow, leave about 3-4 inches," the stricken paramedic instructed.

"Really? That high up?"

"Yes! It's probably spreading up my arm as we speak, and if you drag your feet any longer you're gonna have to chop off my whole damn arm!"

The frazzled, wiry man in filthy scrubs shifted his footing to a stable, wide stance and choked up firmly on his grip. Looking one more time at this poor man's muscular forearm, he realized aloud as he began to lift the ax, "This may take more than one whack."

"JUST DO IT!" Dave pleaded even as the ax was in motion.

Sam drove the blade home in one smooth, arcing stroke. The sound of crunching bone was nearly lost over the sound of the ax blade striking the metal running board with a loud TWANG!

Thankfully, it only took one whack.

Dave's severed forearm rolled off the running board and flopped lifelessly onto the street. The young paramedic screamed in pain and dropped to the ground briefly before rising back to one knee. He looked up and Sam and simply said, "Thanks." Wincing in excruciating pain, he then turned to Hicks saying, "Grab the tackle box … see what we have left to patch me up."

Sam stood there speechlessly, ax hanging limply in hand, trying to absorb what had just transpired. His mind was completely detached as he watched Hicks open up the paramedic's tool kit and wrap Dave's bloody stump tightly in fresh gauze, and then draw out a syringe and a vial to administer some sort of pain killer.

Looking around in a daze, he admired how the blazing inferno cast an orange glow on everything around them, and how the large fire truck seemed to be shielding them from most of the heat. His eyes drifted down to a large puddle along the curb, and he finally noticed that there was an open fire hydrant spewing water into the street.

Numbly, he walked over to it and leaned the bloody ax against a nearby telephone pole. He collapsed down on all fours and stuck his entire head into the stream of water, drinking deeply as he rubbed the grime off of his face and soaked his hair. It was divine.

Returning to his feet, he picked up the ax and thoroughly rinsed the blade in the stream of water, and then wiped it clean in a patch of overgrown grass.

"We've got company!" Hicks called out.

Three dark figures were stumbling out from a blind alley. As they drew close, the orange blaze illuminated their sorry state: mutilated, decaying faces and blood stained "Taco King" uniforms.

"We gotta go guys!" Sam warned the men, "I think they see us!"

Hicks was hunched over Dave, working feverishly to control the bleeding. "It's going to be another minute, he's bleeding pretty bad!" Blood was soaking through the gauze as fast as Hicks could wrap it in another layer.

"We don't have a minute! Here they come!" Sam was ready to run off on his own, but these two paramedics were in a bad predicament. His mind was racing through his options.

Oh crap, oh crap ... should I stay or should I go? The ugly one, 'Hicks,' is as good as dead, but Dave still might have a chance. Arghhh ... and they'll be screwed if I run off with their ax ... I don't think I could live with myself if I did that.

"I'll try to slow them down, just get Dave ready to move!" Sam called over his shoulder as he began walking toward the ghouls in a slow, deliberate pace, trying to plan his ax strokes. If the blade became lodged in one of their skulls, the others would be on him before he could rock the ax head loose. Conversely, if he missed, the momentum of an over swung ax would throw him off balance, leaving him open for those things to counter. Even if he *did* hit his mark, it would take him a moment to recover from the swing, leaving him vulnerable to the other two. This would not be easy.

He was closing to within 10 yards of the ghouls, who were walking three abreast. Sam thought it would be wise to hit them on the flank, or the enfilade, so his intended victim's body would provide a barrier from the other two, hopefully buying him enough time to free the ax if necessary and keep moving before these Taco King thugs could grab him.

He raised the ax high over his shoulder and charged, juking to the left and chopping the left-most zombie. Thankfully, the ax head blasted through the zombie's face without becoming lodged, so he ran past the group, circling wide and to the left to keep his distance. Once he ran about 20 yards past the group he turned around to survey the results.

His victim lay on the ground convulsing as the other two were slowly turning, trying to locate the man who just sprinted past them. Before they spotted him, Sam charged again, continuing on a circular course. At the last moment he veered wide to the left and swung the ax again, connecting under the thing's chin and viciously decapitating the ghoul where it stood. Its head bounced and rolled awkwardly before coming to a stop beneath one of the few working street lamps.

Running past the fast food lackeys again by another 20 yards, Sam stopped and turned with his ax cocked back, ready to strike. The first ghoul was still writhing on the ground with its face cleaved nearly in two. The second ghoul was lying headless in the street, and the third one was still turning in a slow circle, unable to track the quickly moving prey. Sam was about to charge in for the kill, but the dead

110

man finally caught sight of him and let out a howling, bone chilling, moan.

Sam glanced over his shoulder to the fire truck and saw that Hicks was now helping Dave to his feet. "Are you guys ready to move out?" he called back to them.

"I think so ... almost! Just buy us another second!" Hicks responded.

The last ghoul standing was hobbling forward aggressively now, moaning with anger. Sam began to back pedal as the Taco King employee approached. He wore a different colored uniform than the other two, and his name tag read, "Leroy Jenkins, Assistant Team Leader."

Sam slowed his backward pace as he assumed a batting stance, holding the ax high above his right shoulder. He continued backing up slowly, but allowed the ghoul to close the distance, waiting for the thing's head to reach the perfect range. Then like a kid at T-ball practice, Sam swung for the bleachers, lodging the ax deep into Mr. Jenkins head.

He let the ax fly free of his hands, allowing the body to fall to the ground as Sam backed up a few more steps to keep his distance from the infected man. Assistant Team Leader Jenkins was down but twitching with an ax in his skull and its yellow handle pointing skyward. Sam leaned forward and grabbed the fiberglass handle, wiggling the weapon free of the man's head. He reared back and gave the man's cranium another chop for good measure, and then did the same for the first ghoul.

Walking over to inspect the body of the third, he saw the man's decapitated head move on its own, rolling two feet before coming to a rest on its side. Sam's stomach began to turn as he realized the severed head was still "alive," still moving. Its jaws gnashed at the air and its tongue lolled around in its mouth. Briefly paralyzed by the sight, the trance was broken when the dead thing's eyes moved, making definite eye contact with the horrified man. He turned and fled for the fire truck.

"We have to go, guys! Who's got the keys to this truck?"

"What?" Hicks responded, "This isn't our truck, we're Paramedics."

Dave had his head down and was cradling his bloody stump, but looked up to add, "We had to abandon our ambulance a couple

111

miles east of here. Those things swarmed us when we responded to a call at a liquor store. They ... they tore up Hicks pretty good before we got away." Dave suddenly winced in pain and his knees almost buckled. "Are you sure you're not a doctor?"

"No, man, I'm an MRI Tech. *You* guys probably know a lot more about first aid and patching up wounds than I do." Sam looked back over at Hicks. He was a young guy, maybe 21, but looked haggard, and he appeared to be on the verge of a mental breakdown. There were at least a dozen bite marks covering his arms and face. "How are you doing, man? Do you feel ..." Sam hesitated to say it, "... sick?"

"I ... I can't tell, but ... but ... but I'm freaking out! Those *things*, they're ... *zombies*, right? That's what Dispatch said. Zombies! If that's true, then I'm infected, too! Right? That's how it works in the movies! I'm going to get sick and turn into one of *them!*" Hicks said as he pointed up the street. Several people were in the road and coming this way, many more than an ax could take care of. They were slow, but making their way directly toward the fire truck.

"Oh, man, this is bad," Dave said.

"Agreed! We have to go! I'm trying to make my way to Michigan Ave, do you guys know how to get there?" Sam asked.

"Sure, we can take Warren to Trumbull. Follow me!" Dave managed to say, despite the obvious pain he was in.

The three men ran from the burning street corner, distancing themselves from the impending host of zombies. As they rounded a corner, Sam looked up to read the street signs: Mt. Elliott and Warren.

Warren was another dimly lit, one way street with multiple charred and abandoned homes. To their relief, there were no pedestrians (i.e. zombies) to be seen, however, a pickup truck was sitting idly in the middle of the road. Its headlights were on, its doors were wide open, and wisps of thin blue smoke were coming from its rattling tail pipe. The men slowed their roll, but continued advancing toward the vehicle. It appeared unoccupied.

"This is too good to be true," Hicks said.

"Don't jinx us!" Sam and Dave said in unison, then looked at each other, saying "Jinx!" once more in unison.

The truck was a gray, rusty old Ford pickup with several faded Red Wings stickers in the back window. The engine was running, and they could hear music coming from the cab, The White Stripes singing

"The Big Three Killed My Baby." Sam approached first with the ax and peered into vehicle. The interior light was on, showing that the truck was empty save for a few crumpled fast food bags. He also couldn't help but notice there was an old spinner knob bolted to the steering wheel.

Sam waved the other two guys over, and they looked around the street for any sign of the driver, but he was nowhere to be seen. Hicks got the bright idea to call out for the missing driver, yelling to the empty street, "Hey! Whose truck is this?"

The response was immediate: several moans and the sound of breaking glass.

Dave slapped the back of Hicks' head as they all piled into the truck, sliding into the vinyl bench seat, Hicks behind the wheel, Dave in the middle, and Sam riding shotgun with his ax.

Briefly disoriented by the three floor pedals and lack of a gear shifter, Hicks stammered, "W-wait a sec … this has a clutch but no gear shifter?" Then a look of abject horror slowly raked across Hicks' pimpled face, "The gear shifter … it's on the *column* … OH, NO! THREE ON THE TREE!"

Although it is no longer common, many manual shifting automobiles used to have the gear lever mounted on the steering column as a three speed manual, with the clutch on the floor as usual. These were discontinued in the United Stated during the 1980's, however some countries still use this layout, nicknamed 'three on the tree.'

"You've got to be kidding me!" Dave said.

"Come on, Hicks! Don't you know how to drive stick?" Sam asked.

"Hell yeah, but not like *this!* This thing is … obsolete! Who the hell still drives three on the tree?"

"Well jump out and let's switch! My dad's Bronco shifted like this!"

The two men performed the fastest Chinese Fire Drill on earth, running around the front of the truck and handing off the ax in the process. Sam slid into the driver's seat, depressed the clutch, and eased the lever backwards then down and into first gear with an awful grind. He gave it some gas and eased off the clutch, and the truck took off.

The paramedics cheered and slapped Sam across the back. It

was great to be back in a moving vehicle. The jubilant men rolled down the windows to allow the cool night air to fill the cab.

Hicks yelled over the music, "Now what the hell is that thing on the steering wheel?"

Sam looked down at the large, yellow knob bolted onto the wheel and answered, "It's called a 'spinner knob.' It's attached to a ball bearing so you can hold it and turn the steering wheel with one hand. I think they're illegal now, because if you get in a wreck it could punch a hole in your chest. That's why they also called them 'suicide balls.'"

The streets here were desolate, so their path was mercifully unimpeded for several blocks. Sam turned the volume down on the radio and switched the old tape deck from 'cassette' to 'FM.' He then turned the plastic dial until he found the local NPR station, with the familiar voice of NPR newsman Aaron McDowell sounding as smooth as ever:

> "... reports coming in from the surrounding metropolitan area cite few incidences of violence, with the exceptions of Dearborn, Dearborn Heights, Inkster, Ypsilanti, and Ann Arbor. However, this appears to be a rapidly changing situation and we are receiving conflicting reports from officials. Facts are difficult to verify at this time, but what we do know is this: Police and Medical Examiners in Detroit and several other major cities throughout the country report that the recently deceased are *returning to life*, and violently attacking those who come in contact with them, *cannibalizing* their victims. I know this sounds hard to believe, and even I find it hard to believe what I am reporting, but we have hundreds of first hand reports that corroborate this seemingly improbable fact: THE DEAD ARE COMING BACK TO LIFE, AND ATTACKING THE LIVING. The Governor has declared a state of emergency, and is advising all residents in the Detroit Metropolitan Area to *stay indoors*, and to avoid any contact with the recently deceased."

Sam suddenly turned the volume down and sat up alert at the wheel, "Whoa, guys … what do we have here?"

Standing under the streetlight at the next corner was a middle aged black man, with a middle aged paunch filling his unbuttoned polo shirt to capacity, casually toting an AK-47 assault rifle over his shoulder.

Downshifting to second gear, he slowed the truck with the engine's compression but had no idea what this gunman's intentions were and therefore didn't want to stop.

As they approached the well-lit intersection, blaringly loud jazz music filled the night air, and they saw two groups of older men sitting nonchalantly at tables on the sidewalk in front of some old five and dime store. They were playing cards and drinking, and all were heavily armed.

The old man in the polo shirt casually took a drag off his cigarette and waved as they passed. The three men in the truck waved nervously in response, craning their necks to look back at these crazy, brave, S.O.B.'s.

"I feel sorry for any zombies who show up on *their* street!" Hicks rightly observed.

"No kidding, man. Those boys aren't playing," Dave agreed with a chuckle.

Sam raised an eyebrow and glanced over at Dave, saying, "Wow, Dave, you sound surprisingly well for a man who just got his hand chopped off. Are you doin' okay?"

Dave grinned a pie-eyed grin, replying, "Dude, I am feelin' fan-frickin'-tastic. That cocktail Hicks shot me up with should keep me feelin' no pain for at *least* another hour. By then we should be at the hospital and I can get this thing patched up." He held up his stump proudly.

Shifting uneasily in his seat, Sam asked, "Hospital? What hospital? St. John is the other way, and you *don't* want to go there. Everyone there is either dead or a zombie."

"No, man. The Detroit Medical Center is straight ahead, I think Warren runs right into it a few blocks after Woodward. You can just drop me off at that corner."

"What? You *are* high, man! First of all, I'm not going to 'drop you off' and make you walk anywhere. And secondly, well, if the DMC is that close, they've certainly been inundated with bitten and infected people as well, and are probably *swarming* with zombies!"

"Wait a second, guys," Hicks interrupted, "I think we have another neighborhood watch ahead."

There was a group of young men with flashlights and handguns standing in the street up ahead. As the truck approached, the young men signaled for them to stop. Sam obliged, and the men all approached with their flashlights trained on the truck.

Hicks raised his hand, saying, "Stay in the truck, I'll handle this." He opened the truck door and stepped out with the ax flung over his shoulder.

The armed men took one look at Hicks' bloody, chewed-up state and drew their weapons. A man who appeared to be their leader took a big step back, saying, "Whoa-whoa-whoa! You been bit!?"

"Well, yeah, but …" Hicks began, but was peppered in mid-sentence with a hail of bullets to the face! His entire head disintegrated in a pink mist.

"OH, SNAP!" Dave screamed, "PUNCH IT!"

Sam flung the wonky gear lever back into first and floored the old Ford. Its tires squealed as the truck's rear end wavered before gaining traction and launching forward. The young gunmen dove out of the way as Sam and Dave raced away down Warren.

"God bless America! The whole city's gone trigger happy!" Sam mouthed off.

"Just keep going!" Dave yelled, suddenly sounding a lot more sober, "Don't stop for *anybody!*"

They barreled down the road, pushing the truck for all that it was worth, blowing through stop signs and red lights. Warren gradually changed from abandoned residential to sparsely populated industrial, and they began seeing isolated zombies roaming in the street, forcing them to slow down and weave defensively. As they neared I-75, more and more zombies could be seen in people's gated yards and meandering through parking lots. They also began encountering more abandoned vehicles in the road, but had the good sense not to stop and check them; this truck was moving along just fine.

Gripping the spinner ball with white knuckles, Sam wove the gray Ford through a tangle of wrecked cars and past a particularly gruesome accident. A car was flipped on its back and burning, with several burning zombies pinned beneath it. They clawed futilely at the truck as it sped past, seemingly impervious to the flames.

Slowing down as they crossed the I-75 overpass, they were discouraged by what they saw. Beneath them, the highway was completely overrun with the living dead. Traffic had ground to a halt and was buried beneath a river of writhing, mutilated bodies, fighting to get into the cars that were still occupied by the living.

Suddenly another helicopter buzzed by directly overhead, slow and low. Sam and Dave waved frantically out the truck's windows, trying to hail the passing chopper, but it was useless. Its large searchlight was surveying the highway, and it continued flying south, toward Downtown and the Auto Show.

"Just keep going!" Dave urged, "They'll never see us in all this chaos. Midtown's straight ahead, we'll be at the hospital in no time."

The old Ford pressed on, cresting the I-75 overpass and entering a more lively part of town. Midtown is home to Wayne State University, the DMC (Detroit Medical Center), the DIA (Detroit Institute of the Arts), the Detroit Science Center, The Detroit Masonic Temple, Woodward Avenue, and the Cass Corridor. It is a heavily populated area that has retained a vibrant economic and cultural bustle, managing to avoid the typical problems of urban blight that have affected much of the city.

There were enough cars on the road here that Sam actually felt compelled to resume obeying the traffic laws, and he stopped at a red light. There were people running down the sidewalk, mostly college students judging by their age and clothing. Several businesses were rolling heavy steel shutters down over their windows. Shutters such as these have become a cost of doing business in the city. They serve well to prevent break-ins, smash-and-grabs, and the looting that can accompany the occasional riot. Those businesses that didn't have the forethought to install such shutters were now boarding up their entrance ways with plywood.

The car behind him honked, because he had not noticed the stoplight had turned green. Sam waved apologetically through the back window and threw it in first gear. Dave was not so courteous and offered a middle finger instead.

They drove past the Detroit Science Center, and noticed the pedestrians were looking increasingly frantic. There was an old, ornate clock mounted prominently on the side of a building: 4:15am.

"This is too much to handle at four a.m. without a cup of coffee. If I see a drive thru that's open, I'm gonna have to stop," Sam said in all seriousness.

"You can hit the cafeteria when we get to the hospital ... wait a second ..." Dave twisted his head around to look behind them. "I think we passed the hospital ... crap, it's somewhere *south* of here, off of Mack Avenue ... take a left here on Woodward!"

Sam threw his hands up incredulously, "Dude, there's *no way* I can get over into the left lane! I thought you were an ambulance driver! You don't know where the *hospital* is?"

"Hey, man, I'm from the suburbs; Livonia. I just volunteered to come out and help with the riot. When I got here, they paired me up with Hicks and sent me to answer a call from a liquor store. The next thing I know, we're running through frickin' Armageddon getting our asses chewed off by zombies! I don't really know my way around here; I only come downtown for baseball games and concerts. Without my GPS I'm screwed. But I think the hospital is *that* way." He pointed with his stump. "And I'm not an *ambulance driver*, I'm a *PARAMEDIC*," he added, sounding genuinely offended.

"Alright," Sam said checking his blind spot, "I'll try to get over."

The traffic at the intersection of Woodward Ave. was the worst he'd seen off the highway. The light ahead was green, but traffic was not moving.

Woodward is one of the main drags that run north and south through the center of Detroit. It boasts the first mile of paved highway in the world, the first modern traffic light, the original Model T factory, and the site of the annual Dream Cruise, which celebrates the days when muscle cars had impromptu drag races up and down that very boulevard.

Sam was tapping his hands on the steering wheel impatiently, "Come on ... MOVE, people! Sheesh!"

"Whoa ..." Dave sat up alertly, adjusting his sleek prescription glasses, "Look over there." Again, pointing with the stump.

Several elderly people in hospital gowns were making their way across the street, lashing out at passing cars.

Sighing nervously, Dave looked down and adjusted the bandages on his arm, then elevated it to help control the bleeding.

118

"That's not a good sign. Those patients are probably coming from the DMC, and they're obviously infected. Let's just try to drive by the hospital, and if it looks too bad to stop we'll turn south and head to Corktown."

"Corktown? Is that where the old Tigers Stadium was?" Sam asked.

"Yeah, right there on Michigan Ave. The stadium's gone now, but the field is still there. That's the road you were looking for, right? Michigan Ave.?"

"Yeah, that's the only other route I know to get home without taking the highway."

Corktown was once a proud Irish enclave within the city of Detroit. It was established in the mid-1800's by a group of Irish immigrants who fled their homeland during the Great Potato Famine. Most of the immigrants who settled there hailed from Cork County, Ireland, which is how the neighborhood acquired its name.

They sat through three green lights before traffic started moving again, the whole time watching cars swerve around the elderly patients in the middle of the road.

"Why is everybody driving *around* those freaks?" Dave wondered. "Someone needs to run them down!"

Sam chuckled, slowly easing the truck along with traffic. "Nice bedside manner, buddy."

"No, seriously! They're obviously infected; you'd be doing them a favor! And the longer they roam the street, the more likely they're going to infect someone else!"

"Dang ..." Sam thought for a moment, "You're right. It's just ... they look like someone's *grandparents*. But... they are eventually going to bite *someone* if they don't get put down soon. And technically, they're already dead, right?"

They looked at each other with mischievous, childlike grins.

"It's almost our turn to go," Dave said, rolling up his window with the old fashioned hand crank, "Let's do this! Buckle up!"

"Already am," Sam nodded.

The car in front of them was now entering the intersection, and it accelerated sharply, swerving around the cluster of deranged senior citizens.

Sam gripped the spinner ball tightly, pointing the wheels directly at the group, "Here we go. Brace yourself!"

119

The truck's muffler rattled as Sam floored the accelerator, barreling straight into the crowd of seniors, mowing them down while sending a couple airborne!

Sam stopped the truck, and they looked back through the rear window to inspect the damage. Twisted and broken, the elderly zombies seemed unfazed and were already trying to rise to their feet.

"Back over them!" Dave yelled enthusiastically, "Put 'em down for good!"

Sam threw the truck in reverse, and the old pick up bounced and bumped over the maimed, crumpled, geriatrics, yet they were still moving.

"Again!" Dave cheered.

Grinding it back into first gear, he roared the old Ford up and onto the pile of crushed zombies, parking triumphantly on the mound.

Sam and Dave were laughing hysterically, even as steam began to pour out from under the hood. Suddenly the passenger door was yanked open and a policeman grabbed Dave by the sleeve, yelling as he drew his pistol, "You demented sons o' bitches! Get out of the truck!"

Without thinking, Dave back-fisted the cop in the face and slammed the rusty door closed, yelling, "GO, MAN! GO!"

The truck bounced down the pile of bodies and took off as the cop opened fire, shattering the rear window. Sam swerved evasively, pulling up onto the sidewalk and away from the congested intersection.

Speeding down the busy sidewalk, Sam laid on the horn and plowed forward, forcing pedestrians to dive for cover.

"You just punched a cop, man! What the heck were you thinking!? We could have *told* him that those were *zombies* we just crushed!"

"I don't know, man, it was reflex! That guy shouldn't have snuck up on us like that! I thought he was one of those infected jerrys (geriatrics)!"

Blue lights started flashing across the interior of the cab as a police cruiser pulled in behind the truck, sirens blaring.

Sam eased on the brakes, saying, "Let's stop and talk to these guys, we could really use their help ..." His words were cut short as bullets began pinging off the bed of the pickup.

"Jiminy Crickets! These jokers are *shooting* at us!" Sam

shrieked, crouching low in his seat.

"Aw, *come on!*" Dave pleaded rhetorically out the missing back window, "It was an *accident*, for Christ's sake!" Obviously, he was still heavily medicated.

Utter chaos lay ahead at the next intersection. There was an overturned police van blocking Warren, and the sidewalk ahead was filled with a rioting crowd. Packed tightly on the sidewalk, these people would be unable to dodge the approaching Ford.

"Look out! Those aren't zombies!" Dave gripped the dash board with his one remaining hand, "Quick, turn left here! On Cass Ave!"

Sam cranked the wheel hard, hopping off the curb and sliding sideways to make the turn. Wayne State University's 'Old Main' building dominated this corner with its beautiful brick and limestone walls. Its clock tower was in flames, and dozens of unscrupulous characters were looting the building, carrying out computer towers and flat screen monitors.

The police cruiser easily made the corner onto Cass, and pulled up aggressively to the truck's rear bumper, resuming fire. The front windshield shattered, raining glass down into their laps and releasing a torrent of wind through the cab.

Sam jerked the steering wheel hard to the right, hopping the curb and landing back onto the sidewalk with a violent bounce. The guys heard a loud thump in the pickup truck's bed. They looked inquisitively at each other, and then over their shoulders. In the bed, an ancient looking man wearing a blood soaked hospital gown was rising to his feet and lurching toward the open rear window! The two men screamed like school girls as Sam began swerving the truck erratically from side to side, trying to shake off the creepy old man.

The police car remained hot on their tail, but stopped shooting when the old man surfaced. Apparently he landed in the truck's bed when they plowed through that pack of rabid seniors.

Pedestrians continued to dive for cover as the old truck zig-zaged through the campus grounds, tearing up turf and knocking over trash cans. The smoking, roaring, reckless pursuit crossed several streets and sidewalks. In the blur of passing people, Sam began noticing *infected* people among the crowd, several wearing hospital attire.

"ZOMBIES IN SCRUBS!" Sam screamed.

121

"I KNOW! I KNOW! FORGET ABOUT GOING TO THE HOSPITAL! JUST SHAKE THIS GUY OFF!" Dave said, crawling up on the dashboard to distance himself from the old man who was reaching through the back window.

Ahead on the sidewalk was a small set of concrete steps, a three foot drop.

"Hold on tight!" was all Sam had time to say.

The truck launched over the steps, catching a brief moment of air before landing hard. Sparks shot out from beneath the truck and the old man was once again airborne, coming down directly onto the hood of the police cruiser as it bounced down the steps. The cruiser swerved left then right before smashing squarely into an old maple tree head on. The chase was off.

"Woo-hoo! You are the *Wheelman*!" Dave cheered, offering his stump in a high five motion (before thinking better of the idea).

"Well," Sam said modestly, "I *do* play a lot of videogames."

They turned down an alley, which led to a less congested street. The truck's steering wheel was now shaking violently, and steam continued to roll out from underneath the hood. There was zombie blood splattered across the truck's crumpled grill and quarter panels, and the windows were shot out, but the old Ford soldiered on.

"Um," Dave said, looking at the steering wheel, "I think we blew a tie rod."

Sam glanced down briefly at the shuddering wheel, then back to the road. His stressed-out face slowly morphed into a huge grin, and the two had a couple chuckles that grew into a good, hearty, belly laugh. "I think we blew out a lot more than *that*, man!"

Fighting with the steering wheel, Sam tried to reestablish his bearings. "So where are we now? Any idea, Dave?"

"I have no clue, man. No GPS, remember? But if I had to make a guess, I'd say the *bad* part of town."

"Yeah, good point."

Sam squinted as they approached the next intersection, and then groaned in frustration as they passed it. "Man, half of these streets have no street signs! How do people find their way around here?"

"Here comes one," Dave said, leaning forward and adjusting his glasses. "Rosa Parks Blvd., turn left here!"

"No can do, it's a one way street."

"Screw it! Do you realize how many traffic laws you've already broken? If any cars come our way, just pull over until they pass."

Sam slowed to a stop and looked down the vacant street. "Well, I guess this counts as a justifiable emergency. Besides, I actually hope we *do* get pulled over; I'd rather be locked safely in the back of a police car than tooling around in *this* death trap."

He signaled with his left turn blinker before turning onto the residential street. Good fortune was with them, as there were no zombies or traffic to be seen.

"Doesn't Rosa Parks still live in Detroit?" Dave asked.

"Actually, I think she passed away kinda recently, maybe two or three years ago." Sam thought for a moment and chuckled, "Do you remember when those two punks broke into her house?"

"What? No!"

"Yeah, I heard it on NPR. Apparently they didn't know it was *her* house, it was just their bad luck, a random break in. When she confronted them, one of the guys recognized her and said, 'Hey, aren't you Rosa Parks?' She said she was, but they still roughed her up and stole some things out of her house. They *whole city* was on the lookout for those two jerks. I mean, *come on!* She was in her 80's! And she's *Rosa Parks!* SHE is one of the people personally responsible for those two kids having the rights and freedoms that they enjoy today. They're just lucky the *police* found them first, and not the good people of the City of Detroit!"

Sam glanced down at his gauges and cleared his throat, "Ahem … uh, oil light's on … and the temp's running hot."

"Great," Dave said, and began rolling his window back down. "Crank the heat all the way up, it'll help pull heat from the motor."

Reaching down, he slid the temp lever all the way to the red and the fan lever to 'high.' He then clicked the radio back on:

> "… is expected to address the nation from the oval office any moment now, and we will be covering the address live as it happens. Pentagon officials have confirmed that we have lost all contact with our forces in South Korea, and are assuming that the 'worst case scenario' has happened. They would not elaborate beyond that, but have stated that the Chinese military

has launched no fewer than 12 intercontinental ballistic missiles on multiple targets throughout the Korean Peninsula, making this the largest nuclear strike in human history. Chinese ambassador Vu Thon Jiang stated that Beijing *cleared* these launches with Washington prior to deployment. Currently, there are 28,500 American military personnel serving in South Korea, and as of now their fate is unknown. Japan is already reporting increased levels of radiation in both air and water samples, however, they are not yet at levels that would pose any significant health risk."

"Turn it down," Dave chimed in, "we have company."

Two blocks ahead the street was filled with the infected, silhouetted starkly by the fires of several burning structures. Fortunately, they were heading away from the truck, moving south en masse.

Sam put the truck in neutral and coasted to a stop. He then reached down and pushed in a long, plunger-type knob, killing the headlights. "Hmmm … not good. Where do you think they're going?"

"No idea, but there's a lot of them."

As they sat there contemplating their next move, the truck's engine began to make an unhealthy, rhythmic knocking sound.

"Dave, my man, we're going to be walking soon. How's your arm?"

Dave gripped his arm carefully and adjusted the bandages. "It hurts, but not as bad as it should. I'm still feeling pretty high right now. Whatever the hell Hicks gave me is doing the trick, but if I don't get a re-up soon, this may get real bad real quick. I need to get this looked at, *STAT*."

And with that, the truck stalled out. Sam tried repeatedly to crank the engine, but no luck. The motor would not turn over, it was surely blown.

"Alright, that's it. We've got no time to waste, so let's check the truck for anything useful and *go*. Anything in the glove box?"

Dave popped it open and did a quick inventory. "Registration, proof of insurance, napkins, a couple packs of ketchup, and … hey! A road map!"

"Wait a second! Ketchup!?" Sam blurted out desperately.

Dave looked at him sideways, "Um … yeah. Ketchup."

"Thank god! I'll split it with you!"

"Ah, no thanks. Why? You want 'em?"

"Yes, man! I haven't eaten in two days!"

"Here," Dave said, "They're yours." He handed over a fistful of crumpled, fancy ketchup packets.

With shaking hands, Sam opened each packet carefully and licked the wrappers clean, savoring every drop. Meanwhile, Dave unfolded the map and plotted their course.

"Well," Dave said after some thought, "Rosa Parks will take us straight to Michigan Ave., but if we can't get past that crowd of zombies, we can hop back over to Trumbull, heading south."

"Alright, let's do it."

They abandoned the old Ford in the middle of the road, and headed south toward the fires, trying their best to maintain stealth, sprinting from covered porches to parked cars.

As they neared the raging fires and infected mob, they discovered the source of the zombies' interest: a large, limestone church that was illuminated by the surrounding blazes. Like many churches in Detroit, this building stood like a medieval fortress, an impressive structure of brick and stone with towering ramparts, conical spires, and covered parapets. Surrounding the building's stone walls, an army of the dead lay siege, twenty bodies deep or more. The orange hue of the surrounding blazes conjured up a scene from Excalibur, or Lord of the Rings. And above the roaring flames and tortured moans came the beautiful sound of a gospel choir, the soaring voices of the faithful. This old church was filled to capacity with parishioners seeking refuge from the dead. It was a powerful scene to behold.

"Wow," Sam said with wide eyes. "Those folks are either hopelessly trapped, or they really *did* find salvation in that old church."

"Those folks aren't *trapped*; they're sitting pretty! There is *no way* those zombies are gonna breach that huge oak door, and most churches that size keep a well-stocked kitchen. All they have to do is wait it out. Too bad we can't get past all those sick fools to join them."

"I don't know, Dave. You're going to need some real medical attention soon, so 'waiting it out' might not be the best option. And besides, my wife is pregnant and due any day now. I really need to get home to them, ASAP."

"What do you know? My wife Lisa is six months pregnant, too," Dave paused and looked down at his severed forearm, "And she is gonna *freak* when she sees this."

"Well, look at the bright side: it might just get you out of some diaper duty."

Dave laughed humorlessly, "No, not likely. She'll just mention that chick that was born with no arms but had several kids, and managed to change diapers and drive a car with her feet."

"Hmmm …. she's got you there."

Sam looked back up at the monolithic, fortified church, bathed in flickering orange light, surrounded by a sea of clawing hands. "We have to get away from here. What do you say? Should we cross over to Trumbull?"

"Yeah, there's no way we'll sneak past this mob. Let's go. Maybe we can cut through someone's yard." Dave unfurled the map once more, holding it up to read by the firelight. "Let's see… we're at the corner of Rosa Parks and Martin Luther King Blvd., so according to the map … Trumbull should be three blocks east of here."

The men backtracked till they found a home with no fence and cautiously crept around to the back yard. As they crossed the lawn, Sam suddenly raised his hand, signaling for them to stop. In a hushed voice, he said, "Someone is over there, I saw movement, maybe we should …"

BLAM! BLAM! BLAM!

Dave dropped to the ground cursing. "I'm hit! In the leg!"

"Crom's Teeth! They think we're zombies!" Sam turned to the direction of the gun shots, "HOLD YOUR FIRE! WE AREN'T ZOMBIES!"

From the dark porch, a deep sounding, 20-something male voice responded, "Then you better get the hell outta my yard 'fore I shoot you again!"

"AW COME ON, MAN! YOU JUST SHOT MY FRIEND! HE'S A PARAMEDIC! WE NEED HELP!"

The man's response was merciless, "I done told you once!"

BLAM! BLAM! BLAM! *Click ... click ... click* "Aw, *shoot*! Hand me them bullets, Trey."

126

Six shots and out, the overzealous jerk had to reload. The two men took this opportunity and ran for their lives, with Dave limping along painfully.

"Crap!" Dave said as he was huffing along, "I think that cocktail is finally wearing off ... 'cause my leg hurts like a biotch!"

"Just keep going!"

They ran though several more yards, crossing two streets and ducking down in a driveway on the third, presumably now on Trumbull. Sitting down with their backs to the wall, Dave doubled over and began to vomit.

Sam gave him a moment to compose himself, and then asked, "How bad are you hit?"

"Bad enough," Dave replied as he began tearing off his pant leg to inspect the wound. "Just above the knee. It looks like it went in and out, straight through."

Dawn was beginning to break, but there was not yet enough light to see the full extent of his injury, so Sam powered up his cell phone to provide a working light as Dave used his torn pant leg to wrap the wound and try to stifle the bleeding. He looked up at Sam and raised his stump, saying, "Do you mind helping me with this knot?"

"Oh! Of course, no problem, man. Here ..." Sam held the phone with his teeth as he cinched the knot tight.

Dave grimaced painfully and began to dry heave, eventually pulling it together and saying, "It's not bleeding too badly, so I don't think they hit my femoral artery *or* my femur; I'm pretty lucky. But it feels like someone is pounding it with a sledge hammer, and my stump is on *fire.*"

"Tell you what," Sam said, "I'm gonna sneak down to the next intersection and confirm our location. You wait right here. With any luck I'll find some help or another car to steal and we can get the heck outta here! Just sit tight and save your strength. I'll be right back."

Dave simply nodded and continued to nurse his wounds.

Inching out into the street and looking south, he could see headlights several blocks away, and the bright lights of the Motor City Casino beyond that. He hoped to flag down a car, so he began to jog south.

Coming up to the first traffic light he found a massive three way intersection. The street sign confirmed that he was at the corners

127

of Trumbull, Grand River Ave., and MLK Boulevard, but what commanded his attention was the glorious neon sign of Taco King. Sam was painfully hungry, and was seriously contemplating the moral implications of breaking into a fast food chain, when unexpectedly, he saw movement inside the building. It was human, alright, and he appeared to be ... *mopping?*

He crept closer to the parking lot to get a better look. Sure enough, a young man in baggy pants was finishing mopping the floor. Sam watched as he wrung out the mop in a bucket, walked over to the front door, twisted open the lock, and pulled the chain on a neon sign that flashed 'open.'

You have got to be kidding me ...

The employee then walked back behind the counter, which was an elaborate affair of bullet proof glass with a swiveling window to dispense the food. He appeared to be prepping the cook line, without a care in the world. Sam looked both ways, and then ran across the parking lot and into the building.

The cook barely looked up, mumbling in a bored, scripted tone, "Welcome to Taco King, can I take your order?"

Sam was speechless.

"W-w-wha? You ... you've got to be kidding me! You're open!?"

The cook finally made eye contact, stared blankly at Sam, and repeated his scripted spiel as if he didn't hear Sam's question, "Welcome to Taco King. Can I take your order?"

"You're joking, right? Don't you know what's going on out there?"

The obviously dull employee looked out the window with a glazed expression and stared back at Sam, saying, "Um, we opened at six. Can I take your order?"

Sam's jaw dropped. "Listen, dude, there's a *riot* going on! It's not safe, you need to get out of the city!"

The young cook looked out at the deceptively empty street and then rolled his eyes, saying, "No, *you* listen up 'dude,' if you're not gonna order somethin' you need to leave. I gotta lot of work to do, and no time to talk crazy with some bum."

Taken aback, Sam looked down at himself and his general

appearance. His long hair had not seen a brush in *days,* and was beginning to clump into wild dreadlocks. His scrubs were stained with black soot, mud, and blood. And worst of all, he still *reeked* of that moldy Petri dish of a bed, with a few days of B.O. to sweeten the deal.

"Look, man, I know I probably look like a bum, but I've been on the run for three days. And I know this must sound crazy, but the city has been overrun with *zombies*! You've got to get out of here and find someplace safe." Upon mentioning the word 'zombie,' Sam had lost all credibility in the young taco cook's mind.

He pointed angrily to the front door, saying gruffly, "You best get the hell outta here if you ain't gonna order nothin'. My slack-ass morning crew hadn't shown up yet, so I got things to do! Now git!"

"*Of course* they haven't shown up yet! There's a frickin' zombie apocalypse in progress out there! Wake up, man!!!"

The taco merchant looked out the window, beholding the peaceful, quiet morning, and then glared back at Sam, huffing, "Are you ordering food or not?"

Sam threw his hands up in frustration, "FINE! I'll order something! I'm frickin' starving." Looking up at the menu, his eyes lit up as if it were the second coming, "You ... you have cappuccinos!?"

"What size." The kid answered flatly, more as a statement than a question.

"Heck, *any* size! Large!"

"What flavor." Again, without emotion or proper inflection.

"Flavor? No flavor, please, just a cappuccino ... but I will take a packet of honey if you have it," Sam added with a hopeful, kid-in-a-candy-store tone.

The cook sighed, "You *have* to pick a flavor."

"Oh ..." Sam was at a loss for words ... this was highly irregular. "Um, what flavors do you have?"

The kid sighed again before robotically listing the choices like a prerecorded message, "Quad Mocha, Faux Vanilla Crème, Spicy Santa Fe, and Hazelnut Toffee Crisp."

"...*Spicy Santa Fe?*" Sam wondered aloud, not believing that this man could be serious.

As he pushed a few buttons on the cash register the kid mumbled, "Alright, large Spicy Santa Fe. Anything else?"

"Oh, wait! God, no! *Not* Spicy Santa Fe! Sorry, I was just

thinking out loud … in shock. Um, I'll try the vanilla, please."

Spicy Santa Fe cappuccino? Dear god, what an abomination!

Hunger pains were returning with a vengeance as Sam poured over the menu. The smells and sights were like a slice of heaven. His eyes were welling up with joy as he placed his order, a chorus of Angels singing in his head.

Halleluiah! Halleluiah!

"Wow, man … I'll have a bean & rice burrito, with guac and sour cream … and two soft shell chicken tacos, please."

"Will that be all." The kid's words seemed to be directed into the ether, not posed as a question, but just a reflex to hearing a series of food items spoken in sequence.

"Yes, please. That'll be all."

The taco merchant turned without saying a word and went to work preparing the order. Sam began pacing nervously, and then walked up to the front windows to survey the street. Looking down the long boulevard, he noticed the telephone poles were all askew and poorly maintained. And before his eyes, one by one, the streetlamps were turning off as the sky waxed from dawn to early morning. There was no traffic at all and no zombies to be seen.

No wonder this kid is oblivious to the riot, it's pretty quiet over here. Sam cast his gaze to the empty parking lot. *Hmm, no car. He probably lives close and just walks to work. I only wish I had made it all the way to Mexicantown, I could have got some REAL Mexican food.*

Mexicantown was another neighborhood of Detroit, near the bridge to Canada. It is mostly populated by, as the name implies, Mexican immigrants. The Mexican cuisine in that area is marvelously authentic and reasonably priced.

"A'ight. That'll be nine-fiddy," Taco Guy mumbled, in a voice that says 'I hate my job.'

Sam strode back to the counter and placed his Debit Card in the

130

revolving bullet proof glass thing. He was well and truly salivating, almost to the point of nausea.

The kid picked up the card and swiped it in the charge terminal… and then swiped it again. Nothing. Scratching his head and staring vacantly at the card, he stated to no one in particular, "This ain't American Express, is it? Cause we can't take American Express."

No response seemed expected, but Sam felt obliged to answer his question. "No, man, it's a Visa Check Card. You can treat it like a normal credit card."

The kid tried repeatedly to swipe it, finally putting it back in the revolving bullet proof thing and saying, "This card doesn't work. You'll have to pay with cash."

"But … I don't have any cash on me. I mean, there's at *least* a grand in my bank account, but …" Sam looked through the glass at his bag of food and piping hot cup of artificially flavored, instant Faux Vanilla Crème pseudo-cappuccino. This truly was hell incarnate.

"Wait, the phone lines are all down! I bet your credit card machine is down, too! Don't you guys have a backup plan to process credit cards when the system is down? Like one of those sliding machines that make a carbon paper imprint of the customer's card?"

Sam was met with a blank stare. The kid eventually managed to ask, completely off subject, mind you, "Uh … did you used to be a *doctor* or somethin'?

Glancing back down at his blown out scrubs, Sam shook his head in frustration, "No, man, I'm an MRI Tech. But seriously, there is a riot of crazy, sick people going on out there, it's total anarchy! People are *dying*! I barely escaped the hospital alive, and I've been wandering the city trying to find my way home to Milan. I haven't eaten in *days*; you have to help me out here. Please."

"Listen, cuz, there's a soup kitchen down the street. I wish I could help you out, but I cain't. I gotta lot of work to do, the night crew left this place lookin' like a dump, and I got three no shows I'm coverin' for. Now just take off before I have to call the po-lice."

"Arghhh … listen buddy, I'm *desperate*." Sam's tone became very sincere, "Can I *please* just have the cappuccino?"

Taco Guy flippantly dumped the cappuccino, tossed the bag of food in the trash, and yelled, "Get the hell outta here ya bum! I ain't got time for this!"

Sam totally lost it, screaming ferociously at the top of his lungs and banging on the bullet proof glass. He looked side to side like a wild animal before his eyes locked onto the condiment stand. He ran over to it and began filling the little paper condiment cups with sour cream and salsa from the big, plastic pump dispensers, working the levers violently.

"Hey!" Taco Guy yelled, "You can't use the condiment stand unless you buy somethin'!"

"BACK OFF, TACO GUY! I HAVE A CAFFEINE HEADACHE THE SIZE OF YOUR *MOM,* AND I WILL FIGHT YOU TO THE *DEATH* FOR THIS SOUR CREAM AND SALSA!"

Taco Guy made a move to the door like he was going to come out from behind the glass to call Sam's bluff.

"TRY IT, BUDDY! If you dare come out here without a cappuccino in hand, *I swear I will beat you down!"* With piercing eyes, Sam glanced down at Taco guy's name tag. "Listen here, Rod, do you know Assistant Team Leader Leroy Jenkins!? Well I chopped his frickin' head off with an ax last night! *So don't cross me, man!*"

Taco Guy shrank back fearfully from the hazy glass and ran to the phone, trying to dial 911.

"Knock yourself out, Rod; they're not gonna answer. Just go home, lock your darn doors, and turn on the news," Sam said as he walked toward the front door with two fistfuls of sour cream and salsa. Pausing at the door, he sighed remorsefully and cast his gaze to the floor.

"Look, man... I didn't mean what I said about your mom. That was just rude, and I'm sorry. But you need to get out of here; there is some kind of plague or something going on. The hospital I work at was overrun, and it seems to be spreading fast. These people seriously look like zombies, but *whatever* they are, they are violent and contagious. You'll see them soon enough. If you're smart, you'll lock this door behind me and lay low."

Sam walked out across the parking lot and headed back to catch up with Dave. They would have to walk further south if they wanted to find someone who might give them a ride.

Walking cautiously back up the street, he gobbled up the sour cream and salsa, licking the paper cups clean.

I can't believe that joker working at Taco King, he has

132

no clue what's been going on. I feel kinda bad for not being able to talk some sense into him, but I have to admit it does sound completely crazy. Zombies. In Detroit.

But Neptune's Knickers, I was mere INCHES away from a cappuccino ... AND A SOFT SHELL CHICKEN TACO!

His stomach began to grumble painfully, uncertain how to process his meal of straight sour cream and salsa.

The sun was now peeking over the horizon, and the morning was deceptively peaceful. Trumbull was a well maintained residential street, and its proximity to Midtown and the Wayne State Campus made it a relatively desirable neighborhood to live in. Sam was awestruck by the beautiful Victorian homes that lined the street. Each brick home reminded him of a fortified citadel, or a medieval keep, and most were easily a hundred years old or more.

Turning quietly up the driveway where he had left Dave, he froze; the young Paramedic was gone.

"... *tartar sauce!*" Sam cursed under his breath, "This is not good."

There was a small pool of blood on the pavement where Dave had been sitting, and a torn piece of his pant leg that had been used as a temporary tourniquet. Sam looked around nervously, and then crouched down against the wall to brainstorm.

Maybe he went to go take a leak ... or maybe someone chased him off.

A scuffing sound came from behind the home, sending Sam's senses on high alert. Unconsciously, his hands began searching the ground for a weapon while his eyes remained locked on the brick corner. The scuffing sound drew nearer and Sam felt as though his heart may burst.

To his immense relief, it was Dave who rounded the corner, dragging his wounded leg behind him.

"Whew! Dude, I thought you were a zombie! I nearly soiled myself," Sam wiped the sweat from his brow. "So how's your leg?"

Dave grumbled and waved off the question.

"Well, I found a Taco King that's open, but their credit card terminal is down. Do you have any cash? Because dude, I am *famished*… and…uh, dude?"

Dave was plodding recklessly toward Sam with his head hanging low.

"Dave? Hey, man, say something …"

The paramedic lifted his head and belched out a lifeless moan, casting his dead eyes skyward.

In a flash, Sam was gone, running at full speed down the street like a bat out of hell.

Everyone is dead! Everyone!

Sprinting past Taco King, he noticed a bloody man banging on the glass door. Sam had no desire to be a hero, so he continued running south without slowing his pace.

After several blocks, he approached an intersection with a few pedestrians loitering in the street. Common sense began to return, and he decided discretion was the best approach when encountering people, infected or otherwise.

Choosing a parked car to provide cover, Sam surveyed the scene. A slim, 40-something year old male in a blue "Ford Motor Company" windbreaker was lingering in front of a looted liquor store. He had no apparent injuries, but he was swaying in the early morning light with his neck craned at an odd angle, staring into the broken front door.

From the second floor window of a nearby home, a mature woman's voice called down to him in that distinctive Dee-troit dialect, "I see you Earl! Don't you get any ideas 'bout goin' into that store. I'll call the po-lice, I will." She was using her "Mom" tone of voice.

The man turned up to face her with the practiced grin of a charmer, saying, "Shoooot, Mrs.Turner. I'm just takin' a look t' make sure no one's in need a' rescuing! What with the riot goin' on and all."

She scolded back, "I'm sure none a' that liquor needs rescuing, Earl. Now git!"

"Well, the place looks busted up pretty good. I'm just gonna take a quick peek, Ma'am, t' make sure no one is injured an' needs *medical* attention," and with that he strutted cautiously into the broken doorway.

His false sincerity came across quite humorous to Sam, but Mrs. Turner was not amused. "That's it, Earl Walker! I's calling the po-lice!"

Earl poked his head back out, grinning sweetly, "Oh, don't you worry Mrs. Turner, I got this under control!" The old woman disappeared into her window, cursing and talking up a storm to someone else in the home.

After several minutes, Sam heard some commotion coming from the store, and out came Earl, wrestling with a shopping cart that was filled to the brink with bottles of booze. It nearly tipped multiple times as he maneuvered it over the broken glass.

The woman called down threateningly, "I see you Earl Walker! You gonna have to pay for all that!" To which Earl responded with a smile and a wave as he rolled his loot down a side street.

Sam observed the store for several more minutes, finally deciding that it would be worth the risk to enter the store in search for food. The sour cream and salsa he had eaten was beginning to sour his stomach, and he desperately needed something solid to ground it out.

Creeping up the front door, he paused to look back at Mrs. Turner's house. There she stood, stone faced, silently giving him 'the look.' Sam forced a smile and an awkward wave, and then entered the store.

The place was a mess. Empty racks were knocked over, broken glass and busted bottles littered the floor. Slowly working his way to the back, aisle by aisle, he was disappointed to see that the store had been thoroughly looted of edibles. The candy aisle: empty. The potato chip aisle: empty.

What the heck!? Did 'Earl' just clean out the last few morsels?

Upon reaching the back coolers, his spirit sank further when he saw that every shelf was empty … with the exception of a single row of Gatorade! He darted over and pulled one out of the cooler. Twisting off the lid, he turned up the bottle and drank its entire contents while standing there. Grabbing two more bottles, he circled around the back aisle and began making his way to the front when he found an end cap fully stocked with granola bars, beef jerky and nuts!

He pulled off his scrub top, and then removed his t-shirt, tying its sleeves and collar into one big knot, making a grocery sack out of his ripe smelling undershirt. After putting his scrub top back on, he loaded the sack with food and drink, and then resumed his search.

At the front counter, he rummaged through the debris and found a cigarette lighter and some bubble gum. Then glory of all glories, he looked over and saw a half full carafe of coffee. He ran over to the coffee station to assess the situation. The pot was cold, and stained black as tar, but it was a gift sent down from heaven.

He poured a tall cup of the opaque, muddy brew, and doctored it up with a packet of white sugar and a touch of powdered creamer. Anticipating the worst, he considered plugging his nose before sampling the concoction, but decided just to dive in and let nature take its course.

It was harsh and full bodied. Its palate was acrid, stale, and thoroughly scorched from sitting on the hot plate too long. It finished cold and bitter, with a distinct note of burnt carbon. Sam added some more sugar and another sprinkle of creamer, swirled the concoction, and took another pull from the paper cup.

Ack! Nasty instant creamer and processed white sugar... but I guess it'll have to do.

Silently he made his way to the front of the store. Mrs. Turner was still standing watch over the building, but remained silent as Sam stepped out into the morning light. Thankfully, the street was still free of the undead.

Looking south, he saw that he was close to the Motor City Casino, and beyond he could see some traffic in motion, possibly on Michigan Ave. That was where he needed to be. Thumb a ride heading west, and be home in time for lunch.

Eating a granola bar as he walked, he only made it half way down the block when he saw them ... *lots* of them. At least 50 infected people were corralled behind the wrought iron gate surrounding the modern casino's parking structure. Sam froze, granola bar in hand, considering the wisdom of walking past this iron fence. It stood over ten feet tall, and there were no visible gates through which the infected occupants could escape to pursue him. But he would be passing within a few feet of the crowd, which would certainly cause a commotion. There may have been an alternate way, a longer way, to

136

go around and avoid their line of sight, however he could not see it from here. Sam decided to just speed walk past the fence and hope that it held.

He finished off the granola bar and washed it down with his last sip of cold coffee, grounds and all.

Barf! ... that was horrendous.

Holding his T-shirt-sack of groceries tight to his chest, he steeled his nerves and walked double-time toward the casino. The dead casino goers saw him immediately and rushed the iron fence, moaning wildly. As he passed, they went berserk and began reaching for him through the iron pickets, grasping at the air. These penned in ghouls were all well dressed for a night on the town, and now they were dead. Or sick ... or something even worse. Their classy evening wear looked comically out of place in the early morning light, like an undead prom; colorful men's suits of purple and yellow, women with oversized hats. The irony of wearing your Sunday best to go gambling was not lost to Sam's sense of humor.

Over the sound of the moans and the pounding of his heart, Sam heard an engine turn over in the parking structure, followed immediately by squealing tires. Without breaking his stride, he looked over to see a Cadillac Escalade barreling across the lot. Apparently Sam had caused enough of a distraction for someone to make a run for their vehicle.

Several of the zombies turned to pursue it as it sped toward a gate on the south side of the lot. Without slowing, the oversized SUV burst through the heavy iron gate and rolled to a jerky stop. The engine stalled out from the violent impact, and steam began pouring from the damaged grill. The starter whined twice before succeeding on the third try, and the white Cadillac with oversized, overpriced rims took off like a house afire, swerving wildly and turning west on Michigan Ave..

Zombies began to pour through the breached gate, fanning out in several directions, but mostly heading straight toward Sam.

"Thanks a lot, jerk!" He yelled to the SUV as it vanished out of sight.

Running hard, Sam tried to power past the gate but had to zigzag evasively to avoid being grabbed. Zombies were now everywhere.

Unexpectedly, a stocky man with a magnificently groomed white beard and a backpack ran up alongside him yelling, "Hey! Where are you headed?"

Shocked, Sam stammered, "I-I don't know… where are *you* headed?"

"To the train station! Follow me!"

Without hesitating, Sam fell in behind the bald, bearded man as they booked across the street and began climbing a tall chain linked fence that surrounded a huge, empty lot. Hitting the ground, they backed away from the fence as the dead crashed into it.

Sam leaned over with his hands on his knees, trying to catch his breath, "Thanks … thanks, man. I owe you one…" he looked over his shoulder and saw that the bearded man never stopped running, and was now halfway across the vast, vacant lot.

"Crap."

Clenching his sack of food tightly, he ran to catch up with him. Near the far side of the field he passed a mound of dirt and suddenly realized that it was a pitcher's mound. It was THE pitcher's mound, the centerpiece of the old Tiger Stadium! Visions of the 1986 Championship flashed through his head, and he was momentarily star struck to be crossing that hallowed field, which now was no more than a weedy, vacant lot. Ahead he saw that the bearded man ducked into the trash filled remnants of a dugout, so Sam followed his lead.

"Thanks for the help, man. I owe you one. My name's Sam," he said, offering his hand.

"Bryan," he replied, not yet accepting the open hand, "Have you been bitten?"

Sam relaxed his shoulders but left his hand extended, "No, not yet."

Bryan smirked and gripped his hand, "Good. Me neither." He began rummaging through his backpack, producing a Snickers bar. "I was out making a food run when I saw you. Are you hungry?"

"Famished, thanks, but I … uh … 'found,' for lack of a better word, some granola bars and jerky in a looted liquor store." He pulled a "Honey & Oats" granola bar out of his sack, inhaling it in three bites.

The bearded man chuckled as he ripped open his candy wrapper, "Yeah. Me, too. I 'found' a box of Snickers and this new pair of shoes."

Sam looked down at Bryan's feet, "Nice running shoes."

Bryan grinned, admiring his new footwear as he tore into the candy bar, "Well, I would have preferred some steel toes, but these'll do the trick. So tell me Doc, any idea what the hell's going on?"

"Not really …. Zombies, I guess. It's the only explanation that makes any sense. Frickin' zombies," Sam mumbled, now with a mouthful of beef jerky.

"Finally! Someone who's not afraid to say it: frickin' zombies."

"You've got to admit, it does sound crazy. But they do meet all the criteria: rotting flesh, no pulse, bites spread the infection, heads shots are the only thing that'll stop 'em …"

"Well I'm just glad it's the *old-school* zombies: slow and stupid," Bryan interjected.

That comment caused Sam to finally break a smile.

"For real," he agreed, "If these clowns could run and reason, I wouldn't have made it out of the hospital alive."

After a long pause of chewing and reflecting, Bryan looked at the sky, wondering aloud, "Zombies? … Really? Frickin' *zombies*?"

They split a Gatorade and sat a little longer, discussing the epidemic and hoping that staying out of sight would lose the attention of the zombies from the casino.

Bryan cautiously sat up and peeked out of their makeshift fox hole, speaking as he panned the field, "So, have you heard about Korea?"

"Just a little blurb on the radio, but we were interrupted by some zombies… or maybe it was by some gunmen… I can't remember, it's all beginning to blur. I've been on the run for *days*, hiding in burned out stores, old car factories …"

"Old factories, huh? Which ones?"

"Oh, I think it was the old Packard Plant. It was huge."

Bryan nodded, gesturing to his camera, "I've been there. Did you see any fires while you were there?"

Sam was puzzled, "Fires? What do you mean?"

"Yeah, fires. That place is so immense and deteriorating that apparently there's always at least one fire burning somewhere in the building. There's even a web page that someone put up where you can check on the current status, it either says the Packard Plant is 'Burning' or 'Not Burning'."

Sam laughed, "You've got to be kidding me!"

"No, man, seriously. It's full of old wiring, combustibles, heavy metals, plenty of natural tinder; fires just spark up all the time and then burn themselves out. There was a large fire there a couple weeks back that the fire department responded to, but they couldn't figure out how to actually *get* to the fire. They could see huge flames lighting up the night sky above, but the place is a maze, and they couldn't actually find their way to the fire. So, they just stood by in the alley to make sure it didn't spread. It finally burned itself out by morning."

"That is such a shame."

"Tell me about it," Bryan said, laying back against the dugout wall and sighing deeply.

"So," Sam finally said, "You were going to the train station? Why there?"

"I've been holed up there all weekend with a couple other guys. I'm a photographer, and I was working on a project, documenting the urban decay and architectural ruins of Detroit. I ran into some contractors who were doing a survey of the abandoned train station and the surrounding park. Apparently, they are planning to erect a statue of Robocop in front of the building ..."

"Whoa, wait a sec ... did you say *Robocop*?"

Bryan pretended to hold up a gun and replied in a robotic voice, "Your move, creep."

Sam stared at him slack jawed and befuddled. "First of all, that was the worst Robocop impersonation I've ever heard ... actually it's the *only* Robocop impersonation I've ever heard. And secondly, um, why Robocop?"

"The movie took place in a not-so-fictional Detroit, in the not-too-distant future."

"Oh ... ok ... but my question still stands: why Robocop? Aside from being an ironic choice considering the local crime rate, isn't it a little ... I don't know ... silly? I mean, it's *Robocop*."

"Sure, maybe the whole idea of erecting a statue of Robocop is a little tongue in cheek, but this city *needs* to have some fun."

Tipping his head with uncertainty, Sam said, "Well that may be true, but isn't there more important things the City could be spending its money on?"

"It's not going to cost them a dime, the statue's being funded

140

entirely by private donations," Bryan sat up a little straighter, continuing, "People need to see that Detroit still has a pulse, and that people can get together, pool some resources and make things *happen*. Even if it is just a statue, or a park, or a mural."

The sound of a crumpling chain link fence brought all conversation to a halt, and both men sprang up, crouching cautiously on their haunches to peer out of the dugout. A section of the tall fence was folded down to the ground and zombies were pouring onto right field.

"They're coming … which way is that train station you mentioned?"

Bryan looked over his shoulder and pointed to the sky. A few blocks behind them the towering Michigan Central Station loomed large in the skyline. Only its upper floors were visible from the dugout, but its decrepit, ruinous state was already apparent. Every window of the tall building was broken, allowing the morning sunlight to pass through one side of the building and out the other. It provided a hollow, ghostly silhouette of the structure.

"Yikes! Are you serious? That place looks haunted!"

"Only by crackheads and metal scrappers, which are far more preferable to zombies. Let's go!"

The two darted across the field to the far fence and quickly scaled it, finally setting feet on Michigan Avenue, and what they saw was not good. It was pure chaos in the streets. Several cars were overturned, police cruisers were burning, and the few uninfected people that could be seen were running amok, shooting and looting like it was the end of the world. Zombies were roaming the street in all directions, and several immediately took notice of the two men and began to close in on them.

"Quick! Let's cut down this alley, I need to swing by the Gaelic League."

"What? Why *there*? Green beer?" Sam asked as they ran.

"No, I have my camera battery charging in an electrical plug out back."

"What!? Your *camera* battery? Are you kidding me!?"

"Just trust me," the bearded man said.

They ran behind a row of buildings and ducked into the alley. Trash bins lined the back wall of the businesses. Bryan stopped underneath a sign labeled, "Gaelic League & Irish-American Club of

Detroit – PLEASE USE FRONT ENTRANCE." He pulled away one of the trash bins to reveal the wall plug with his fully charged camera battery and a plastic grocery bag filled with hamburger buns.

"Grab those buns, will ya?"

"Sure," Sam said, looking over his shoulder nervously. Several zombies were now entering the alley way, led by a mangled city bus driver.

Bryan pocketed his battery and charger, and then retrieved a rusty shovel from behind the bins. Jumping up, he used the shovel to hook the fire escape ladder and pull it down.

"Whoa-whoa," Sam said, "Where are we going?"

"*Just trust me*," Bryan said as he began hoofing it up the ladder, "I used this same fire escape *twice* yesterday to shake off these bastards."

Cradling his sack of granola bars and the bag of buns, Sam struggled his way up the ladder. A dozen zombies had now filled the alley and were hot on his heels, grabbing at the bottom rungs.

"*Hurry*, man! *Hurry*!" Sam yelled as he bumped into Bryan, half pushing him up the ladder.

They scurried up onto the fire escape landing and had a brief tug-of-war with the zombies below before finally pulling the iron ladder up and out of reach of the their rotting hands.

"Sheesh!" Sam managed to say between gasping breaths, "That was too close, my friend … *now* what?"

"To the roof, I'm going to lure the rest of them into the alley with this shovel."

Rather than ask the white-bearded man to explain himself, Sam followed him up the fire escape steps to the roof of the three story building. Stepping onto the flat, tar paper roof of the old brick building provided an awe inspiring view of the now defunct Michigan Central Station.

"*That* is the train station?"

Bryan gave a bleak grin, "It *was* the train station. Now it's just a hulking ruin, a putrid corpse waiting to be incinerated."

It loomed ominously in the sky: a cold, gray, eighteen story tombstone presiding over the death of Detroit; a lingering ghost from the city's glorious past. It must have once been a magnificent, beautiful building. Built in 1913, it was composed of two distinctly different, almost incongruent structures: the grand, formal train station, and an immense office tower sprouting from its rear.

The main structure was reminiscent of an imposing government building, or a 19th century stone and marble museum. Classical Beaux Art in design, it had a grand entrance, with massive, 40 foot arched windows flanked by stout, Corinthian columns. Protruding from the aft portion of the building was a wide, soaring, high-rise tower, eighteen stories high and as wide as the cavernous lobby. The face of this imposing tower was a grid of broken windows, hundreds of them.

"Dear god ... that building is *amazing*. But look at it, how did someone manage to break *every single window* in the entire building? I mean, look," Sam pointed to the upper floors, "even up there. Every window is broken!"

Bryan shrugged. "It's been that way for years. The last train pulled out in '88, and it's been vacant ever since. The windows have been gone for at least a decade. But before we can make our way there, I need to clear us a path."

Walking over to the front corner of the Gaelic League's roof, Bryan leaned over the edge and began banging his shovel against the brick wall, drawing the attention of the zombies down in the street. After he'd attracted the twenty or so zombies within ear shot, he scooted ten feet in the direction of the alley and repeated the banging. The sick bastards instinctively followed him. They were being worked up into a frenzy by the panging of the shovel, moaning loudly and pawing in vain at the bald man who taunted them from above. As the crowd gathered beneath him, he scooted down again, repeating the process. In less than ten minutes he had managed to lure most of them into the back alley.

"Get ready to make a break for it. We can climb down onto the front awning once the coast is clear."

Sam tip-toed to the front ledge. It would be an easy climb down the awning, and then a short jump to the sidewalk. There were still many zombies in the street, but it looked clear enough to make a run for it. "Brilliant plan, sir."

"Thanks," Bryan said, still banging the shovel over the back alley, "Are you ready?"

Sam took a deep breath before answering grimly. "Sure. Let's do this."

"Okay, here we go!" Bryan dropped the shovel down into the

alley behind the trash bins and then ran across the roof toward the awning. "Crap! Why didn't you tell me there were more out front!?"

"What? Those ones? They aren't *too* close, and they aren't looking this way ... I don't think they're close enough to be a problem ..." he answered, somewhat apologetically.

"Well, I guess we'll find out the hard way. Just drop your bags down onto the sidewalk and follow me." Bryan swung a leg over the side and began to climb down.

Sam dropped his bags as instructed. The buns landed fine, but the make-shift bag he improvised from a t-shirt burst open, scattering his cache of granola and jerky across the sidewalk.

"Darn it all!" Sam cursed under his breath, shaking a fist to the sky.

"Just forget about it," Bryan said as he slid down the awning, "grab what you can and keep moving!"

They landed on the pavement, filled their pockets with what they could reach, and ran like the dickens.

Michigan Ave. was littered with abandoned and burning cars. A late model Lexus was ablaze nearby, with two women inside, surrounded by a dozen zombies. Bryan and Sam raced past, helplessly watching as the two trapped occupants of the car screamed hysterically, forced to choose their brand of death: exit the car and be eaten alive, or burn to death in their vehicle. The driver chose the former, opening her car door and attempting to flee. She was quickly dragged down by three women wearing blood stained hijabs. She struggled to break free, but several more zombies joined in, dog piling the poor woman, viciously biting her face and arms.

In a surreal moment, Sam made eye contact with an old man running in the other direction. He had a Playstation 3 clenched tightly to his chest and fistfuls of loose gold jewelry; apparently he had just looted the pawn shop across the street. The man's eyes bulged with guilt when he realized he'd been spotted, and he shrugged apologetically, not that it mattered given the peril of their situation.

Swerving evasively to avoid the sick, they were startled by a well-dressed, overweight man who ran up alongside them. He was carrying a yellow fiberglass pick-ax and was struggling to catch his breath. The ax looked *exactly* like the one Sam had used to chop off Dave's arm.

"Help!" the man wheezed, "They're crazy … and they're everywhere!"

"Just keep running, man!" was all Sam could think to say, and the big man fell in line behind them.

Leaving the street, they crossed a large, grassy, zombie-filled promenade that lead to the front steps of the towering train station. The entire building was surrounded by an 8' chain-linked fence, and their desperate run across Michigan Ave. had attracted the attention of scores of zombies, who were now converging on the promenade.

As they neared the fence, Bryan called out to the group, "Get ready to toss your things over and climb like hell!"

The men chucked everything they had over the fence: loose granola bars, a Gatorade, the hamburger buns, the yellow ax, Bryan's camera bag. And then the men began to climb like hell.

The fence rattled and jangled as they crested the top, and then hurriedly dropped to the other side, landing safely on all fours. Bryan and Sam jumped to their feet and backed away from the fence. It was then, to their horror, they realized their heavy-set companion was still on the other side, straining to heft himself up and onto the fence, but he seemed unable to break free of gravity's hold. His chubby fingers were entwined in the chain link fence, and with the grace of a rhinoceros, he repeatedly tried to throw a leg up but could never seem to dig a foothold into the fence.

"Come on! Climb!" Sam implored, "They're coming!"

But it was too late; the first few zombies had caught up with him. It was three homeless men in secondhand t-shirts. They grabbed the portly man from behind, pulling him off his feet. With white knuckles, he somehow managed to keep a firm hold of the fence as they pulled his body up into a horizontal position, biting into his fleshy legs. The man screamed in pain, but continued to maintain his death-grip on the fence. Another zombie caught up with the group and tried to join in on the tug-of-war, but was unable to as his fingers were missing, obviously chewed off when he fell victim to a zombie himself. It did not, however, stop him from trying; the fingerless zombie pawed repeatedly at the man's legs, unable to comprehend that his maimed hands could never grab hold.

By now several more zombies had arrived at the fence and were moaning loudly at the men on the other side, snapping their teeth and clawing at the fence.

"Let's get out of sight before they mob this fence!" Bryan said as he gathered up their scattered belongings.

In a daze Sam picked up the yellow ax. The textured grip of the fiberglass handle felt good in his hands, as did the weight of the blood stained head. He looked up at the poor man clinging to the fence: outnumbered and cornered, pleading for them to stop. It was a slow, horrible death, indeed. Looking back down at the ax, he wished that he could put this poor man out of his misery.

"Snap out of it!" a voice called out from behind the building.

It was Bryan; he had run around to the east side of the train station and was waving his hands frantically for Sam to keep moving.

Sam took one last look at the overweight, dying man who was no more than three feet away from him. The guy's lower half was already a mutilated, chewed-up mess. His pants had been completely shredded away, exposing his mangled legs and genitalia. It was gut wrenching to watch this living, screaming man being torn apart, muscle from bone. There was no way to save him, so Sam turned and ran.

Rounding the corner, he caught up with Bryan and followed him toward the side entrance of the building, the old "Street Car Entrance". The large double doors had been ripped from their hinges and stolen years ago, so the two men stepped inside.

"Jeez, Bryan," Sam gasped, "this place is *incredible!*"

The Street Car Entrance was where the building planners assumed most of the passengers would be entering the station, so they appropriately made it a grand affair (however, with the development of the automobile, this entrance was rarely used; most passengers arrived by car through the less glamorous "Carriage Entrance" on the far side). Inside, the stone and marble walls formed a long hallway, an Arcade, rising 28 feet high with beautiful coved ceilings. The empty shops lining the Arcade had been gutted, but had a few telltale clues that spoke of their past: a few barber chairs, some corroded soda fountains, old magazine racks, old signage for cigars and pharmaceuticals.

The two men crept down the long, dimly lit Arcade, cautiously peeking into each shop before they dared pass its doorway. It was slow going, but they didn't want to take any chances.

"Man, this building is frickin' *terrifying!* I feel like it could swallow us up," Sam whispered.

"Wait till you see the Main Lobby, it's as big as a football pitch in there."

"A what?"

"A football pitch, a *soccer* field."

"Oh, gotcha."

On the right hand side, they passed a broad, debris-filled staircase that spiraled up into inky darkness. Sam raised his hand, signaling Bryan to halt, whispering, "Hey man, maybe we can get up on the roof to see how clear Michigan Ave. is heading west. That's the way I need to go to get home."

Bryan shook his head, "You don't want to use that stairway without a flashlight. There's a better lit stairway in the Concourse."

"Excellent. Lead the way, sir."

"But first we have to stop by the Mercury Room to meet up with Kenny and Jason."

"Those are the two contractors you were talking about?"

"Yeah. They seem like decent guys, just a little freaked out about the whole 'zombie' thing."

"A little freaked out, huh? Imagine that. What's the Mercury Room?"

"It's the old restaurant. We've been camping out in there and the adjoining Reading Room."

The Arcade led directly to the Ticket Office, which was a series of bank-teller style windows flanked by four massive columns; each was easily 4 ft. in diameter. These beautiful marble columns were defaced by poorly drawn graffiti (an anarchy symbol and a crudely drawn penis).

To the right of the Ticket Office, the hall opened up into the train station's crown jewel, the cavernous waiting room.

"Wow …" Sam stood speechless for several moments, jaw agape. "I … I feel like we just discovered Atlantis … or the lost city of gold!"

Bryan nodded, "Impressive, isn't it?"

The main waiting room was an expansive architectural marvel, inspired by an ancient Roman bathhouse. It measured 234 ft. long by 98 ft. wide. The marble walls were punctuated by stout, 21 ft. tall Doric columns that supported the graceful Guastivino arches of the 55 ft. vaulted ceiling. Natural light filled the room through four gargantuan windows, measuring 40 ft. tall. The main front entrance was also framed by two 'smaller' windows, measuring 21 ft. tall.

147

Even in its ruinous state, the room permeated a grand sense of importance.

"Dude, how could the city allow this building to rot away? This place is *magnificent!* I've been to Grand Central Station in New York, but *this* place blows it out of the water!"

Bryan let out an indifferent laugh. "Funny you should mention Grand Central, because Michigan Central was designed by the same guys. But you shouldn't be surprised by this city's failings, this place is a socio-economical train wreck. Murder capital of America, corrupt and ineffectual city leaders, crime, poverty, drugs, you name it. Heck, Detroit has *thousands* of vacant buildings. To them, this is just one more."

"Yeah, but *look* at this place! How can they let a place like this rot on the vine?"

"Welcome to Detroit, man."

Sam took a few steps toward the towering front windows. "It looks like our antics at the fence drew a crowd."

Outside, there were scores of zombies crowded at the fence, a mutilated cross-section of the local population: African Americans, Arab Americans, several Hispanics, and a couple whites. They were whipped up into a frenzy, moaning loudly and attacking the poorly maintained fence like rabid dogs.

Bryan took a look, saying, "Jesus … that fat is guy still moving. He's buried under a pile of them, but … he's still moving."

After a moment of watching in silence, Sam looked down at the ax and asked, "I wonder how long it takes to die from being bit to death? That poor guy …"

"Well we need to go. They seem to know we're in here, and I don't like how that fence is buckling. If they get through the fence, we're screwed." Bryan pointed to the gaping front doorway, "There's nothing to keep them from getting in the building."

They backed away from the window and proceeded past the Ticket Office into the Concourse. Golden shafts of dusty sunlight illuminated this enormous room, pouring in through dozens of copper framed skylights. Nearly as large as the waiting room, the Concourse measured 204 ft. long by 78 ft. wide. Its stately walls were made of light-colored brick, laid in Flemish bond with terracotta accents. A wide ramp sloped down to the passenger gates. It was easy to imaging the ghosts of travelers filling this majestic room.

Strangely enough, in the middle of the vast open room sat a single elementary school desk, illuminated by a column of dusty sunlight. Bryan stopped and pulled out his camera. After a moment to compose and meter the shot, he snapped off a few pictures of the old, wooden desk.

"Nice," he said, as he reviewed the digital images on the back of his camera. Then, "Okay, the restaurant's this way. Let's go."

A passageway in the northwest corner led directly into the Mercury dining room, which was yet another once-beautiful room, with a vaulted ceiling of caen stone and magnificent floors of Welsh quarry tile. At some point in the room's history, a drop ceiling was installed that foolishly must have hid the architecturally significant ceiling, but now all that remained of that poor decision was the metal framework.

"Hmm, they're not in here, so they're probably up front in the Reading Room," Bryan whispered.

"Reading Room? You seem to know a lot about this building, Bryan. You've been in here before?"

"Yeah, it's a bit of a hobby. We call it urban exploration, sneaking into abandoned buildings and photographing them. This building's become one of my favorite haunts. But I've also snuck in here long ago, back in the 90's. There were a couple raves here."

"Raves? Wow, I forgot about those."

Bryan smiled, "There are a *lot* of things I've forgotten from the 90's …"

They tip-toed on past a small café and into the next room, which was a more modest, well lit room in the front corner of the building. Two men were standing in the front window, looking out at the mayhem on the fence.

"Hey, guys, I found a live one," Bryan said.

The two men spun around, brandishing hammers.

"Easy! Easy! It's just me," Bryan pointed over to Sam, "This is Dr. Sam."

"No, I'm not a doctor, I'm an MRI Tech," Sam corrected.

"Whatever," Bryan continued, "We're going up on the roof to get a better vantage of the street. You guys want to come with?"

The taller one, Kenny, answered angrily, "Did *you guys* attract all this attention to the fence? It's damn well about to collapse!" His fists were clenched, and he looked a lot like Frank Zappa in a hard hat,

149

with side burns and a handle bar mustache.

Bryan shrugged, "Hey, it wasn't like we planned it that way. I barely made it back with my tail intact."

Kenny glared at Bryan and Sam, nostrils flaring.

The other guy, Jason, intervened, "Well, we'll be safer up there anyway. If they bust through that fence, this place will be crawling with 'em. Let's just grab our things and move to higher ground." He was short and stocky, built like a jock.

They collected their things and followed Bryan to the Concourse where they found a broad, graffiti filled staircase that led to the second floor. Weaving through a debris strewn labyrinth of hallways, they passed several dark elevator shafts and ultimately reached a utilitarian stairway that led all the way to the roof.

This smaller stairway was made of pressed sheets of rusty metal, sheathed in a crumbling layer of cement. Kenny stepped forward to inspect the stairway's integrity, tapping various points of the structure with his hammer.

"Well it looks like hell but it seems solid. Just watch your step."

The group cautiously ascended to the roof, which was easily accessible due to yet another missing door.

The cityscape before them painted a grim picture. Looking west, black plumes of smoke were filling the sky. A particularly large column of smoke seemed unnaturally metallic blue, as if coming from a burning chemical plant. To the east, downtown Detroit was in flames, nearly obscuring the skyline. To the north and south, there were dozens of isolated house fires, streaking the sky with ribbons of black smoke.

"Christ … look there," was all Kenny could muster to as he pointed to the Ambassador Bridge. The bridge was packed tightly with a burning convoy of military vehicles: Hummers, Armored Personnel Carriers, and ¾ ton trucks, all facing the city of Windsor, Ontario. On the Canadian side of the smoldering convoy was an imposing concrete roadblock. Large floodlights and hastily built gun turrets were perched above the barrier, with guns pointing toward the American side.

Sam furled his brow in disbelief, "Is that the Canadian Army pointing guns at Detroit? What … what happened? *How* did this happen!? Is this real!?"

150

"That must have been the explosions I heard last night," Bryan said. "It sounded like we were under attack. I guess we were. Ha, I guess we still are," he added, pointing to another surge of zombies coming from Downtown.

Suddenly, two military helicopters roared overhead. Moving at a steady rate of speed, they descended to no more than 50ft above the street and began dropping teargas canisters on the crowded street below. Sickly, gray-green smoke began to rise from the canisters, but it seemed to have no effect on the crowd.

The younger looking construction worker, Jason, asked, "Why are they using teargas? They need to blow those bastards sky high!"

"They're still acting like this is just another riot," Bryan said. "They don't seem to realize this one is different."

"It's not too different," Kenny puffed. "I was only a kid in Dearborn during the '67 riot, but we had frickin' *tanks* rolling down our street to keep the peace. That's what we need: some big-bad-men who aren't afraid to get things done and some *tanks.*"

"Well, Kenny, *there's* your tanks," Bryan said, pointing to the bridge.

Sure enough, there was a burning tank among the military convoy. Their hearts sank.

Another loud helicopter approached the train station's roof, slowly passing by the men at eye level before pulling up and hovering just above them. Its bright maize and blue paint job easily identified it as the University of Michigan Hospital's "Survival Flight" chopper. The guys began waving their arms for help as they were blasted with wind from the prop wash.

A loud voice hailed them from the helicopter's bull horn, "You on the roof, are any of you injured?"

The men looked at each other briefly and then back at the chopper, shaking their heads "no."

The voice asked again, "How many people are with you?"

Shielding their faces from the roaring wind, the men held up four fingers.

"Roger that," the voice said, and then asked, "You, in the scrubs, are you a doctor?"

Sam shook his head and yelled, "No, I'm an MRI Technologist!"

The voice boomed, "Say again, I did not copy that."

151

Sam cupped his hands and yelled even louder, carefully mouthing the words, "NO! M-R-I TECH!"

"Oh … roger that. Stand by," the voice said, and then went silent for several moments while the chopper hovered in place. The crew was obviously in discussion with each other.

Finally the voice returned, "Stay where you are. We are only taking wounded at this time. We will radio your position to the authorities. Do you copy?"

The men nodded, and the helicopter tipped forward and pulled away.

"Wait!" Kenny yelled in vain at the chopper. "What a load of crock!" he screamed, throwing his hands up in the air as the aircraft flew away. "They're just going to *leave* us here!?" He stomped around and kicked a loose brick off the side of the building, then turned and pointed at Sam, "And *you!* I thought you said you were a *doctor!*"

Raising his hand to correct him, Sam stated "Actually, I never said that I … was …" he allowed his words to taper away as Kenny stormed off.

Bryan shrugged his shoulders, "You should've lied to those guys in the chopper. It might have got you a free ride home."

"Naw, I don't think so. They probably would've dropped me off with a gymnasium full of bite victims."

"Oh, right. That would be bad," Bryan agreed.

Sam walked over to the edge and surveyed Michigan Ave. as it headed westbound. A fog of teargas still hung in the air, but was having no affect whatsoever on the majority of the crowd. The only ones who were fazed by the gas were the *uninfected* people who were now blinded and unable to breathe, thus being rendered defenseless from their zombie attackers. They watched as several gas-stricken civilians were dragged down and eaten alive.

"Friendly fire," Bryan murmured between taking pictures, obviously disgusted but unable to pull away from his camera.

"Jeez, guys, we are so screwed," Sam realized aloud. "This neighborhood is totally overrun, and there is *no way* I'll be able to take Michigan Ave. home. Maybe I can commandeer another truck and try to take the side streets south of here."

Another surge of zombies was pouring into the street, this time coming from the west, most of which appeared to be Arab-American.

"Whoa," Jason the construction worker chimed in, "it looks like church just got out at the Mosque. See? Half those folks are wearing head scarves!"

Bryan chuckled grimly, "They must be coming from Dearborn, it's just a few miles away. It's the largest population of Arabs outside of the Middle East."

"Seriously?" Jason said in disbelief. "Dearborn, Michigan?"

"Yeah, it's been like that for decades. Syrians, Lebanese, Palestinians, Chaldeans … they've done a good job at keeping up the place. And the food there is fan-tastic."

"What are Chaldeans?" Sam asked.

Bryan raised his camera and zoomed in on the riot below, answering as he snapped off a few more pictures, "Iraqi Christians … but there are a lot of Muslim Iraqis here, too."

Having regained his cool, Kenny walked back and rejoined the group. He pulled off his hardhat and ran his fingers through his long, curly dark hair.

"Sorry I flew off the handle, guys. It's just that …," he paused, trying to find the right words, "I mean … frickin' *zombies?* In *Detroit?* This whole thing is just too damned crazy."

The group shrugged collectively, saying things like "you got *that* right," and "no worries, man, we're all a little freaked out."

Kenny looked back down at the street and saw the large Arabic addition to the mob. Shaking his head, he pulled out a cigarette and lit it with an old fashioned Zippo. Blowing a long stream of smoke though his nostrils, he said, "Damn, looks like they got Dearborn, too."

Perched high atop Michigan Central Station, the exhausted men watched helplessly as the few remaining people in the street were dragged down and torn apart.

Bryan finally looked out from behind his camera, bewildered, "I can't believe how crowded the street is. I mean, this part of town *isn't* densely populated, so where are all these people coming from?"

"No clue," Kenny said, clearing his throat loudly and spitting off the side of the tall building, "but this building provides a commanding view of the area. When I stepped away to cool off … I saw a couple people heading this way, creeping up the train tracks."

"Were they inside the fence?" Jason asked nervously.

"I think so, but it was hard to tell. You can't really see the entire fence line because of our angle."

Bryan stood up, "Let's take a look. Most of the tracks don't access the station anymore."

They walked the south edge of the roof, and sure enough, there were three women on the tracks. They were on their hands and knees looking under a train car. Suddenly, they sprang to their feet and took off screaming, running directly toward the station. A moment later, two men hobbled around the corner of the boxcar and began to pursue them, plodding along with stiff arms raised and an awkward gait.

"Bryan, do you know if *those* tracks are on this side of the fence?" Sam asked.

"Unfortunately, yeah," Bryan said, pointing to a section of the rail yard, "That whole part of the rail yard is enclosed within the fence."

"Crap," Kenny grumbled, "so those broads are leading them straight to us."

As they watched, another man stumbled out from behind the boxcar and collapsed on the ground. Bloodied and injured, the man dragged himself along for several feet and then slumped face down in the dirt, unmoving.

The fleeing women continued toward to train station, disappearing from view as they reached the concourse. The pursuing zombies reached the concourse shortly after.

Sam rubbed his weary eyes and let out a long sigh. "I'm going down there to help them. Who's with me?"

Kenny let out a long, "Pfffffftt," shaking his head. "Knock yourself out. I'm staying right here."

Jason and Bryan looked at each other, neither one speaking up.

"*Really*, guys?" Sam pressed. "No one?"

Bryan winced for a moment before finally relenting. "Ah, dammit. I'll go. Somebody let me borrow a hammer."

"Not mine!" Kenny scoffed before looking over at Jason expectantly.

"What?" Jason asked, "*My* hammer? Sorry man," he said, turning to Bryan, "No offense, but if you don't make it back, I'll be screwed without it. I … I'm not parting with my hammer."

"Whatever, man," Bryan said as he kicked a loose brick from its crumbling mortar. He picked it up and gave Sam a nod. "Let's go."

Sam hoisted the yellow handled ax over his shoulder and fell in behind Bryan as they hustled down the stairs.

Several floors down the white-bearded man froze mid-step, raising his hand to signal silence. Pausing at an open doorway, they trained their ears in the direction of a long, sterile hallway. It resembled the hall of a grand-yet-simple art deco hotel, but it had been exposed to decades of windowless Michigan winters, and every door in the hall had been kicked in years ago.

A loud thump echoed from far down the hall, followed by a long, scraping sound. Moments later there was another thump, followed by more scraping.

"Someone's down there," Bryan whispered, glancing around the stairwell. "Well the floor numbers aren't marked, but this is probably the 5th or 6th floor. Let's remember that on our way back up."

Sam nodded with fearful eyes, clutching the ax handle tightly.

"Come on," Bryan whispered, continuing down the stairs with a heightened sense of urgency.

The stairway terminated at the 2nd floor, so the men had to go down a hall and around a corner to reach the elevator shafts and the wide staircase that led to the ground floor.

They paused at the final staircase to peek down into the Concourse and do some reconnaissance. Catching his breath from descending 13 flights of stairs, Sam realized that Bryan was hardly out of breath.

"You sure do have good cardio for an old guy."

"Old guy?" Bryan whispered, "Dude, I'm 35. Don't let the bald pate and white beard fool you, I have vitiligo."

"*Vitiligo?* Isn't that what Michael Jackson had?"

"Pshhhh, no. That's just a load of B.S., what that man had was an identity crisis and a screwed up childhood. But he could sing and dance, I'll give him that."

Both men went silent as loud footsteps came pounding by, dangerously close yet out of sight. Due to the acoustics of the empty stone building, it was difficult to pinpoint the direction of the sound. Listening intently, other sounds could be heard in the building, coming from the Arcade. Possibly footsteps, possibly rats or pigeons; it was hard to tell. They waited a few moments longer, but heard nothing more.

155

Sam spoke up, in a whisper, "That running sound *had* to be them. I have yet to hear a zombie run as fast as that."

"You're probably right. Let's circle around back near the tracks, and then do one pass of the Arcade. If we don't see them, then I say screw it: back to the roof. Deal?"

"Sounds fair enough. Let's just be swift and silent; like ninjas."

"Like ninjas," Bryan agreed, nodding very seriously.

They stepped down the final landing into the open Concourse and a rotting, snarling man stumbled forward onto Bryan, grabbing him by the shirt!

"EEEEEEEEEEEEEEK!" Bryan and Sam screamed like pre-teen girls at a slumber party.

Bryan thrashed around convulsively, managing to shake the man loose, and then he took off running toward the train tracks. Sam ran the other way, toward the Arcade, still screaming in an embarrassingly high octave. His girlish screams had attracted attention, and the sound of footsteps and moans began to converge on him from several different directions, echoing through the vast corridors.

Stopping and turning by the old soda fountain, Sam held his ax high as his eyes darted to all the dark nooks and crannies. The empty building was now alive with sound: hungry moans, footsteps, glass breaking ...

"BRYAN!" Sam yelled, desperate for help.

Tall, dark shadows began moving along the Arcade walls as a pack of diseased zombies emerged through the Streetcar Entrance. Sam took position in the center of the wide hall, trying to decide how to face these creeps, but saw two more coming from the direction of the Concourse ... and another from the Barber Shop ... *he was surrounded*.

His heart was bursting in his chest and his mind was in full blown panic. There was no way he could fend off this many of them at once, especially with this unwieldy ax. This wasn't like a Bruce Lee movie, and he was no Bruce Lee. He was going to die here.

The first of the bunch came within reach. It was a man wearing nothing but white cotton briefs, and Sam swung the ax with all his might. The heavy blade connected with the man's temple, knocking him into the dark stairwell Bryan had warned him about.

156

THE STAIRWELL! YAY!

Sam leaped over the brief-clad man and stumbled up the first few steps. They were a horrible tripping hazard, strewn with large slabs of marble, broken loose from the vandalized marble walls.

Ten steps up, he reached the first landing which was literally pitch black. He could tell that the staircase turned left and continued upward but he had zero visibility. Looking back down, there were several zombies clumsily making their way up the first steps. It was absolutely horrifying.

My lighter! The one I looted from the liquor store!

He reached into his scrub pocket and produced the plastic Bic lighter, attempting to strike it several times. The flint sparked, but there was no flame. He shook the lighter frantically and tried again, but still no joy. Pressing the "gas" button on the lighter, he held it up to his ear to listen: there was no hissing sound.

NO! YOU'VE GOT TO BE KIDDING ME! IT'S EMPTY!?

He continued to flick the lighter in rapid succession, over and over, illuminating the stairwell one frame at a time which produced a terrifying strobe effect as the zombies drew near.

Sam screamed involuntarily again as he turned and made his way up the second flight of stairs. He tripped, and stumbled, and recovered, and tripped again, struggling to hold on to the ax while simultaneously working the lighter. The burled wheel of the plastic lighter spun and spun, providing only brief sparks of light but ample amounts of pants-crapping terror.

At the next landing the stairway turned left again and ascended into more darkness. There was no other light source in sight, and to complicate matters, someone had dumped piles of trash and debris in this unused stairwell, making it nearly impassable.

Recklessly high-stepping through the trash, Sam kept checking over his shoulder, watching with each strobe of sparks as the zombies stumbled their way up the stairs in a graphic series of still images.

157

Again at the next landing, the stairway turned left. Thankfully, there was a dim glow of light ahead which provided a glimmer of hope and a target to run toward.

His right foot then landed awkwardly on something soft and wet, and Sam slipped hard into the wall. On the dark stairway beneath him, something large moved and moaned, grabbing at his pant leg.

Sam screamed yet again, and dropped his lighter so he could wield the ax with both hands. He swung blindly, striking only the hard floor. Unable to see his target, he frantically hoisted the ax back over his head, chopping again and again and again, searching for the zombie on the stairwell floor. His first strike clipped the wall, and the second swing met only trash, but the third found something meaty, and the fourth found more meat, and the fifth finally struck what felt like a hard shelled gourd. Even without light to see, he knew that he just crushed a man's skull.

The ax pulled free, and Sam danced up the last few steps into a dimly lit room. There were several dark elevator shafts, and two halls leading away. Choosing the best lit hall that seemed to lead back toward the other staircase, he ran at full speed, fleeing from the moaning stairwell.

This was another hall that was reminiscent of a grand hotel, running the length of the building with dozens of brightly lit rooms on either side. Each doorway had been smashed open, revealing abandoned office spaces with glassless windows and the smoldering skyline outside.

At the end of the hall, Sam turned and kept running, turning again and again, looking for the main stairway. He was out of breath and his legs were about to give out, so he stopped to think things through.

As he stood there panting, he could hear quiet footsteps approaching, slowly getting louder, but moving very fast; obviously not a zombie.

That sounds like ... the stairs!

Running toward the source of the sound, the stairway came into view just as Bryan came flying up them.

"Doc! You're alive!" was all Bryan said as he flew past, continuing up the stairs.

Sam fell in behind him, but was unable to keep pace. His legs were spent and his adrenaline was crashing, so he plodded up the stairs as best he could. When he reached the top and stepped out onto the hot roof, he found Bryan sitting against a shaded wall, telling Kenny and Jason about the zombies in the building.

Staggering over to the group, Sam propped his ax against the wall and collapsed on the roof next to Bryan. In a daze, he pulled out his cell phone and powered it up. The screen turned on, but the battery was flashing "empty," so he wasted no time and composed a quick text message.

"hi babe. its real bad out here. i'm still in detroit, in the train station on michigan ave. its gonna be a long walk home. r u guys ok?" send.

A moment later, Jessica replied, "Yes, we're fine! But please be careful! There are zombies in Ann Arbor now, at the mall, and there was one here at the gas station in Milan. Police are closing our street off at the highway, so you'll have to take side streets. Are you ok?"

"just tired and freaked out. i think these really are zombies. its horrible babe. i cant wait to get home." send.

She responded immediately, "The President said they ARE zombies! For real! From Korea! It's like a disease. Stay away from them, they will try to bite you!"

Sam was too exhausted to smile at her gross understatement, but he chuckled on the inside.

Yep, they definitely bite.

He continued typing with his thumbs, "my cell phone is going to die soon. please take care of simon and the baby. try to text my parents and amanda. i will be home as soon as i can." send.

She replied, "Your mom & dad are fine, so is your brother. Florida hasn't had any zombies yet. And Amanda is safe, she went to the Air Force base near Salt Lake, but she said she loves you and to aim for the head. Not sure what she meant … but I'm sure you do."

Sam's chapped lips cracked painfully as he grinned from ear to ear. He and his 19 year old daughter, Amanda, share a passion for videogames. Therefore, she has been trained since birth that headshots are the only way to kill a zombie … at least on the Playstation.

"she is so awesome :-) tell her that i …" before he could finish his thought, the screen went black as his cell phone powered down from a dead battery.

DANG IT!

He snapped the phone closed and dropped it in his shirt pocket.

160

Bryan was wrapping up his update on the status of the building, and it was obvious that Kenny and Jason were not thrilled.

When Bryan concluded, Kenny stood silent for a moment, staring up into the smoke filled sky. There were perhaps a dozen helicopters in the air, circling the city, hovering near rooftops, and evacuating the injured with ropes and baskets. He finally spoke in a threatening tone, pointedly accentuating each word, "We need to flag down another helicopter. We'll tell them Bryan here's got a broken leg. And we'll tell them that *that guy* ..." he pointed to Sam, "... is a doctor. We need to get off this building." He wolfishly looked around at the rooftop and continued, "Help me find some stuff to spell 'HELP' on the roof."

Bryan and Sam looked at one another nervously, trying to feel out Kenny's vibe. He was beginning to lose it, and the guys were beginning to wonder if Kenny might actually try to break Bryan's leg to make their story believable.

Reluctantly, the men all returned to their feet and began gathering loose debris. Thankfully, there was no shortage of trash, and very quickly they had "H-E-L" spelled out in large, 20ft letters. Gathering refuse for the last remaining letter, Bryan unfurled a large, moldy, silk cloth. It was a flag.

"Hey guys, check it out. It's the flag of Detroit," Bryan grabbed the corners and spread his arms wide to display the flag. An amused grin spread across his face, and he asked, "Do you notice anything ironic about the imagery?"

The other men stopped to view the flag. It had a quartered background, with symbolism representing France, Great Britain, and the United Stated (the three countries that have controlled the city at different points in its history), and a seal in the middle depicting two women, one of which was weeping over the burning city skyline, one of which was presiding over its rebuilding.

Sam was taken aback, "Is that an image of the city... *burning?* On the city flag? Seriously?"

"Yep," Bryan chuckled grimly. "But it has nothing to do with the riots, or Devil's Night. Detroit actually burned to the ground in 1805, the *entire* city. Only one building was left standing, it was the only building made of brick."

"Dang," Jason said, "I didn't know the city was that old."

Sam's penchant for useless knowledge chimed in, "Oh yeah,

161

the sign on Mack Ave says 'Detroit City Limits founded 1701'. So I guess that would make it over a hundred years old at the time it burned."

"And what does *that* say?" Jason asked, pointing to the inscription on the seal.

"Not sure ... it looks like Latin." Bryan said.

"Let me see," Sam offered, "I took Latin in high school."

Bryan cleared his throat, saying in jest, "Nerd alert."

Blowing off the comment with a grin, Sam struggled with the words for a moment. "Speramus Meliora ... we hope for better things ... and ... Resurget Cineribus ... it will rise from the ashes? That's a pretty grim slogan. Probably not the best motto for attracting tourism, either."

Nodding in agreement, Bryan unceremoniously bunched up the moldy flag and used it and some old tarps to finish spelling the letter "P" in "H-E-L-P."

The group stood there for a moment, admiring their makeshift distress signal while looking to the sky, hoping to catch the attention of another chopper. Dozens of helicopters now dotted the sky: bright orange and white Coast Guard choppers, local news choppers, gray military choppers, and Wayne County Sheriff choppers. Several appeared to be engaged in roof top rescues; others were combing the freeways, or hovering near particularly large fires.

Sam rubbed his temples, saying, "I can't believe how much of the city is burning, there are fires *everywhere.*"

"Actually, it doesn't look much different than Devil's Night," Bryan said with another smirk. "Well, with the exception of Downtown," he corrected, pointing to the blazing skyscrapers along the Detroit river.

Sam puffed, "That might be a *wee bit* of an overstatement, sir."

Bryan raised an eyebrow, "You, obviously, haven't been around on Devil's Night. On our worst year we had more than 800 fires that single night, with a couple more on Halloween and the night after. *Eight hundred.*"

"What!? No way." Jason said in disbelief.

"Yes way. Detroit *invented* Devil's Night, and we go all out. Mostly it's just kids vandalizing vacant buildings, but some of it is landlords torching condemned property to collect on the insurance. Some of it is local folks burning down crack houses. A few years ago,

Mayor Archer tried to put a positive spin on it, calling it 'Angel's Night', and organizing neighborhood watches to keep an eye out for arsonists. It *has* helped, there's only been a few hundred in recent years." Bryan looked out across the city skyline, sizing it up, "I'll bet that's only two or three hundred burning right now."

"Only a couple hundred, huh?" Sam smirked.

Suddenly, Jason perked up and pointed toward the Ambassador Bridge. There was a grey helicopter flying directly toward them at a slow, steady rate, broadcasting its approach with a steady *whup-whup-whup* sound.

The men began jumping up and down and waving their arms, calling for help.

`The helicopter was a CH-47, a twin rotor Chinook. It was *huge*, probably as long as a city bus. It passed overhead and then banked sharply, circling wide over the train station.

The guys cheered wildly! They had been spotted!

Then without warning, Kenny turned toward Bryan and blasted him in the knee with his hammer, shattering his patella and grotesquely hyper-extending the joint. Bryan dropped like a sack of potatoes, screaming painfully as his lower leg dislocated backwards.

"What the heck was that for!?" Sam screamed in shock, hoisting up the ax defensively.

"Just shut the eff' up, Doc, and go along with it! This is our ticket out!" Kenny snapped, before turning back to the helicopter and waving for help.

The grey chopper slowed to a hover in front of the building, and the pilot made eye contact. He used hand jive, and clearly mouthed the words, "Is anyone injured?"

Kenny and Jason mouthed "Yes" and were pointing animatedly toward Bryan, who was writhing on the ground in pain. Sam just stood there with a dumbfounded look on his face, ax in hand.

There seemed to be some confusion between the pilot and co-pilot. After a brief discussion the chopper rose 20ft and hovered over the building. Four ropes unfurled and eight heavily armed men fast-roped down onto the roof.

Fanning out with perfectly choreographed precision, half of the men secured the rooftop and stairway, the others rushed the group with machine guns drawn, barking commands to drop all weapons and lay on the ground.

The four men complied, lying face down on the roof, hands on their heads.

A square jawed soldier went around to each man, securing their hands and ankles with zip ties, while another soldier followed behind him sticking black, adhesive thermometer strips to each of their foreheads, similar to what you stick onto fish aquariums. The color on the strip changed like a mood ring, illuminating the number "98". He then checked his watch, and used a black marker to write the current time on each man's forehead. It was in military time: 1442.

"What the hell are you jack-boots doing?!" Kenny cursed, straining against the zip ties, "That man needs medical attention! And that other hippie is a *doctor*!"

The soldiers ignored his words, quietly convening around a tall, rangy man who appeared to be in charge. Sam was positioned closest to the soldiers and listened in.

"Sir, I thought there were no casualties on this building, just evacs."

"Affirmative, that's the report we were given," their leader said calmly.

"Well, we're stuck with them now. Air support won't pick them up until they pass quarantine ... unless we can commandeer a civilian craft to air lift them out."

"Negative on that. We don't want to draw any more of the Canadian's attention to this rooftop; a daylight insertion was crude enough. What is the casualty? Bite victim?"

"Negative, sir. The bald guy claims he was hobbled in the knee by the mouthy-one, with a *hammer*. He says it was a ploy to get a medevac; it seems they were passed over once by a life flight since they had no injuries at that time, so loud-mouth decided to produce some injuries, to ..."

"Got it, got it. That would explain the report we received," the man paused and shook his head, "The stupid bastards would be on a flight home had they remained uninjured till we got here. Hand me the radio.

"This is Lone Wolf to Wolf's Den, Lone Wolf to Wolf's Den, do you copy?"

Static crackled for a few brief moments, before a voice responded, "Lone Wolf, this is Wolf's Den, we copy loud and clear, over."

"Wolf's Den, this is Lone Wolf, LZ secured. We have oh-four civilians in custody, oh-one casualties. Injured does NOT appear hot. Blunt trauma to the knee, no bites. I say again, NO BITES. Quarantine began at ..." he glanced over to the writing on Bryan's forehead, "... 1442 hours. Request civilian extract at 0242 hours. Over."

165

"Roger that, Lone Wolf, civilian extract at 0242 hours. Proceed as planned, over."

"Copy that Wolf's Den. Over and out."

The man handed the radio back and walked over to the zip tied men. A medic was busy splinting Bryan's knee, and Kenny continued to curse and protest.

"Alright, listen up. My name's Colonel Toon, retired, but you can call me Colonel Toon." He pointed to Kenny, "Since *this* genius decided to hobble your friend, you are now stuck on this roof for the next 12 hours. My air support won't pick up any injured civilians unless you've gone through a 12 hour quarantine, so here we are. That thermo-strip on your forehead will warn us if you develop a fever. To the best of our knowledge, individuals exposed to the infection will develop a fever within 3-6 hours. If you're still clear by 2am, we'll radio for a flight out. Any questions?"

Bryan tried to get up, snarling at Kenny, "You stupid son of a …"

"Easy, tough guy, easy," the medic said, holding Bryan back.

Colonel Toon added, "Yes, you *will* remain quiet and cooperative. *All* of you."

"Sir!" said a soldier who was perched with a rifle on the ledge, "You may want to see this."

The Colonel gave one last look at the four restrained men, reinforcing his orders clearly before walking away, "*Quiet* and *cooperative*. Do that for the next 60 minutes, and I'll remove those ankle ties. Just play along, and you'll all be on your way home soon."

He walked over to a man who handed him a high powered rifle with a large scope. They appeared to be glassing the Ambassador Bridge, and were visibly affected by what they saw.

Without taking his eye off the scope, the Colonel called out, "Beeker! Front and center."

A young man loaded down with electronic gear stepped forward, "Sir?"

"Who's in contact with the Canadians?"

"That would be CENTCOM, sir."

"Get them on the horn. Tell them we concur: the bridge is overrun and their roadblock has been breached. Tell them we need verbal auth to drop ordinance."

"Yessir."

166

Beeker took a bulky, desert tan radio off his back, dialed in a few settings, and began chatting away in military jargon.

Sighing deeply, Colonel Toon returned the rifle and walked over to the quarantined men. He sized each man up before directing his questions to Sam.

"You: are you the MRI Tech?"

"Um … yeah. How'd you know?"

"Not important. What do you know about this building? Is anyone else inside?"

"Yeah, zombies … *lots* of them. The ground floor is crawling with them, so is the stairwell by the Arcade … and we heard something on the 5th floor, probably more zombies."

"*This* stairwell?" the Colonel asked, pointing to the open doorway.

"No, but there are probably some in there, too."

The Colonel chewed on his thoughts for a moment, and then began issuing orders, "Garner! Lacey! Recon that stairwell for hostiles, but *do not* engage unless you have to. I want claymores deployed on the top three landings. And *don't* get yourselves painted into a corner. Cline! Welty! Scatter that HELP sign and do a secondary sweep of the roof. Look for any other points of entry, and keep an eye out for defensible positions; we may need to fall back if they rush the roof. Beeker, what's the ETA on our drone?"

"It should be on station by 1530, sir."

"Good enough. Keep me apprised of any more delays. What about CENTCOM?"

"They're still talking to Ottawa, Sir. Negative on the heavy ordinance, but they are trying to negotiate aerial gunships."

"Christ," the colonel mumbled as he pulled out a pair of high-tech field glasses to survey the bridge again. "Mark my words, Beeker, they'll change their mind once they see the drone's video feed. There are too many on the bridge to neutralize with machine gun fire, and we'd end up destroying the bridge in the process." He paused, rubbing the tension out of the back of his neck. "When you get them back on the horn, you tell them we won't need to blow the *whole* damn bridge; just knocking out 20 feet of tarmac will stop the foot traffic. And get me targeting coordinates on that middle span."

"Already done, sir."

"Good work, Beeker. Not bad for a Chair-Force Sergeant,"

167

Col. Toon taunted his man, referring to the Air Force's reputation for cushy, sit-down jobs. He then resumed a dead serious tone and addressed his men as a whole, "*Stay sharp*, boys. Remember the ROE (Rules Of Engagement): if they are bitten, put them down. Two shots to the head, no exceptions. If you encounter any hostile civilians and cannot determine their infection status, take out their knee, no hesitations. Got it?"

"Hoo-ah!" the men barked in unison.

"Good. Hop to it."

The men fanned out, going to their assigned tasks. The Colonel went back to his rifleman and continued to observe the bridge while fielding various incoming radio calls.

After about 20 minutes, he rose to his feet and approached the quarantined men, carefully eyeballing their thermometer strips from a distance. All read "98" in large, green font.

"MRI Tech, how are your boys doing?"

Sam lifted his head off the hot rooftop, pieces of fine gravel stuck to his cheek. "Oh, no complaints … except for the whole 'hog-tied' thing."

The Colonel paused for a moment, carefully evaluating each of the prone men before speaking. Thankfully for the group, Kenny managed to hold his tongue.

"Well you boys have been as quiet as a mouse, and I thank you for that. Trust me; we have *no* interest in keeping you in our custody. You are *not* under arrest, but you *are* under medical quarantine. We'll be flying you out the moment they give us clearance, until which time you will be under the full protection of my men and resources. Understood?"

The group nodded, a little more jovial than before.

"Good. Based on your 'injuries,' I don't foresee any of y'all turning into zombies any time soon. I'll send someone over in a minute to cut those ankle restraints and give y'all some water. But let me make this clear: you will stay sitting on your *asses*, in a seated position. If anyone rises to their feet, they will be shot in the leg. I repeat: *you will be shot in the leg if you do not remain seated.* Is that clear?"

Kenny lost it, and began cussing up a storm.

Col. Toon gave him the look of doom, "Except for *you*, Frank Zappa. You will remain prone and hog tied until we can hand you over to local law enforcement." He strode over to Kenny who continued spewing a colorful stream of expletives. Producing a roll of black duct tape, he wrapped it several times around the belligerent man's mouth.

"Can you breathe?" Toon asked without emotion.

Kenny's struggling and mumbling seemed like a sufficient enough response. The Colonel looked back at his men, who were all diligently working away. "Well, my boys are busy, so I'll get y'all squared away." He flipped open a Gerber pocket knife and cut the zip ties from their ankles, helping each man up into a more comfortable seated position.

"Thanks, sir," Sam said. "So, you guys are *Air Force*?"

The Colonel paused, caught off guard by the question, and then grinned, "No, just Beeker. He's a Forward Air Controller, or FAC. Garner and Lacey are Rangers, the rest of the guys are Navy."

"What about you, sir? You look a little young to be retired ... or to be a Colonel for that matter."

The Colonel raised an eyebrow, "Are all MRI Techs so deductive?"

"Well," Sam blushed with false modesty, "I *did* go to Community College."

Colonel Toon's face slowly creased with a broad, amused grin. "Name's Col. Dan Toon, USMC retired. I'm now a civilian advisor to the United Stated government."

Sam's eyes lit up, "No way, you're a *spook*? Sweet!"

Toon laughed, "No, no. Not C.I.A., just a civilian advisor; a *contractor*. We're here to assess the situation on the ground and keep peace with the Canadians, we're not on any 'covert mission.' But *if* we were ... I wouldn't tell you, or else I'd have to kill you."

Sam, Jason, and Bryan looked at one another, shifting nervously in a moment of sweaty, uncomfortable silence.

"*Joking, joking.* Sheesh! Relax, boys."

Bryan spoke up, "Not funny, sir."

The Colonel looked him up and down, "How's that knee, son? Can you bear weight?"

"Don't know. I don't want to get shot in the leg for trying."

"Smart man," the Colonel said. "Once we get this rooftop secured, I'll send a man over to help you up so you can test it out." He turned to walk away, but paused and looked back at Sam. "MRI Tech:

let me know when your boys are hungry. I'll pass around that bag of buns you were carrying."

"Alright, will do."

He gave a curt nod as he strode away.

"Why'd he choose *you* to be teacher's pet?" Jason mumbled under his breath.

"Not sure."

Sam furrowed his brow and gave it some thought, finally saying "I bet that first helicopter radioed back our information, and it got passed along to *these* guys. That would explain how he knew I was an MRI Tech. And he probably figures that a square, upstanding professional trapped on a roof during a zombie apocalypse has no reason to mislead the men who seem prepared to rescue him."

Jason shifted on his rear, "These jar heads aren't here to *rescue us*. They're up to something, some kind of covert, black ops crap. I don't trust them," he glared sharply at Sam, continuing, "Maybe I should have chosen a more 'upstanding' profession, then *I* could play boss."

Sam shook his head, "Dude, I have no desire to 'play boss', I just want to go home."

"Well *tag*, you're it."

"Hurmph ... no thank you," Sam said, squinting up to the sun, trying to guess the time of day and wondering how Jessica and Simon were faring back home.

After a few moments, he sighed with resignation and looked back at the quarantined group. Bryan was trying to get comfortable against the wall.

"So Bryan, you said you've been sneaking into this building to shoot photos?"

"Yeah, I've been here a lot recently. It's a magnificent old building, there's a lot of history here. Presidents used to speak here on the campaign trail, from the back of those Presidential train cars, waving to crowds. Charlie Chaplin passed through here with much fanfare ... and heck, every soldier from Michigan who fought in World War II departed through this station."

"Seriously?" Sam stared off in the distance, momentarily caught in a daydream. "Y'know, after Pearl Harbor both my grandma and grandpa enlisted in the Marines. They must have passed through here, too."

170

"I'm sure they did," Bryan said, "This place was a major artery during the war, shipping out planes, tanks, and men."

"And *women*," Sam interjected, "Like I said, my *grandma* was a Marine."

"That's true, women, too," he conceded. "Detroit was fully mobilized back then; they stopped producing cars entirely and re-tooled their factories to help with the war effort. This city was a big deal, man." He let out a puff of air and continued, "Ya' know, had the Germans developed the Bomb *first*, Detroit would've been on their short-list of nuclear targets."

Colonel Toon heard the tail end of that comment and walked over. "You boys talking about Korea?"

"No, sir, Detroit," Bryan said, "But I did hear something about Korea on the radio. What happened? I've been out of the loop for the past couple of days. Did China really drop the Bomb on them?"

The Colonel dropped to one knee and removed his helmet, "Yeah, son, they did. North *and* South Korea. The entire peninsula was... overrun with these walking corpses, and has subsequently been reduced to a fine ash." He paused for a moment. "Millions are gone... including a lot of Americans."

The quarantined men were speechless.

"And I suppose I should get you up to speed on *our* situation. We've lost radio contact with Selfridge Air National Guard Base, which was where our Team deployed from, and where our chopper returned to. We do have a Forward Operating Base, or FOB, set up at the Detroit Metropolitan Airport, however, the only contact we can establish with Metro is a young Airman, a mechanic, who's trapped in a small chopper on the flight line. He doesn't know how to fly the damned thing, and he estimates at least a hundred corpses have the bird surrounded... most of which are dead military personnel. He believes the entire Airport may be overrun, but he could not confirm it."

"Son ... we're stuck up here?" Jason asked.

"For the moment, yes. There *are* more aircraft inbound to Metro, but we can't be sure they'll have a safe harbor when they get there. We're also monitoring civilian chatter on the radio, and are considering hailing a Coast Guard chopper that's been in the area."

All heads turned as the two men who were assigned with checking the stairway returned to the roof. They moved quickly, and the expression on their faces was not reassuring.

"You boys just sit tight," Colonel Toon said to the bound men in a fatherly voice, "We've got lots of ammo, and multiple contingencies to fall back on. We'll get you off this roof."

He rose and debriefed the men from the stairwell, Lacey and Garner. The report was full of more bad news: there were scores of zombies just a few floors beneath them, in the stairwell and the adjacent hallways. And, according to the two Rangers, they weren't just shambling around; they seemed riled up and on-the-move.

After convening with the rest of his men, the Colonel returned, taking one last look at the green "98" on everyone's foreheads. He then pulled out his knife and cut each man free of the zip ties (with the exception of Kenny, who finally got his ankles freed, but had to keep his wrists bound).

"Grab your gear and get to the far side of the roof, *quietly*. There are several geeks in the stairwell, and they are closing in on us. My men deployed booby traps, *claymores*, at the top three landings, and you won't want to be nearby when they start popping off. Chief Petty Officer Welty tells me there's a hole in the roof over there. We'll make our stand at that hole. If things get bad, we'll drop down into the building and fight our way out from there."

The four civilians were sober with fear, rising to their feet and nervously gathering their belongings.

"Uh, sir? What about my ax?" Sam asked hesitantly, "Is it OK if I grab that, too?"

"Yes," the Colonel nodded, "Axes and hammers. Let's just hope you won't need them before the night's through."

They all ran to the far side of the roof and turned to face the stairway. The military men fanned out into a defensive line, guns trained toward the open doorway. The sniper and his spotter took up position on the ledge, continuing to observe the bridge, while the Colonel and his FAC got back on the radio to update "Wolf's Den" of the situation.

Kneeling down and staring intently at the open stairwell, Sam became acutely aware of a rumbling in his bowels. There could be no worse time for a bathroom break.

Dang it ... I need to find a place to GO ... and soon!

172

He spoke up quietly, "Sir ... psst ... Colonel Toon, I need to go to the bathroom."

Toon, who was still conversing on the radio, simply said, "Hold it."

Grimacing, Sam replied, "Don't know if I can, sir ... I think I haven't pooped in two or three days, and it's feeling pretty urgent."

"Christ, son ... number *two*?"

"Yeah ..."

"*How* urgent?"

"Um ... I think I'm crowning. I gotta go *now* ..."

The Colonel dropped his head and grinned, "Couldn't pick a better time, could you." He glanced around the rooftop, finally saying, "Well, we can't afford the luxury of *modesty,* so just hover over that hole in the roof and fire at will. Do you have paper?"

Sam pulled out his copy of *Marine Sniper* and began ripping out the first few pages, causing the group to chuckle and shake their heads.

He looked down the dark hole they were positioned around, it was a 10' drop into a dingy corridor. "Hmm, guess it will have to do," he said as he dropped his trousers and did his business. As he tossed the last bits of paper down the hole, a bloody face peered up from below and began to moan violently.

"Aghhhhhhh!!!" Sam leaped away from the hole with his scrubs around his ankles, dancing around in a panic to get them back up and tie the draw-string.

The soldiers laughed hysterically, heckling the poor man and slapping their knees as Sergeant First Class Lacey leaned over the opening and put two bullets in the zombie's brain with a silenced pistol.

"*Not funny*, guys! That scared the crap out of me!"

"*Literally!*" Garner laughed.

Snickers continued as they all settled back into position, returning their attention to the stairway. As the laughing subsided, the tension returned. Slow hours ticked by, sitting in silence, waiting for a claymore to blow, but it never happened.

The sun was beginning to dip toward the horizon, and the temperature had dropped to the mid 50's, which was mildly unpleasant in scrubs. Cold and exhausted, Sam pulled his arms into his shirt sleeves, tucked his mouth and nose into his collar to trap the heat from his breath, and then curled up on the roof for a nap.

Surrendering to sleep, his mind drifted into a peaceful, sepia-toned dream:

It was late November, 1944, and a tall, young woman gazed dreamily out the window of a Greyhound bus. As the bus entered the city limits of Detroit, her mind was in faraway Pearl Harbor, and Paris, and the South Pacific. *Anywhere but Flint, Michigan,* she thought. There was nothing left to keep her here; her mother had passed away a few years earlier, she had never been very close to her father, and there were no young men left in the town. She'd go to the public dances and dance with her girlfriends, but all the boys were away to the War. She was tired of Flint and wanted to see the world, and the Marine Corps seemed like a great way out. The Corps had finally broke with tradition, and began enlisting women 21 years and older in 1943. Her cousin had joined with the initial group of girls, and had the most wonderful stories to share, but Joanne had to wait another year until her 21st birthday.

Reaching its destination, the bus pulled into the carriage entrance of the towering, vibrant Michigan Central Station. It was lightly dusted with a coat of fresh snow, but was bustling with activity. From here she would travel to Paris Island, NC, for Marine Corps Boot Camp.

The passengers, mostly men, disembarked the bus in an orderly manner, and waited patiently as the driver began unloading their baggage. Hers was the last piece of luggage on board: a small tan suitcase. She had been instructed by the Marine recruiter to pack light, clothes and toiletries only; everything else would be provided for them.

Leaving home for the war, saying goodbye to Michigan and goodbye to her father, enlisting in the Marines; it was a bold, liberating move for a young woman during the 1940's. Her father's embrace as she boarded the bus in Flint was the first time in her life that she recalled the man giving her a hug. It was time to venture out into the big world. She was a tall, beautiful, tough Irish girl, and she was going to War.

BOOM!!!

The building rattled as a large explosion ripped Sam from his sleep. A growing plume of dust belched from the stairway, and the men all shifted to battle positions.

"The first claymore," Toon said calmly. "They're three floors down ..."

BOOM!!! The second claymore was tripped.

"... correction: *two* floors down. Beeker, direct the drone to the rail yard, have them locate an E&E (escape & evade) route. We can't wait for a chopper."

"What do you mean?" asked Bryan, "We're *walking* out?"

"No choice. Don't you worry about your knee, Garner there is a pack mule, he'll carry you out."

Shaking off the fog of sleep, Sam collected his things and tried to regain his bearings. His bones ached from laying on the hard rooftop, he was cold, scared, and confused, but knew he had to be ready to run at a moment's notice. Pulling himself together, he took a good look around. The night sky was stained with smoke, and illuminated by the now-familiar orange glow of burning buildings. His companions were huddled behind the line of heavily armed sailors, soldiers, and airmen. Everyone was nervously preparing themselves for the inevitable assault of corpses.

After many long, tense minutes, audible moans began to emanate from the stairway.

"Here's the scoop," Toon whispered to the group, "when they emerge from the doorway, we will put them down with controlled fire, *head shots*. I don't want any of you to panic or do anything stupid. We will hold this line and continue firing until I determine otherwise. If-and-when I decide it's time to bug out, Welty and Lacey will drop down the hole to clear the way for our retreat. Stay close, and we will work our way down and to the rail yard. CENTCOM said there's a National Guard contingent about 2 klicks west of here past a small train bridge. *That* is our rendezvous point. Understood?"

BOOM!!!

The rooftop access seemed to explode as the final claymore was tripped, blowing rubble and dust into the air. The men's ears were ringing as they nervously strained to see through the thick screen of smoke.

A soldier next to him raised his rifle and fired two controlled rounds: CRACK ... CRACK ....

"Who's firing?" Toon Yelled, "What do you see?"

"Me, sir, Sergeant First Class Lacey. We got Zeds on the roof," a square jaw soldier said nonchalantly.

All the men trained their rifles toward the plume of dust as dark silhouettes began to emerge from the smoke.

"Single shots only; *no* bursts! Fire at will!" Toon barked, and the big, bad men began dealing death.

Crack! ... Crack! ... Crack! ... Crack! ...

Loud shots rang out, each 'crack' sending a corpse to the ground, only to be back-filled by two more.

Crack! ... Crack! ... Crack! ... Crack! ...

"They keep coming!" Garner yelled.

"Keep your head, Garner! Slow and controlled!" The Colonel yelled back over the firing.

Crack! ... Crack! ... Crack! ...

A seemingly endless procession of zombies continued to pour out onto the roof.

"There's too many of them! Let's get the hell out of here!" Kenny yelled, but the soldiers paid him no mind.

Crack! ... Crack! ... Crack! ...

The men were systematic: aim, fire, reload, repeat.

Crack! ... Crack! ... Crack! ...

Fallen bodies began to pile up at the doorway, causing a traffic jam of advancing zombies, each jockeying to the front of the pile only to receive a bullet to the brain, and become another corpse on the pile.

Crack! ... Crack! ...

Crack! ... Crack! ...

Crack! ...

Crack! ...

176

"Stay sharp!" Toon continued to encourage his men as the firing tapered down.

Crack! ...

Crack! ...

"Alright, hold your fire!"

The shooting stopped, and the men surveyed their work. They had inadvertently piled high a large, horrific, berm of rotting bodies, effectively blocking the doorway. A few unidentifiable parts in this pile of meat were still moving, but nothing that seemed to pose an immediate threat.

"Check your weapons and look sharp!"

On cue the men methodically locked-and-loaded their weapons before re-training their sights back on the berm. As the ringing in their ears began to fade, it was replaced by a chorus of moans coming from behind the pile of corpses. All eyes were nervously locked on the pile, anxiously anticipating the inevitable breakthrough.

"Beeker! What's the status on that drone?"

"On station, sir. The pilot reports that no helicopter support is available, and our only corridor of escape is behind the building, on the rail line. He also said the National Guard contingent that's west of us is struggling to put down a large mob of Zeds. He recommends linking up with them and fighting our way out on foot."

The pile shifted, and several lifeless corpses slid down the berm. Infected faces pushed through the top of the pile, moaning angrily...

CRACK! CRACK! CRACK!

Three craniums burst open by three well-aimed shots, briefly silencing the moans. Within seconds, more heads and hands began to push through the top of the pile.

CRACK!

CRACK!

"Our position here's untenable," Col Toon announced in a loud-and-clear tone. "Lacey! Welty! Drop down that hole and secure the room below! The rest of you: prepare to move out! We'll fight our way down the closest stairs, and make our way to the rail line. Remember: the National Guard checkpoint is two klicks west of here, *that* is our rendezvous point if any of you get separated."

"What the hell's a 'klick'?" Kenny asked.

"Kilometer. Now shut up and do as you're told."

K-RACK! The sniper's rifle boomed as another head exploded in the pile of corpses. He re-chambered a round in his bolt-action rifle and ...

K-RACK! Another head vaporized into a pink mist.

"Go! Go!"

Chief Petty Officer Welty and Sergeant First Class Lacey donned their Night Vision Goggles and dropped into the hole.

"Awwwww ... Christ!" Lacey cursed as soon as he hit the floor, "Who's bright idea was it to use our E&E route as a latrine?"

"Stay on task, soldier! Is the room clear?" Toon snapped back.

"Affirmative, sir. Room's clear, but I can hear Zeds down the hall."

The Colonel turned to his men on the roof, "Pair up with a civilian and provide escort. Garner, you have the injured man." He then turned to address the civilians, "You won't be able to see once we're in the building, and there is likely to be a lot of gun fire. I want you to hang on to the ruck-straps of the soldier you're paired with and follow his lead. You will maintain *strict* silence and *total* cooperation if you want to make it out of this building alive," he paused, taking a moment to make eye contact with each man individually. "Now *GO!*"

One by one, they climbed down the hole and into the dark room, carefully passing down the wounded photographer, Bryan. Colonel Toon was the last man to go, and he paused to take one final shot at movement in the pile ... CRACK! ... and then dropped down into the building.

Without the benefit of Night Vision Goggles, the four civilians were essentially blind and struggled to orient themselves in the dark, musty room. It had a hard tile floor, and unfortunately smelled of fresh feces. Minute amounts of ambient light penetrated the blackness from an adjacent window, not enough to appreciate the room's dimensions, but enough to make out the corpse on the floor.

The military men quickly secured the room before pairing with their civilian charges. After a few tense moments of getting organized, they all fell in line and were ready to move out. At Colonel Toon's signal, Welty and Lacey moved forward to scout ahead, clearing the next room and positioning themselves strategically to provide covering fire for the group's advance. Again at Toon's signal, they all followed in single file, pausing once more for the two point men to advance and clear the next room.

They continued to leap frog from room to room, finally coming to a stop in a long hallway that echoed with the moans of the undead. The soldiers dropped down into a tactical firing position, and began to communicate silently using a series of hand signals.

The soldier who was paired up with Sam, a Spaniard by the name of Sgt. Cline, whispered to him, *"The stairway's at the end of this hall, on the left, but there are at least a dozen zombies blocking the path. We're going to open fire, so hold on tight and be ready to move."*

Sam nodded nervously in the dark, tightening his grip on the man's backpack. Strain as he might, he could not see the zombies down the hallway, but he could sense them. The smell of rotting bodies was becoming strong, and their moans were absolutely terrifying. He had no choice but to hang on blindly and follow this man into ...

BLAM! CRACK! CRACK! CRACK!

The building erupted in rifle fire, illuminating the hall with brief bursts of orange light and thoroughly ruining what little night vision his eyes were beginning to gain. Sam struggled to look over Sgt. Cline's shoulder and down the hall, but he flinched with the bright flash of each gunshot.

As quickly as it started, the firing suddenly stopped. Sgt. Cline rose to his feet and began to move forward at a good clip, practically dragging Sam behind him.

Holding on tightly with one hand and clenching his ax in the other, he struggled to keep his balance in the dark. It was a helpless feeling; the building was pitch black, his ears were ringing, and flashes of light were burned into his eyes from the bursts of gun fire. His nose was overloaded with the smell of sweaty soldiers, spent gunpowder, and the stench of bloated corpses. All he could do was hold on tightly and entrust his fate to the man in front of him.

CRACK! CRACK!

Two more shots rang out from ahead, but the group's pace never slowed.

At the end of the hall they rounded another corner, and the shooting resumed. Sam crouched behind Sgt Cline with his eyes closed, trying hard to preserve his vision. He listened intently through the gunfire and could hear bullets chipping away at the marble walls and bodies collapsing to the floor.

The shooting petered out, and there was a quiet discussion at the front of the line, something about 'the stairway', and then they were up and moving again.

They hadn't walked more than three paces when there was an outburst of cursing at the front of the line. The soldiers stopped abruptly and began yelling, "Hold your fire! Hold your fire!"

It sounded like there was a physical struggle going on, a wrestling match, and a soldier began yelling, "Pull him off! The bastard's trying to bite me!" Then came a yelp of pain, a loud thump, and some more commotion.

CRACK! CRACK!

Two gunshots rang out, and then Colonel Toon's voice rose above the others, "Protect your eyes! I'm going to kick on the lights!"

Sam closed his eyes tightly and the soldiers all flipped up their Night Vision Goggles as the Colonel turned on a bright LED light that was attached to the barrel of his gun. Garner, the man who had been carrying Bryan, was down on the ground, bleeding from his leg. A now-headless zombie lay next to him, and Bryan was crumpled up against the wall, grasping at his injured knee.

"What the hell just happened!?" Bryan cursed.

"The man who was carrying you just got bit," Lacey said as he inspected Garner's wound. "It's deep," he added, turning to the Colonel.

Col. Toon closed his eyes briefly and took in a full, deep breath, letting it out slowly. "Garner," he said in his fatherly tone, "How do you want it?"

The soldier looked up at him without fear said, "I know the drill, sir. Two in the head, no exceptions. That being said, I'd like to propose a more sensible exit. Leave me here to cover your back-trail. Once I hear y'all making your way down the stairs, I'll fall on my own sword."

Kenny stepped forward and blurted out, "*Wait* a cotton pickin' minute... you guys had flashlights this whole time? Then why the hell are you parading us around in the flippin' dark? We need to get *out* of this damned building and ..."

"Pipe down, scumbag," Toon interrupted, "If I can see them

180

but they can't see me, *I win*. The light would surely draw their attention; we don't want that."

Suddenly a pack of zombies stepped into the bright hallway, shielding their eyes and turning inquisitively toward the well-lit group. The soldiers instantly dropped into firing positions, opening up with deadly accurate fire. The entire pack seemed to drop as one, devastated by fatal head wounds.

Moans erupted from several doorways, and another wave of infected corpses were drawn into the hall. The soldiers put them down mercilessly, sending the entire second wave of bodies to the ground within seconds. Behind them, another group of zombies ambled into the hall, only to be mowed down again with ruthless precision, and then another. A seemingly endless procession of zombies followed behind them, each wave replacing the ranks of their fallen, effectively cutting off the group's escape with the growing piles of headless corpses.

"Goggles!" Toon ordered, and turned off his flashlight, sending the room back into darkness that was punctuated only by chaotic bursts of muzzle flash.

The men were all barking at one another to tighten up and regroup, and in the ensuing commotion Sam lost his grip on Cline's backpack.

Groping around blindly in the dark, he backed himself into a doorway. He desperately needed to link back up with the group, but did not want to approach the muzzle flashes for fear of being shot, so he stood his ground in the strobing darkness, clutching the ax handle and brandishing it high in the air.

Broken chips from the marble wall were peppering him in the face as the soldiers laid down an increasingly dangerous level of gun fire. It sounded as though more and more zombies were filling the hallway from every direction.

"Keep moving! Fight your way to the stairs!" the Colonel bellowed over all the noise.

A rotting hand grabbed Sam from behind, and he turned, swinging blindly. The ax head bit into a meaty shoulder, knocking the creature over. Raising the ax high, he brought it down hard into what felt like an abdomen. He pulled it loose and took a wide stance, vainly trying to see in all the chaos. Zombies continued to find their way into the hallway, drawn to the muzzle flashes like moths to a flame.

181

"AGHH! I'm bit!" a soldier yelled. It was Beeker.

Another soldier began to scream in panic, "Get him off me! Get him off me!"

Sam felt around helplessly in the dark, unable to find his bearings, and unable to link up with Cline or any other soldier; he was cut off from the group.

A clumsy hand began tugging at his ankle and he instinctively brought the ax down hard, crunching through a boney forearm. Another set of hands gripped his shirt, pulling him off balance and bellowing a rancid smelling moan right in his face! Sam roared out of fear, blindly cross-checking its teeth with the ax handle as he turned to run. He didn't make it more than two steps before he tripped over a fallen body and face planted brutally into the marble wall.

His mind was dazed and blood gushed from his nose and mouth as he slid awkwardly to the ground.

The remaining soldiers continued to fight effectively, but they were hopelessly outnumbered and being attacked from all sides. Sam could vaguely hear them barking commands and firing hundreds of rounds like a buzz saw, but it all blurred together like a hazy dream.

As he regained enough strength to lift his head, he could see several dark silhouettes circling around him. He gripped the fiberglass handle tightly and rose to his unsteady feet, wildly swinging the ax in huge, arcing motions; the classic, ineffectual 'windmill' technique.

A glancing blow knocked one of the silhouettes down, but the next swing became tangled in the arms of another. A brief tug-of-war ensued, and as Sam pulled the ax free he lost his footing and fell backwards down the stairway, tumbling end over end, knocking over zombies like bowling pins.

The fall hurt like hell, but he managed to hang on to the ax. Screaming in pain and swinging like a berserker, he fought his way back to his feet and blindly tripped down the next flight of stairs.

Colliding with bodies in the dark, he continued to bounce and slam-dance his way down several flights. Banged up and broken, feeling as good as dead, he had nothing more to lose and decided to chop, push, and fall down the stairs as far as his luck would carry him, caution be damned. Eventually he would be grabbed and bitten like every other soul around him, so why bother cowering in the dark?

Against all odds, he bumbled his way down into a dimly lit landing with an open window. He plowed his way forward and looked out, where the smoky orange night sky was like Hades on earth. Below him was a 10 ft. drop to the rooftop of the Carriage Entrance, so he recklessly dove out the window, smashing face first into the black, tar paper roof, knocked out cold. TKO.

With a sore back and a busted face, Sam's dry eyes opened in a painful squint. He was alive, and looking at the rising sun.

"Uuuugh ..." was all his mouth would allow him to say.

He pushed himself up from the gritty rooftop and looked around in a daze. The city still burned, but the old train station seemed silent. Slowly, the previous night's events returned to him.

Those soldiers, I wonder if any of them made it out alive? He forced a smile. *It was only dumb-luck that I bounced my way down the stairs and out that window.*

Groaning like an old man, he stood up and gave himself the once over. His right shin and shoulder were banged up pretty good from falling down the stairs, and he may have broke his nose *twice*, once while face planting the wall, and again when he dove through the window and onto the roof. His mouth was swollen, and his beard was caked with dried blood. His cell phone and bag of food were gone, but he still had his book, tucked securely in his waistline. More importantly, the yellow handled ax lay at his feet.

Memories of the previous night came crashing into his mind and he suddenly felt very exposed. A disoriented rush of fear passed over him, and he snatched up the ax, holding it high as he looked around in a confused panic. Fatefully, he had crash-landed on an odd spot of roof that was tucked away from view, no more than 20 ft above the ground. He could hear moans coming from the Carriage Entrance, but they seemed unaware of his presence.

Still feeling confused and vulnerable, he reared back with the ax and looked up at the window from which he dove. The open, gaping frame was quiet and empty, like all the other windows in this towering building. He breathed a sigh of relief.

Good ... no zombies.

He recounted his reckless flight down the stairs, and his desperate jump from the window above. It wasn't much of a fall, but his form was bad and he landed all wrong. Reaching up, he felt his face to survey the damage more thoroughly. His nose was busted *good*, and had apparently been bleeding all night as he lay there, because his beard and scrub top were thoroughly crusted with dry blood. His eyes felt puffy and swollen, probably black, and he had a painfully fat lip. Lastly, he peeled the black thermometer strip off his forehead and watched it as the green 98 faded away.

No broken limbs, no permanent damage... and I'm alive... but what about the others? Did they make it out alive? I know Garner was bitten... and Beeker. He shook his head, snapping himself out of the morbid thoughts that ensued. *I just have to carry on. Colonel Toon said to meet up on the train tracks, two kilometers west of here. So that's what I'll do.*

He eased into a *big* morning stretch, trying to wake up and clear his mind without the benefit of coffee. His back ached and his body felt broken, but he had to loosen up and figure out a way down off this roof.

Creeping up to the edge, he was relieved to see that it would be an easy climb down; the ornate brick and iron architecture offered plenty of good hand holds. Visually scanning the immediate area, he started to plan his escape route. There were several zombies loitering nearby, but they were oblivious to his presence. The rail yard was inaccessible from here, so once on the ground he would have to hop the tall chain link fence, cross the street, and sprint about 70 yards south to reach the train tracks. The tracks were high on an overpass, but there was a set of concrete steps that let up to them. That route would have him contending with at least three zombies before he reached the tracks.

He sized them up carefully: two of the zombies looked like they were brother and sister. Both had been horribly mutilated and were probably not very mobile, so he felt confident he could out run them. The third was a very obese senior citizen, and therefor probably not much of a runner, either.

He did a few more stretches to limber up his aching body and took a few deep breaths to wake his lungs and steel his nerves, trying hard to think *everything* through.

I only get one chance, so I can't mess this up. I need to

185

carefully plan each step; chess tactics. What was that acronym Clarence taught me? S-A-L-U-T-E? Size ... Activity ... Location ... U ... U? What was "U"?

Unexpectedly, he heard a meaty 'smack' sound from behind.

Turning to investigate, there was an African American man lying face down on the roof, clumsily trying to push himself up on all fours. Before the guy could right himself, another person fell directly on top of him.

Sam looked up to see several zombies recklessly crawling out of the window above him. They had spotted him, and were salivating like a pack of wolves.

Smack-smack! Two more zombies dropped down onto the others. A queue of zombies began to follow one after another, like lemmings, landing hard on the rooftop only a few feet away.

He quickly tossed his ax off the side and began climbing down the ornate wall as fast as he could. Rock climbing had taught him that climbing *down* any route is much more difficult than climbing up. It's hard to plan your hand and foot holds since your eyes are topside but your goal is beneath you. The first few feet were challenging, but he eventually reached a sturdy brick pillar and slid down the remaining few feet. His heart was racing, but no one on the ground seemed to notice his descent, so he scooped up the ax and ran to the fence.

Approaching the fence gave him a more comprehensive view of the area, and of the hundred or more zombies still loitering in the promenade in front of the station, a few of which noticed him immediately and began to circle around to the Carriage Entrance.

Sam tossed his ax over and scampered up the rattling chain link fence. The jangling drew more unwanted attention, but he had no choice but to climb even faster and louder. Clearing the top, he did a controlled fall to the ground, grabbed the ax, and took off running.

The three zombies that stood between him and the tracks began to hobble toward him, but he weaved around them without a second thought and sprinted toward the concrete steps. Curiously, the train bridge had a large graffiti portrait of Andre the Giant, with the word "Obey."

At the top of the steps, there was another small fence that he hurdled effortlessly before stepping onto the tracks. These tracks led west, slowly curving out of sight to the south. Holding the ax close to his chest, Sam broke into a slow, low-impact jog. He wanted to pace his run as efficiently as possible; there was a lot of ground to cover and he wanted to make good time, but he also didn't want to run out of steam. He needed to keep a little energy left in reserve, just in case.

He cautiously slowed to a stop where the train tracks crossed over another interstate highway. Like the others, it was nothing more than a dead parking lot, full of stranded cars and meandering corpses. Sam kept low to avoid being seen, and made his way across the bridge.

At the other side, there were two bodies lying motionless on the tracks.

Sam stopped and crouched low to the ground, watching the bodies for several minutes before deciding to proceed. He crept up to them slowly and took a good look.

It was two young males, both teenagers. They appeared dead, as in *really* dead, not zombie-dead. Both had been shot multiple times, but there were no head shots. Their back packs had been ransacked, with the contents scattered around haphazardly. Sam poked each kid with the ax and then stood back to wait for a response, but there was none. The bodies laid there, still as a ghost.

Apprehensively, Sam thought:

I need to play it safe, be redundant so I can survive an occasional oversight in my judgment. I gotta make sure these kids are REALLY dead. He hesitated briefly, and then though: *Just do it, don't think about it.*

Strolling up to the bodies, bold as brass, he lifted his ax and brought it down hard on the first kids head, crushing it like a melon. Pulling the blade free, he turned and crushed the other kids head, too, trying hard not to humanize them.

It's just parts, nothing more. And THESE parts may be infected. Just carry on and get through this day; there will be time later to go insane.

He rummaged through their backpacks, but the boys had already been picked clean. The only item he found any use for was a dirty white t-shirt. He tied it to the end of his ax to use as a white flag, hopefully preventing him from being mistaken as a zombie and shot when approaching the National Guard outpost.

Moving along, he passed several residential blocks, occasionally making eye contact with zombies who were corralled within fenced yards, but none of them could pose a threat so he didn't even bother to hide or be evasive.

Rounding the slow bend of the tracks, a large sign came into view, propped up on the tracks with a pile of cinder blocks. It had the word "STOP" stenciled in huge red letters on a 4x8 sheet of plywood, with more words in smaller font stenciled beneath it.

Cautiously slowing to a stop, he read the fine print:

ALL RAIL LINES CLOSED BY ORDER OF NATIONAL GUARD - FIELD HOSPITAL AHEAD – APPROACH SLOWLY AND IDENTIFY YOURSELF – REPORT ALL INJURIES UPON ARRIVAL

Stapled to the bottom of the board were two sheets of paper. The first was printed on National Guard letterhead and defined "Martial Law." It cited several legal references and sounded pretty broad. It also defined the terms "civil unrest," "riot," and "curfew." The second page was on CDC letterhead, and it gave recommendations to avoid communicable diseases and other such things that had nothing to do with this outbreak.

Elated to have found the National Guard post, he took a good look around, but there was absolutely no one in sight. The tracks continued to turn gently to the left and out of view, vanishing from sight half a mile ahead.

It must be further ahead, around that bend...

Not wanting to get shot, he decided to heed the sign's warning and approach *slowly*, so he resumed his advance at a walking pace with his white flag held high, continuing west down the tracks.

His heart rate slowed along with his pace, calming his nerves and giving him time to stop and smell the roses. A haze of black smoke hung in the morning air, providing a fragrant bouquet of burnt rubber and charred wood, with a suspicious hint of chemicals and heavy metals.

I love the smell of Detroit in the morning; it smells like ... house fires.

It was eerie to walk in this bubble of "calm" considering the terrifying night he had managed to survive. To the north, gunshots continued to echo throughout the city as they had all night, but this stretch of town seemed to be a little quieter.

He finally rounded the bend and was elated to see several tents and military trucks spread out across the tracks! Jumping with joy, he waved the white flag high in the air, grinning from ear to ear.

Curiously, no one stepped forward to greet him, nor were there sentries standing guard. Looking more closely, he saw a corpse on the tracks between himself and the large, green tents. It was a soldier, lying face down in full combat gear. Sam decided to circle wide around it, but gawked at it curiously as he passed. It was a big man, a redhead, who somehow looked quite familiar.

Sam's foot scuffed the gravel as he walked past, and the corpse opened its eyes, awkwardly pushing itself up onto its knees... it was Sgt. Garner, and he was most assuredly a zombie.

Sam took off running toward the tents, waving the white flag wildly and yelling, "There's a zombie on the tracks! Help! There's a zombie on the tracks!!!"

He ran into the camp uncontested, and was overcome by the stench of death. There were bodies lying in piles, covered in flies and stacked like cords of wood.

"HELP! Is anybody here?" he yelled.

In response, moans called out from around the camp, and several corpses began to animate. Looking back, he saw that Garner was now entering the perimeter and charging straight for him, chugging along like an undead juggernaut.

Sam ran for the nearest truck, it was a tan Humvee. He jumped in and slammed the door closed, desperately looking around the interior, trying to figure out how to start the engine. Somewhere he'd heard that military trucks don't need a key to operate, and now was his chance to confirm that story.

His eyes raced across the dash. There was a placard that read:

WARNING: PRIOR TO STARTING, ENGAGE PARKING BRAKE AND SHIFT TRASMISSION TO NEUTRAL.

189

The brake was already set, and the transmission was already in "N", so that was easy enough. To the left of the steering wheel was a clunky, rotating switch with three settings: 1) ENG STOP, 2) RUN, and 3) START. He flipped the switch to START ... *but nothing happened.*

Looking out the windshield, he could see Garner barreling toward him, and he began to panic. Frantically, he fumbled around with the switches on the dashboard, finally finding one that simply said "ON". When he flipped it, an orange light that said "WAIT" turned on over the starter switch.

WAIT? Wait for WHAT?

Garner finally caught up to him and began banging on the door as several other zombies joined in, surrounding the vehicle on three sides.

Sam looked down at the dash board just as the orange "WAIT" light blinked off. A little confused, he tried the starter again and the truck cranked over, purring with the rattling sound of an old diesel motor.

"Woo-hoo!" he yelled triumphantly, as he released the hand brake and threw the transmission into "D".

The truck lurched forward, effortlessly rolling over Garner and the other unfortunate zombies who were in his path.

With a beaming smile, Sam turned the big truck west, swerving around several more zombies in military garb and bouncing over a few others as he continued on down the tracks. The feeling of being alive, in a bad-ax vehicle, and on-the-move was exhilarating. The fuel gauge only read ¼ full, but that was fine. He would ride this thing until the tank ran dry.

Bouncing along down the train tracks in his newly acquired Humvee, the exhausted MRI Tech found a brief moment of peace and security. The big truck was a blast to drive, and he had always wanted to get behind the wheel of one. There was surprisingly little room for passengers, and very few creature comforts. The two small front bucket seats were separated by a high center console that seemed to be 3 or 4 feet wide. The interior was stamped sheet metal, painted desert tan, with brown vinyl seats that had been patched up with duct tape. The dash was all business, no frills, with several utilitarian looking levers and knobs, and the heater looked like a metal dryer-vent that was probably just pulling in heat from the engine compartment. No radio, no A.C., and the steering wheel looked like it came off an old tractor; it was a very spartan rig, indeed.

With his life not being in immediate danger, and being in a truck without FM radio, he had the luxury of quiet time, time to reflect on the whole situation.

What in the world is going on? Nuclear war in Korea ... a plague in Detroit... the dead are coming back to life ... The whole world has gone crazy. God, I only hope Jessica and Simon are OK. The radio mentioned an outbreak in Ann Arbor, which is only a stone's throw from home. At least my first-born made it to the Air Force base with her ma and stepdad. Hope they're doing OK, too.
Whoa ... what's this?

Ahead he saw a large convergence of tracks, with a train stopped at the junction. The train's engineer had already spotted the approaching Humvee, and had his arm out the window, waving a red handkerchief. Sam pulled up alongside the train engine and rolled down his window.

"Christ, son! What happened to you?" The engineer asked, "You don't look military. You some kind of doctor?"

"No, sir, I'm an MRI Technologist."

"A *what*?" he asked, twisting his face.

"Oh ... nothing," Sam said, shaking his head, "it's not

important. Are you doing alright?"

"Better than you, I imagine. You aren't one of those *cannibals*, are ya?"

Sam knew what he was implying. "No, sir," he said, wiping the dried blood from his mustache and beard, "just a little banged up. I'm trying to make my way back to Milan, avoiding the roads if I can. Do you know if I'm on the right track?"

"Milan, huh? I'm not so sure you want to go *there*, I hear that everything between Ann Arbor and Toledo's been overrun by these *cannibals*."

Sam's eyes turned hollow and his heart sank. He looked down at the steering wheel, gripping it tightly.

Seeing his reaction, the engineer asked, "You have family there?"

Sam could only nod in response.

"Well," the man took off his hat a scratched his head. "... you'll want to take this line going south. Once you see the fork near I-75, you'll cross over to the line heading west. About, oh .... 10 or 15 miles beyond that you'll pass the Airport. Just keep on following that line, it bends southwest as you pass through Belleville, and then goes on through Milan."

"Thanks, friend. Where are *you* headed?" he asked somberly.

"*Nowhere*, for now. The National Guard came by and shut us down. We can't move until told otherwise. I was hoping *you* were coming along to tell me I could get under way."

"No, sir, not me. But I have to tell you, I passed a National Guard roadblock on the tracks a few miles back ... and they were all dead. All of them. You may want to disregard those orders and find someplace safe. Back in Detroit, it was every man for himself."

The engineer put his hat back on and took a big pull from a ceramic coffee mug.

Sam's eyes lit up, "Hey, man, is that coffee?"

"Yeah. Want a cup?"

"Does a bear crap in the woods!?" Sam responded with enthusiasm.

The conductor chuckled, saying, "Hold on, I'll pour you a cup," and then he ducked away into the engine compartment.

Sam stepped out of the truck, ax in hand, and climbed up the side of the train. Waiting patiently at the window, he used this high vantage point to take a good look around. Smoke loomed on the horizon, but no zombies were within sight.

"Hope you don't mind black," the conductor said, offering him a steaming Styrofoam cup.

"No, sir! And *thank* you!"

He carefully blew on the cup before taking a slow, purposeful sip, allowing the coffee to linger on his palate for a moment before swallowing.

"Ahhhhhhhhhh ..." His body tingled from head to toe, and his olfactory region went to work, analyzing and deconstructing the humble brew:

A very thin, medium-light roast, delicate and mellow ... He took another small, ritualistic sip, closing his eyes and clearing his mind. *Hydrolyzed and earthy ... slightly acidic ... instant to be sure.*

"Dang, son, you really seem to be enjoying that coffee. You want me to give you a moment alone?"

Sam opened his eyes, smiling, "No, that won't be necessary. However, that may be the second best cup of instant I ever had."

"*Second* best, huh?"

"Yeah, second best. When I was in school I did some work at an archeological site in a remote part of Peru, the Atacama Desert. Surprisingly, for being one of the largest coffee producing countries in the world, you couldn't find a cup of fresh brewed coffee to save your life; all they had was instant Nescafe. But I'm here to tell ya, after a few days of working in the desert, that morning cup of Nescafe tasted like mother's milk."

The engineer looked down at his mug, swirling the brew with a skeptical look, mumbling, "You don't say?"

Realizing that this was the wrong audience for a lecture on the finer points of instant coffee, Sam decided to keep the conversation more relevant. "So, have you heard any recent news reports? Do you know what's going on?"

"Riots, cannibals, Koreans eating Germans, Chinese nuking Koreans ... not sure what to believe."

"So ... you haven't *seen* any of them yet?" Sam asked.

"Who? Koreans?"

"No, *zombies*."

"What? You mean like the ones they found in Roswell?"

"No man, those were aliens. These are *zombies*. You know: flesh eaters, Night of the Living Dead, Resident Evil ..."

"Pshhh," he waved his hand in disbelief. "I heard some crazy stories on the radio, but ya can't believe everything ya hear. Engineers've been reporting people walking out onto the tracks, deranged and suicidal like, not even flinching as the train runs them down. While I'm sure there's some truth to their stories, I like to see things with my own eyes before I start deciding what's a zombie, and what's a cannibal, and what's a Korean."

Sam lifted his ax, showing the blood covered blade. "Trust me friend, I've seen them with my own eyes, these are *zombies*. The sooner you wrap your head around that fact, the better your chances for survival."

The engineer leaned away apprehensively, politely saying, "Well, I've appreciated the company, young man, but maybe it's about time you headed on your way."

Smiling, Sam hopped down off the train, saying, "Trust me, sir, these people are dangerous. And I assure you, they are dead, but infected with something that makes their body get up and move around, acting out violently. If you see any of them, stay out of sight."

He climbed back into the idling Humvee and shifted into drive, but before he drove off, he felt obliged to give this man one last piece of advice. "Hey, sir! One more thing: when it comes time for you to defend yourself against one of these zombies, aim for the head. You have to destroy their *brain* to kill them."

The poor engineer looked at Sam like he was crazy, with his wild hair, blood soaked beard, black eyes, and tattered scrubs.

"And thanks again for the coffee!" He raised the Styrofoam cup, saying "Cheers!" before continuing on down the tracks.

The engineer's directions were easy to follow, and Sam managed to put several uneventful miles behind him. Interstate 75 was a graveyard, as were the suburban neighborhoods he passed along the tracks. The devastation of south-east Michigan was apocalyptic. It was unbelievable to see how far this plague had spread in a matter of days.

> *I guess if one zombie infects three people, and they each infect three people, and they infect three people, this thing could spread exponentially. And all those helicopters that were evacuating the injured, they were just helping the sickness spread farther and faster.*

The railroad tracks meandered along to the west, eventually paralleling I-94 by a few hundred yards to the south. Sam was feeling the need for a bathroom break, so he brought the truck to a stop and stepped out to do his business. After shaking it off, he climbed up onto the roof of the truck and took a good look around. I-94 was completely snarled with abandoned vehicles, with corpses wandering aimlessly between the cars. Farther ahead he could see the hangers and terminals of the Detroit Metropolitan Airport. He remembered Col. Toon saying that a young Airman was trapped in a helicopter on the flight line there, surrounded by hundreds of zombies...

> *That was only yesterday. I wonder if that guy is still alive ... trapped in the helicopter ...* The thought gave Sam the shivers. *Maybe I'll be able to see when I get a little closer.*

He hopped back into the truck and got situated, then grimaced when he noticed that the fuel gauge was pointing to "E." Having no choice but to carry on, he followed the tracks as they passed between the airport and the interstate. There were several military aircraft on the runway, surrounded by hundreds, if not *thousands* of zombies. If there were someone alive in one of those helicopters, there would be no saving them.

Several zombies from both the airport and the highway took

notice of the moving Humvee, and were instinctively drawn toward it. Even though Sam knew that they would never catch up to the truck, it was terrifying to know that he had been spotted, and he stepped on the accelerator, pushing the big truck faster down the tracks.

Fear and reality were returning to him as pondered his fuel situation. He was now passing landmarks that he recognized, and was probably within a half hour drive of home, but this truck's poor fuel economy all but insured he wouldn't make it home without refueling.

As he neared Belleville Lake, the tracks veered south-west, leaving the suburban sprawl behind and entering more wooded farmlands.

Ultimately, the inevitable happened and the truck began to sputter and misfire. It limped along for another mile, and then finally crapped out. Starved of diesel, the big truck rolled to a stop.

He sat silently in the truck for several moments, hands on ten and two, trying to dig deep and rouse enough courage to get out and start walking. He did not want to leave the safety of this truck, but thoughts of his 3 year old son entered his mind. Simon and Jessica were at *home*, and the world was falling to pot around them. There could be zombies at their door *right now*.

His blood began to boil and he jumped out of the Humvee, ax in hand as he started jogging down the tracks.

After a few miles of jogging, Sam was feeling gassed-out, and slowed to a walking pace so he could catch his breath. It was a hot, sunny morning, and he was parched. He had seen a few homes along the way, and was tempted to stop at the next one he saw with hopes of finding some water. That cup of instant coffee managed to kick the caffeine headache that had been plaguing him for days, but he still felt dehydrated, malnourished, and beat up.

The tracks eventually crossed over a two-lane country road. From this crossing he could see a modest ranch home with a well maintained lawn only a few hundred feet away. Desperate for water, he crouched down along the roadside and tip toed toward the home for a closer look.

There were two cars in the driveway, and the porch light was on. Quietly, he stepped into the tree line so he could approach the home unseen. Once he reached the edge of the yard, he darted across the lawn and flattened himself against the wall, catching his breath and trying to still his heart which was pounding in his chest. He crept up to the closest window and peeked inside.

A man and a woman were standing in the living room, swaying ominously. On the TV was graphic news footage, zombies attacking a police barricade in front of the Capital Building in Washington DC.

Sam ducked back down to collect his thoughts. These people were obviously dead, so he needed to keep moving before he drew their attention.

Sneaking around to the back corner, he spotted a garden hose coiled up neatly in a flower bed along the back wall. Anxiously, he crouched low and snuck over to the spigot, twisting the rusty handle. Sparkling water trickled out of the green rubber hose.

He took a big slurp from the hose but recoiled in shock, spitting out the water and gasping! The water from the hose was piping hot from sitting in the sun. Being a quick learner, he let it run for several seconds, cautiously testing the temperature with his hand until it reached a suitable temperature.

After drinking deeply, he peeled off his shirt and hosed himself down, washing the blood from his face and soaking his long hair. It felt so great he wanted to hoot with joy, but wasn't *that* stupid.

As he wrung out his scrub top and pulled it back over his head, he continued to pan the yard for trouble. It was a nice yard with a large patio and volleyball net. Behind the net was an old metal shed with several bicycles visible.

"*Perfect,*" he whispered under his breath.

Moments later, he was heading southwest along the tracks, pedaling a newly commandeered mountain bike, holding the ax across the handle bars like a kid would a baseball bat. Never one to steal another man's bike, he felt that this was a different. The owner was dead. Dead... but walking.

This world doesn't make sense anymore, he thought to himself.

Another road-crossing lay ahead, and a yellow Jeep was stopped in the middle of the lane. Again Sam pulled off of the tracks, and cautiously circled the abandoned jeep with his mountain bike, surveying the scene.

The driver side door was open, and no one was inside. On the back of the truck was a pink sticker that said "Runner Girl." There were long, black, skid marks that trailed 20ft behind the truck. Its hood was dented and covered with blood. The engine was off but the headlights were on, though very dim, as if the battery was nearly dead.

Piecing these clues together, he concluded that the truck had slammed on its brakes while trying to avoid hitting something, presumably a zombie. The driver got out to investigate, and was attacked. A chill ran down his spine when he realized that the driver and pedestrian's infected corpses could still be nearby.

Hopefully "Runner Girl" was a fast runner.

He scanned the tree line for movement, but saw nothing, so he took a quick moment to search the Jeep. There was nothing much of use, but there was a fast food cup in the cup holder with a few sips left in the bottom. Picking it up, he swirled it then took a sip from the plastic straw. The warm liquid was nothing more than melted ice, with trace amounts of root beer, but in would help keep him hydrated for a few more miles. The keys were in the ignition, so he gave them a turn.

The truck made a clicking sound but would not start; there just wasn't enough juice in battery. Disappointed, he carried on.

Miles rolled by, quiet and uneventful: trees, farm fields, a few houses, and more trees. Eventually he came across a two lane road that he recognized, so he turned onto it. Leaving the railroad tracks behind, he shifted the bike into high gear, allowing him to make much better time on the paved, two-lane road.

Eventually he turned west onto Main St, and was now within a few miles from home. Elated, he pedaled along with renewed vigor, singing songs in his head, anxious to see his family.

There was one more overpass to cross, US-23, after which he would be in the town of Milan. He slowed down as he approached it, and peered down the on-ramp. There was an abandoned police barricade, and he could see that the highway was snarled with parked cars. Zombies were visible, milling about along the roadside. This exit was only a few hundred yards from his home, and it did not bode well.

Cautiously cresting the overpass, an odd sight came into view: there was a long freight train stopped on the tracks which crossed Main St., completely blocking the road. Someone had turned it into a makeshift wall, securing sheets of plywood down its entire length, effectively blocking the spaces in-between the railroad cars and beneath them. Painted on the wall were the words "Don't tread on me! Locals ONLY!"

It was then that Sam noticed an American flag posted on top, and a man with a scoped rifle pointed directly at him.

Being a local, and this being *his* street, Sam waved to the man and flashed a non-threatening smile as he approached the train.

"Hold it right there, Hippie," the man called out, "We're not taking any refugees here, so just turn back around."

"I'm from Milan, sir. My name's Sam Elkins, I live right here on Main St."

The man in hunter's camouflage looked at him dubiously. "Oh you do, huh? Let's see some I.D. ..."

"Man, I've spent the last few days trying to walk home from Detroit. I've lost my wallet, my phone, my car, my keys ... everything. But I swear to you, I live just a few houses down this street. Can you see the funeral home from up there? Well I live right across from it, in that little green house."

199

The hunter looked over his shoulder. "You mean the house with the pregnant girl and the boy?"

"Yeah! That's my wife Jessica and my boy Simon!" Sam's emotions were bubbling over from speaking their names aloud.

The man thought for a moment, and then asked, "Have you been bitten or scratched by anyone?"

"No, sir. I've got a broken nose, black eyes, busted lip, swollen hand, banged up knees and shins, sore foot ..." he paused to give himself a pat down, saying as if he just now realized it, "... but somehow, someway, I managed to chop and kick my way through the whole darn city without a single bite or a scratch."

The man thought for a moment, looking Sam up and down, and then asked, "Are you some kind of doctor?"

An amused smile softened Sam's face as a wave of exhaustion washed over his body. His head began to spin and spin as if he were about to pass out. Awkwardly he struggled to dismount the bicycle but was unsuccessful, and he toppled over. Chuckling deliriously as he lay on the ground, he mumbled, "No, man ... I'm a Magnetic Resonance Imaging Technologist."

The hunter put down his rifle and began to lower a ladder, saying, "My name's Paul Storm. Toss that ax to the side, I'm coming down to help."

Weakly, he threw his ax into the street as the hunter climbed down.

"I've got to check you for bites. Show me your arms and legs."

Sam obliged, rolling up his pant legs and holding out his arms. Satisfied, the hunter picked up the ax and helped Sam to his feet. They climbed up the ladder, and from high atop the train he looked down onto Main Street. Moving vans lined the old, residential street, and the men who were loading them had rifles slung over their shoulders.

The hunter pointed to the little green house, confirming, "That one's yours?"

Sam smiled and nodded.

"Do you know Carol? Your neighbor?"

"Yeah, of course."

"Well go talk to her. She has your boy."

Sam paused, asking intently, "Wait ... what? What do you mean?"

"Just go see Carol," the man insisted.

Sam tossed his ax to the ground and carefully climbed down the leeward side of the train. He wanted to stop and kiss the ground, but the hunter's words were disconcerting, so he broke into a jog, running toward his home.

What did he mean? Why is Simon at Carol's house? And where is Jessica?

As he neared his front yard, he was stopped cold in his tracks. Across the street from his house, in front of the funeral home, there was a mound of charred corpses piled high. The horrible pile smelled like burnt pork.

"Sam!" a woman's voice called out from behind him.

He looked around but didn't see anyone.

"Up here! On the roof!" It was Carol, his neighbor. She had a beach umbrella and chairs set up on the roof.

[DADA!] Simon screamed from beside her!

"SIMON!"

Tears began to roll down Sam's face as he rushed Carol's front porch, climbing the banister like a monkey and pulling himself up onto the roof. He scooped up his boy and squeezed him tightly.

[Dada I missed you so much!] the boy screeched in toddler-speak.

"I missed you, too, buddy. I missed you, too," he said, holding his son close, sobbing quietly.

Carol stood by and had a sorrowful look about her.

"Is everything okay, Carol? Where's Jessica?"

"Well ..." Carol stalled for a moment, searching for the right words, "She went into labor last night. Maybe we should talk in p-r-i-v-a-t-e," she said, nodding toward Simon.

Sam gulped hard and tried to compose himself, "Oh... of course ..."

The last thing he wanted to do was let go of his boy, but he could see in Carol's eyes that something was gravely wrong.

He kneeled down to Simon's level and looked him in the eyes, "Hey buddy, Daddy's gonna talk with Carol for a minute, so be a good boy and go pick out some toys for us to play with."

Carol's teenage son, Peter, chimed in, "Yeah, Simon, come on! I'll help you pick out some toys."

201

[Oh! Okay!] Simon said, then looked to his Dad, saying, [But you stay *right here*, Dada, and don't go to Detroit. I will be right back with so many toys.]

"Okay, buddy. I'll wait right here," he replied, patting his boy's head.

The two boys ran across the roof and climbed into a second floor window, giving the grown-ups time to talk.

Carol handed Sam a bottle of water, and then offered him a lawn chair.

"So," she began, "Jessica's water broke yesterday during lunch. We'd heard that the hospitals in Ann Arbor weren't safe, so she labored at home as long as she could, but... things stopped progressing. She was fully dilated but in a *lot* of pain, and she felt like something was going wrong. The baby just wouldn't come out. My sister knows a midwife named Rosalyn that lives over on Platt Rd., so we took Jessica there and brought Simon home to spend the night with us. She was apparently doing better, and the labor was moving along, but ..."

"But? But what?"

"We went to check on her at sun up, and ... sometime during the night the house was overrun. The front door was wide open, there were zombies in the yard and in the house. There were too many of them to try going inside. We circled the block several times, but didn't see Jessica."

Sam stood up with fire in his eyes, saying, "Where did you say? Platt Rd.? Which house is it?"

"Wait, Sam," Carol stood up and put her hand on his shoulder, "No offense, but you look exhausted. My brother is on his way over, maybe you should rest up until he gets here. The two of you can go check it out together."

Sam stared down at the blackened pile of bodies across the street. He had fought so hard to escape Detroit, and was under the delusion that everything would be fine if he could just make it home. Now he was home, only to find out his pregnant wife was missing... or worse.

"How did this happen, Carol? I've only been gone for a few days," Sam's voice cracked as he spoke.

"Have a seat," Carol said, helping the man ease his broken body down into the lawn chair. "On Saturday morning it was all over the news: a riot in Detroit. By the end of the day they were suggesting that it was related to the riots in Korea, and they started mentioning *bird flu*, and *cannibals*, and *zombies.*

"Late Saturday night we heard there was a zombie in Milan, a woman. No one knew who she was. The police caught her and took her in, but one of the officers was bitten on the arm. No one realized how contagious these people were, and before anyone knew it, the officer fell ill and infected most of the Milan Police Department. The Fire Department stepped up to fill their place, and have been working on evacuating the town, but without ..."

"Wait," Sam interrupted, "*evacuating*? What do you mean? Why?"

"We *have* to, it's spreading this way. Ann Arbor, Detroit, Toledo, the highway ... we're surrounded on three sides. I'm taking the boys to my uncle's farm; it's a few miles west of here. You and Simon are welcome to join us."

"Not without Jessica ... I can't. When do you plan on leaving?"

"Well, as soon as we can, maybe even *today* now that you're back. My brother is bringing his trailer over for us to load up."

Sam looked out at all the moving vans that were being loaded, and then down at the pile of blackened corpses. "What happened to *them*?"

Carol looked briefly, and then quickly averted her eyes from the pile. "Sunday there was a biker funeral across the street. They were out front, preparing to do a military style 21-gun-salute-thing, when a large crowd of zombies came up from the highway. Lots of people were attacked and either killed or infected; it was awful. It turns out the rifles they use for military tributes are only firing blanks, but it also turns out that most bikers carry concealed handguns, and they don't take kindly to having their funerals interrupted. They shot every last zombie, piled up their bodies, and set it on fire. I don't think it was the most appropriate place for a cremation, but I wasn't about to argue."

"And ... no one bothered to clean it up?" Sam asked.

Carol put her hand on Sam's shoulders, speaking more seriously, "Sam, I don't think you understand, *it's not safe here anymore.* Everyone's leaving. The Police are all dead, most of the Fire Department's been infected, every couple hours a few more zombies wander up from the highway. One of them crashed through my front window, Sam. That's why we slept on the roof last night."

"Through your window?"

She nodded sharply, "A man wandered up to the house and started banging on the window. He ... he didn't have any skin on his face. We hid in the kitchen, hoping he would leave. Eventually he broke through the glass and started climbing through the window, so my oldest boy Mark took a cast iron skillet and ... put him down."

Sam slumped down in the chair, holding his head in his hands.

"Why don't you go get cleaned up, soak in the tub for a while. My brother will be here soon."

"Yeah. Thanks, Carol. Thanks for watching Simon. Thank you for everything."

Sam's heavy eyelids eased open, revealing the off-white shower enclosure of his late-80's renovated bathroom. He was up to his cheekbones in cold, soapy water. Apparently he had been asleep for a while, allowing the steaming hot bath to cool.

Sitting up slowly, he could hear Simon playing with Peter and Mark in the other room. His head was still spinning, and he reached up to feel his swollen nose, which was still broken.

Whoa ... how long have I been asleep?

His sore body tightened up in a long, loud, stretch, "Aaaaaaaaghhhhhh ..."

[I hear Dada! He's awake now!] Simon called out.

The boy could be heard stomping his way to the bathroom at full speed. The door burst open, and in he ran like a fireball, screaming, [DADA! You're awake now! Carol said... um... Carol said we have to be *very* quiet, because Daddy is *sleeping*, but now you're AWAKE!]. He then danced around the bathroom.

"That's right, bud. I'm awake now."

[YAY! I am SO HAPPY! Do you want to play?]

"Of course I do," Sam smiled, "Can you hand me a towel?"

[Oh, yeah!] Simon said, realizing that he was getting ahead of himself, [You need to dry your body!]

After drying off and putting on some blissfully clean clothes, they joined the others in the living room. Mark and Peter were playing video games.

"Hey, guys. Where's your mom?"

Mark, the older of the two, looked up, "Outside, helping uncle Tom load the trailer."

Sam smirked, "And you young men aren't helping her?"

"She told us to watch Simon until you got out of the bath."

Peter finally looked up from the video games, asking, "What the heck are those numbers on your forehead?"

He looked over at the large mirror that hung on the wall above his couch. In bold black ink was the number "1442," written in a dead man's hand.

205

Sam rubbed it with his hand, but it didn't even smudge. "Apparently the U.S. Special Forces use very persistent ink."

"What!?" the boys asked with piqued interest, "Special Forces!?"

"Oh ... it's a long story, I'll tell you guys all about it sometime. But I need to go talk to your uncle." He then crouched down to address his son, "Listen up, Simon: I need you to wait here while I go to the store with Tom."

[Aw, but I want to be by you.]

"I know buddy, and I want nothing more than to be by you, too. But, I'll be right back. I promise. I need you to be a good boy and wait with Mark and Peter."

[Aw, maaaaan,] Simon acquiesced, sulking away to his room.

Outside, Sam found Carol and Tom loading his trailer.

"You look like you're feeling a lot better," Carol said as she wiped the sweat from her brow.

"Yes, thank you, but you're being too kind. I look like I've been beat in the face with a frozen turkey," he said, rubbing his swollen nose. "So Tom, Carol said you might be able to give me a ride to the midwife's house."

"Of course," the tall man nodded, "Are you ready to go?"

"Ready when you are."

The two men rolled through the neighborhood in Tom's Silverado pick up, Sam toting his ax, Tom with a hunting rifle. The only cars on the road were heading west, into the wooded countryside and rolling farmlands, away from the highway. A few men were fortifying their homes and boarding up their windows, but most people were loading up their cars and bugging out.

"So, Tom, how far away is this house?"

"It's close, not more than ..."

BLAM!!!

The men were interrupted by a shotgun blast at a passing house. They looked back in time to see a headless body falling to the ground in someone's driveway.

"What was that?" Sam yelled, "A zombie?"

Tom nervously gripped the wheel, saying, "Yeah. There are a lot of them up here by the grocery store."

"By Kroger's? Really?" Sam's voice wavered with a spark of fear, "That's *close ... way* too close."

"Which is why we're getting Carol out of town." Tom reached up and adjusted his rear view mirror before continuing, "Over the weekend, there was a rush on Kroger's, and almost every other store for that matter. The shelves were picked clean, people stocking up and preparing for the worst. Folks were lined up out front and arguing to get inside and get some food before everything sold out. Then someone came out of the store screaming that there were zombies inside, and pandemonium ensued. People pushed their way in against the people that were running out, everyone started shooting and looting. It was *bad*. I drove by yesterday, and there were 20 or 30 zombies out front."

Sam sat quietly for a moment, chewing on his thoughts before he brought up the nerve to ask, "Did you see the midwife's house? How bad was it?"

Tom looked Sam in the eyes, and then returned his gaze to the road. "Bad. The front door was wide open, zombies in the yard, zombies in the house." Tom paused, giving Sam a hard look, before asking, "What are your intentions when we get there?"

Sam throttled the yellow, fiberglass ax in his hands, tipping the blade so he could inspect the cutting edge. "I'm going to look for my wife."

Respectful of Sam's feelings, the tall man waited a moment before asking for clarification. "As you should. That's good." Tom nodded, "But... *specifically*, what do you plan to do? Are you going inside the house?"

The young man's eyes were lost in uncertainty; he honestly didn't know what he planned to do. "I ... I have to know if she is alive. If that means killing every zombie in the house, so be it."

"Zombies ahead," Tom interrupted.

Three men were limping in the street ahead, blood soaked and delirious. The truck glided past them uneventfully, and then turned south at the next intersection.

"Here comes the house, ahead on the left."

They slowed to a stop, casing the house carefully from a distance. Six zombies roamed the yard, and one more could be seen standing in the open doorway. The front bay window was shattered, with its crumpled blinds and curtains hanging out of the broken glass.

Two bodies were face down in the lawn, unmoving.

"Here's my idea," Sam said, "drop me off right here, then pull up right in front of the house. Honk your horn and flash your lights for a good solid minute to get their attention, and then pull away *slowly,* like at a walking pace. Try to draw them around the next corner, then circle the block to meet me back right here. If I'm not back yet, do that same trick again, working to herd as many as you can away from the house. Do you follow me?"

"Yeah, I follow. And your wife, describe her for me so I know who I'm looking for."

"Jessica? Well ... she's about my height, long brown hair, blue eyes ... long and lean, with thin arms and graceful shoulders. She's part Greek and part German ... very pretty. She's nine months pregnant ... or at least, she was the last time I saw her."

"Alright, I'll keep my eyes peeled for her. So, you're going inside?"

"Yep."

Tom reached into his jacket, pulling out a .38 revolver. He opened the cylinder to count the rounds, gave it a spin, and snapped it back into place, saying, "Take this, the safety's off and it holds six rounds. But keep in mind: these things are drawn to loud sounds. Once you start shooting they're all going to converge on you."

"I can't thank you enough."

"Don't sweat it. Carol says you're good people; that's all I need to know."

Sam nodded, tucking the gun into his belt as he hopped out of the pickup truck. Ten paces away he ducked into a hedgerow and vanished from sight.

The Silverado pulled ahead and began honking as planned. The horn had its intended effect, drawing several zombies out from within the home. Tom put the truck in drive and began rolling away, with a dozen zombies in slow pursuit.

Meanwhile, Sam had already jumped the fence and was in the midwife's back yard, peering into an open doorway which lead into the kitchen. A bloody, gray haired woman stood in the middle of the dated kitchen, staring vacantly at the wall.

Not allowing himself to hesitate, Sam rushed inside and buried the ax deep into her skull, sending her to the linoleum floor. Overwhelmed with fear and urgency, he charged ahead into the next room, the dining room. A sick, milky eyed girl slowly turned to meet his gaze, and he chopped her down to the ground, pulverizing her head with two more whacks, ensuring that she was down for good.

Moans echoed from elsewhere in the house, and a large man in overalls burst awkwardly into the room, knocking Sam to the ground. He rolled under the dining room table, and saw the legs of several more zombies stammering into the room. Emerging from the far side of the table, he circled around it and began swinging for the bleachers; he was *all-in*. Blasting thru the room like the angel of death, he lobotomized the first one within reach, then grazed the temple of an old man, then sent the blade deep into a boney shoulder, then clipped the head of another man, then decapitated an old woman, then finished off the old man, then returned to the boney shoulder guy, then kicked a small child to the ground, and then brained the man in the overalls, and then finished off the child on the ground.

The dining room fell silent as he caught his breath, standing ankle-deep in carnage. Moans continued from elsewhere in the home, reminding him that there was no time to stop, so he methodically walked from corpse to corpse, giving each one a final chop to the cranium, a *coup de grace*.

Can't take chances, he thought coldly.

Taking one big breath and blowing it out to focus his "chi," he marched into the front room. On the ground was a crippled, chewed up female crawling across the ground. He split her head in two before continued into the hallway.

The first room on the left was a bedroom, and Sam's world shattered as he tried to piece together the gory scene within. There were three dead bodies piled up under the broken window, all males, with gunshot wounds to the head and splatter marks on the wall. The bed was soaked in blood, and on it was a large turkey roasting pan, containing an umbilical cord and placenta. A badly mauled female body lay at the side of the bed, it was a slender woman with long brown hair.

His legs buckled and he dropped to one knee, eyes welling with tears.

No ... Please, NO ... not Jessica ...

Crawling forward, he delicately brushed the blood caked hair from her face. It had been chewed at mercilessly and was unrecognizable. Looking down at her hand, he saw her wedding ring, the ring he put on her finger nearly ten years ago.

Curling up on the floor next to her body, sanity left him and his mind veered far from this awful room. It was replaced by thoughts of their life together, of their beautiful beginning, and recent troubles, of their first meeting and their engagement.

He had carried her engagement ring halfway around the world, hidden in his backpack as they hiked through Italy and Switzerland. He was nearly forced to propose to her in the airport customs line when the concealed ring set off the metal detectors. The security guard saw the ring and quickly surmised what it was, so he played along, keeping it out of sight from Jessica while he finished searching their luggage. Waiting for just the right moment, Sam proposed to her on a midnight gondola ride in the canals of Venice. It was perfect.

Lost in sorrow, he took her hand into his, holding it tightly to his chest, unable to believe his eyes. He couldn't bear the thought of her final, horrible moments, knowing it must have been filled with terror and anguish. Gently squeezing her hand, he jumped with a start when her hand squeezed back!

Confused and repulsed, he dove away from the corpse and returned to his feet, looking at her mangled, nude body. Her corpse was reanimating, but her face was so badly mutilated that she was blind and unable to see him. Sam was not mentally prepared to deal with this.

A honking horn snapped him back into the moment. It was Tom; he had circled the block as planned, and was now rounding up a second group of zombies from the house.

Sam's eyes darted around the room.

What about the baby? Where is my baby?

Jessica's corpse was trying to rise, a grotesque perversion of the woman he loved, and Sam lost his mind. He charged at her screaming, and sunk the ax head deep into her skull, sending her thin body back to the floor. Sobbing uncontrollably, he chopped three more times, and then began to ransack the room, searching unsuccessfully for the body

210

of his newborn girl.

Motion caught his eye, and he turned to see two infected men wander through the hallway, passing the bedroom without noticing him. Sam peered out to see them round a corner further down the hall. There was a lot of moaning and commotion coming from that direction, so he pulled out the revolver, determined to stalk the remaining zombies down and discover the fate of his child.

Seek and destroy, he thought, as tears continued to roll down his face.

Crouched like a psychotic predator, he snuck down the hall and looked around the next corner. There were four zombies gathered around a closed door, mindlessly pawing at the old wood. There was another open doorway next to them leading into a second bedroom. Sam gripped the pistol tightly and leveled the sights, aiming at the back of the biggest zombie's cranium.

BLAM! (*one*)

The zombie's head burst apart, as the rest turned to face their doom.

BLAM! (*two*)

BLAM! (*three*)

BLAM! (*four*)

A woman's voice began screaming for help from behind the closed door as three more zombies emerged from the second bedroom.

BLAM! (*five*)

BLAM! (*six*)

Out of ammo, Sam tucked the revolver back into his waist line and raised his ax high, cleaving the final zombie's head in two.

Screams continued from behind the closed door, but all movement in the hall stopped. After a good, solid five-count, Sam mustered his nerves and marched forward into the second bedroom. On the ground was a mutilated corpse, dragging itself slowly across the floor. He blasted its skull open with the ax, ending the thing's suffering.

Returning to the hall, he tested the closed door, but it was locked. Knocking hard, he yelled, "Open up! I'm here to help!

"Huh?" came the woman's voice from within, "Are they ... are they gone?"

211

"I don't know, I hope so! *OPEN UP!*" he replied

The door creaked open; it was a bathroom. Inside was a young woman, with long auburn hair and a lip-ring. "Who are you?" she asked.

"My name's Luke Skywalker, I'm here to rescue you."

The poor man's mind was obviously bent, eyes wild and teary. "*What?*"

"Kidding. My name's Sam, I'm the pregnant woman's husband. I'm trying to find my baby, do you know where she is?"

"No ... I don't know ... everything was so crazy! They ... they were everywhere! We need to get out of here!" The young woman was scared to death and babbling.

"I know, but I have to search the house for my baby, do you know if anyone else is still here?"

"No! No ... I don't know! But ... wait, you're the baby's father?"

"Yeah."

"Well, the midwife, she grabbed the baby and ran when the zombies ... they ..." the poor girl broke down and began sobbing, "We need to get out of here!"

"Okay, I know, but ... do you know where she took my baby?"

An infected woman appeared in the hall, drawn toward their conversation.

"OH MY GOD!" the poor girl screamed, "MOM?"

Sam turned to the infected woman, and then looked back at the girl in the bathroom. "Wait ... WHAT?"

There was no time to think, Sam turned his focus back to the approaching corpse and drove his ax deep into her forehead.

"NO! That's my MOM!" the young woman screeched, and began slapping Sam on the back and shoulders.

Confused, Sam turned back to her saying, "Sorry, sorry! She's already dead! These people ... they're not who they used to be! They're dead! I'm ... I'm so sorry."

The girl collapsed into his chest, balling hysterically.

"I'm sorry ... I know ... I know this is hard, but you have to push through it. We can't stop here, we have to keep moving!"

The young woman looked up with big brown eyes, teary and afraid, but she pulled it together and nodded as she dried her eyes with her sleeve.

"Good, let's go."

They crept back through the hall, checking each room and closet along the way. The living room was clear, as was the kitchen, the dining room, and the garage. All clear; no sign of the baby.

"Dang it!" Sam cursed, standing hopelessly in the garage, lost for ideas, trying desperately not to think about his wife. He needed to focus on finding his baby.

"We really need to go ... *please*," the young woman pleaded, beginning to sob again.

"ARRGH. Okay ... okay. Let's go."

They crossed back through the living room and walked out the front door. There were still two bodies lying face down in the grass, unmoving. A wounded zombie limped across the yard, so Sam ran to greet it with the ax.

CHLOP!

It crumpled lifelessly to the ground, as a horn began honking from down the street. It was Tom in his Silverado.

"Run for that truck!" Sam yelled to the young woman.

They hoofed it down the street as Tom stepped out of the truck and raised his rifle to lay down covering fire.

CRACK! The rifle recoiled hard in his arms. He worked the bolt action and took aim again. CRACK! Sam looked over his shoulder and saw a zombie drop to the ground.

Running hard, the two of them jumped into the truck as Tom continued to send bullets down range.

CRACK!

Tom reloaded the rifle and then handed it to the young woman who was now sitting in the middle of the bench seat.

"Let's go!" Sam urged as Tom put the truck in drive.

The Silverado did a hasty three point turn, and then took off down the road.

"You found her!" Tom exclaimed, "But where's the baby?"

Sam shook his head somberly, "No, this isn't her; this is ... what's your name?"

The woman looked back and forth at the two men, still in shock, saying, "Katie ... my name's Katie McDowell."

"Katie," Sam said, "Do you have *any* idea where the midwife would have gone?"

She tried to collect her thoughts, but shook her head, "No, I'm not really sure. There were zombies outside in the street, so we were all trying to be quiet ... But the pregnant girl, your wife, she ... she was screaming with labor pains and the zombies heard her and attacked the house. It was awful, they were busting through the windows, and they came in through the garage ... they grabbed hold of your wife, and my Mom ... so I ran. I ... I locked myself in the bathroom and ... All I could hear was people screaming ... and the zombies, they ... they ..." she broke down into tears, no longer able to keep it together.

Lost in sorrow, Sam stared out the window, unsure of what to do next. He had fought so hard to reach home: running, crawling, kicking, screaming, punching, chopping, falling, bleeding ... but he did it, he made it *home*. He had escaped from Detroit, and was home.

"I'm alive ... and I still have my son," he mumbled.

"Heads up," Tom said, "we have traffic."

A moving van was coming up the street, swerving recklessly between lanes. Behind it, a tan minivan was in pursuit.

"Look out, Tom! That truck's gonna hit us!" Sam yelled, bracing himself against the dash board.

"Stop!" Katie screamed, "Stop!"

Tom swerved hard toward the shoulder, but there was no way he could avoid it. The moving van T-boned his Silverado, flipping it violently.

It bounced once, and then flipped again as Sam's face burst through the windshield and his limp body went airborne. In a blur of pain he watched the cement beneath him scroll by in slow motion, ending in a violent crash of sharp snapping branches and more pain, and then silence. As he lost consciousness, wondering if this is what death felt like, his final thoughts were of his son who was waiting at home, his precious boy who needed his Dada.

Not today, Death. Not today.

THE END?

I hope you enjoyed this ride as much as I did. If so, there is more! Here's a preview of "Riot of the Living Dead" Vol. II:

(spoiler alert: Sam lived)

Day 15 Saturday 1815 hrs

Proudly walking through the woods with three smallmouth bass, a handful of black berries, and a bag full of pansies, Sam reached the edge of the tree line and crouched down in the concealment of the un-mowed, overgrown roadside. Carefully, he surveyed the route home. At the moment there were no zombies in the open street; some had mindlessly parked themselves into the yards of his neighbors, while others moved on in search of prey. Periodically, a gunshot would ring out somewhere in the distance, which helped prod along those who were just milling about. They would mindlessly walk in the direction of the shooting until they arrived at the source, or until something else grabbed their attention along the way.

As he bounced from cover to cover, he paused to reevaluate his route, checking to see if any zeds were on the move. It was at one of these stops that he spotted his orange, 10ft step ladder; it was propped up against the side of his house, *not* in the bushes where he had left it.

His heart raced ... someone was on the roof with his son.

Abandoning caution, he sprinted down the street and anxiously rushed to the side of his house, stopping for a nanosecond to scan the yard for an ambush. All seemed clear, so he dropped his haul of food and raced up the ladder and onto the roof. With a full head of steam he waltzed boldly into his rooftop sanctuary, hammer raised, beast mode: ON.

Coiled next to Simon's books were his empty climbing harness and rope, but no Simon, *he was gone.*

Tears began to well in his eyes as he tore through the campsite. There was no sign of him in the tent, nor under the lawn furniture, nor behind the totes. Turning in circles, he stopped when he saw that his bedroom window was wide open, and plopped on the roof next to it was a faded purple backpack, decorated with rainbow colored Grateful Dead patches.

Oh no, Hippies ... he thought.

Creeping up to the window, he peeked in his bedroom but could see no one inside. Picking up the purple bag, he quietly unzipped it and dumped out the contents. The bag smelled of female sweat and patchouli. It had little more than a flashlight, a dead cell phone, a large wad of cash, and some dirty laundry. Holding a particularly flowery garment to his nose, he drew in a deep breath.

Yep ... it's a girl alright.

So there was at least one person inside, apparently a female. Somehow, the intruder being a woman made the situation seem not as calamitous, but Sam's paternal instincts had him ready to *kill* whosoever had his child. He quickly circled the roof another time, searching for signs of others before storming the house, but found nothing. Was she alone? *Hopefully*, he thought.

He brazenly stepped into the window and looked around, confirming that his bedroom was empty. Moving to the stairway, he peeked down, again seeing no one, so he made his way down the stairs, clutching the hammer tightly. As he reached the bottom, he could clearly hear Simon in the bathroom, casually talking to someone.

[But will you have a skipping race with me?]

There was a quiet groan, and then an unfamiliar female's voice, "Maybe later, Simon. I'm trying to use the potty."

[Oh yeah, I know all about that. You have to listen to yours body when it's time for the pee to come out.]

The woman groaned again sharply; it sounded as though she was having some gastrointestinal troubles.

[Guess what?] Simon carried on, cheerfully oblivious to her distress.

"*What is it?*"

[Daddy pees standing up. Yeah, *BIG* penis,] he explained quite innocently, spreading his arms wide.

The woman began to laugh, "Is that so?"

Standing unseen in the hall, Sam palmed his face in parental disbelief.

Dang it, Simon ... not in front of company ...

"Well why doesn't your Daddy have doors on the bathroom?

Sometimes a girl needs *privacy*."

[Oh yeah! Privacy!] Simon said, holding up his finger and proclaiming, [I *won't* look, and I *won't* peek!]

He turned his back to her, and saw his father peeking in from the dining room.

[DADA'S HOME!] he cheered, and came running to greet him.

The woman in the bathroom jumped to her feet and began wrestling with her jeans, trying to get them up as she dug in her pocket for her folding knife.

"HOLD IT RIGHT THERE! LET ME SEE YOUR HANDS!" Sam barked as he pounced into the bathroom doorway. "Hands out of your pockets! Who else is with you?"

Disregarding Sam's words, the girl continued to grapple with her jeans, finally clearing her hips and demanding, "*How long were you standing there!?*" Her shaking hands rummaged through her tight pockets, eventually producing the small knife. "Get back or I'll stick you!"

Sam grabbed Simon by the arm and tossed him safely into the dining room. "Put the knife down! Why are you in my house?"

The girl stood there with her thighs squeezed tightly together, anxiously shifting from side to side.

Sam raised an eyebrow, "Are you doing ... the pee-pee dance?"

She squirmed sheepishly and whispered, "Um ... no ... Number *two*."

"Oh ... um ... pardon me ..."

Sam backed away into the dining room, but the girl called out, "Go farther away! I ... I don't want you to hear anything," she said with a fair amount of embarrassment.

"Oh ... of course. Sorry." This was all very awkward.

Retreating further, into his living room, he got down on one knee to talk with Simon. "Are you alright, buddy?"

[Yeah, but guess what?]

"What?"

Using his hands to explain, he said, [My friend Sarah pees sitting *down*; she has a *gy-na*.]

"*I can still hear you guys!*" the woman called out from the bathroom, "*Go farther, please!*"

Sam ushered his son away, delicately explaining to him that it's bad manners to talk about penises and vaginas around company.

Waiting for the girl to finish her business, Sam quickly searched the rest of the house, finding no other signs of intruders. This young lady seemed harmless enough. Her diminutive stature didn't pose much of a threat, and she had a soft, feminine presence.

A few bodily noises could be heard coming from the bathroom, followed by her mortified voice, "*Go farther away! Both of you!*"

"SHHH!" Sam implored, running right up to the doorless bathroom, "I'm sorry, but please don't yell! We don't want to attract them to the house!"

Sitting helplessly vulnerable on the toilet and tugging her t-shirt down over her knees, the woman's olive skin blushed red, and she meekly whispered, "*Sorry.*"

"Um ... okay, then ... thank you." Awkwardness returned, and Sam backed away slowly, fading into the living room.

Volume II coming soon...

Sam Elkins is an MRI Technologist who has worked in the Detroit inner city for nearly a decade. His accounts of racism and ruin are based on first-hand accounts and a fair amount of trespassing in the many abandoned buildings that mar the city. He hopes that his debut novel will shed light on the struggles that Detroiters face, and encourage others to invest in this city whose economic fate is directly tied to the fate of the region.

www.ingramcontent.com/pod-product-compliance
Lightning Source LLC
Chambersburg PA
CBHW060323260626
47160CB00007B/2664